Capital Starship

Ixan Legacy Book 1

Scott Bartlett

Mirth Publishing
St. John's

CAPITAL STARSHIP

Cover art by: Tom Edwards (tomedwardsdesign.com)

Library and Archives Canada Cataloguing in Publication

Bartlett, Scott

Capital Starship / Scott Bartlett ; illustrations by Tom Edwards.

ISBN 978-1-988380-11-7

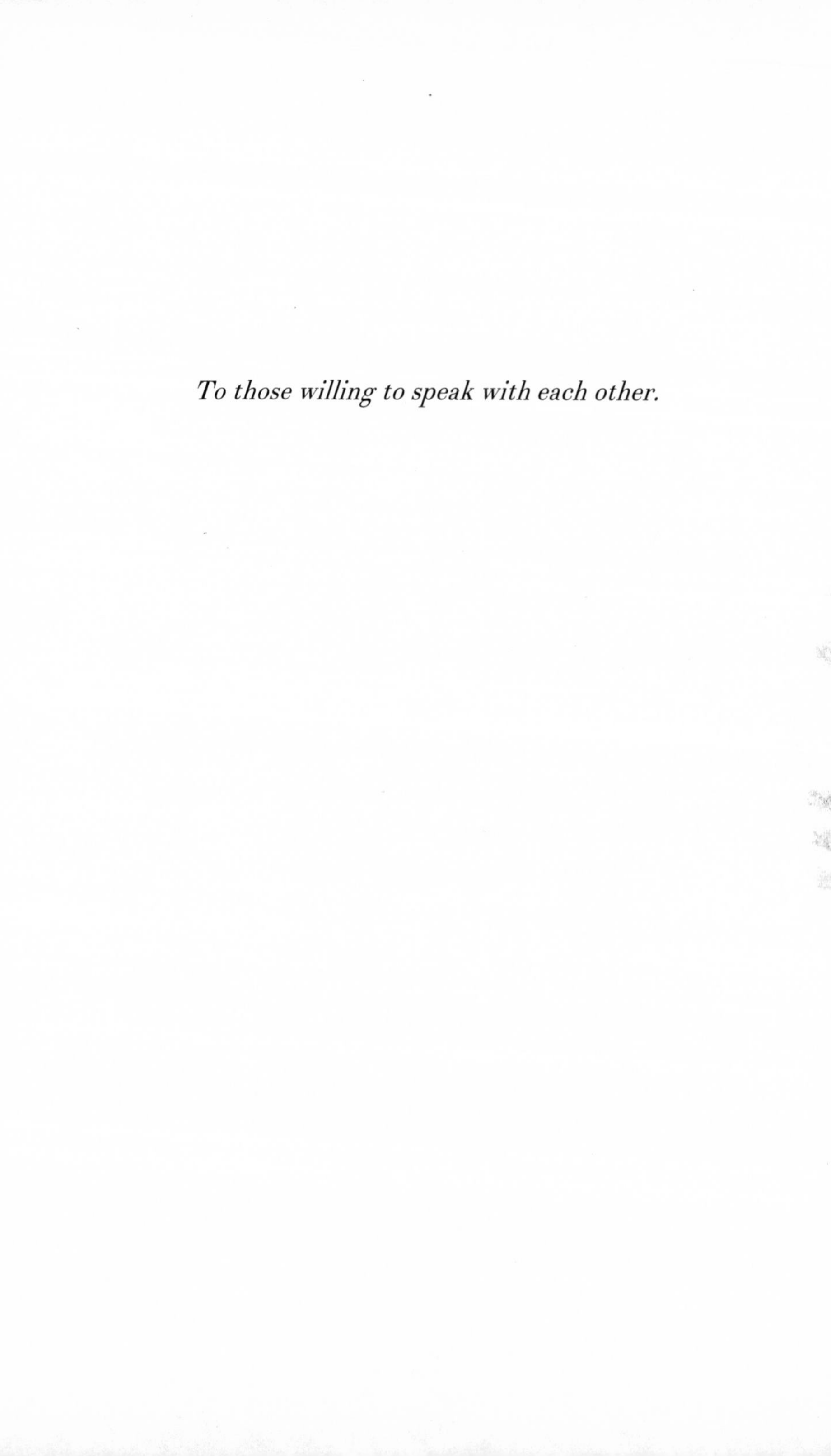

To those willing to speak with each other.

CHAPTER 1

Shattered Peace

The Gok carrier bore down on the IGS *Vesta*, and Captain Vin Husher cursed under his breath. The alien warship was clearly maneuvering for tactical advantage, but until it fired the first shot, there was nothing Husher could do.

With bureaucrats scrutinizing his every move, commanding the largest warship in the Integrated Galactic Fleet counted for less than it should have. He certainly felt less effective as a captain. The voices calling for his removal from the *Vesta*'s command seat seemed to grow louder and more numerous with every passing day, and it took everything he had to continue presenting himself as not only fit for command, but the best man for the job.

Of course, ideas about what "the job" actually was tended to vary dramatically. The way he saw it, his job was to prepare the galaxy for the onslaught he knew was coming. He knew that in his very core, which made it especially baffling when others described his "proper" job as doing his best to render war itself obsolete.

That particular view of his job had gained widespread popularity over the last twenty years, and these days, his every action was held up to a microscope, along with its justification, which he was required to provide in the multitude of reports and statements that had come to characterize his life.

He agreed with civilian oversight of the military. But he also thought that oversight should come from a well-informed, well-reasoned place. Sadly, it rarely did, anymore.

The politicians of the Interstellar Union hadn't seen what he'd seen. They hadn't experienced the ruthlessness of the Ixa in battle, and they hadn't heard the conviction of the Ixan AI named Baxa, when he'd told Husher that he was but one of many superintelligences designed for war. The AI had promised that the others would come soon to finish the job of exterminating all life in the Milky Way.

In the meantime, there was this warship from the Gok, with whom the IU had enjoyed an uneasy peace for the last seventeen years. The Union did everything they could to maintain that peace, including mandating ROEs—Rules of Engagement—that left its own warships at a disadvantage against any Gok ship that might decide to attack.

"They're not acknowledging our transmission request, Captain." The Coms officer almost whispered as she delivered the news. She was Ensign Amy Fry, and she sat two consoles over from Husher's, just ahead and a foot lower. Like every other officer in the CIC, she faced the main display.

"Keep trying," Husher said, his voice tight with strain, even though he was trying his best to seem calm. Though unlikely, the possibility that the other vessel's coms simply weren't functioning would be enough to sink Husher's career if he fired first. Never mind that the Gok was the only species with whom the Interstellar Union had gone to war against during the twenty years since its inception, or that the Gok still steadfastly refused to join the federation that included every other sentient species in the galaxy.

"Sir..." muttered Commander Fesky, Husher's XO, her twitching wings betraying her unease. Not that he needed the indication—he'd served with her since just before the Second Galactic War, and Husher could read his Winger friend like a favorite book.

But that wouldn't stop him from observing protocol. "Easy, Commander. I'm not about to go down in history as the captain who fired the first shot in the renewed Gok Wars." *Even so...* He turned to his Nav officer. "Initiate reverse thrust, Kaboh, engaging engines at sixty-five percent. Let's start inching back toward Zakros' orbital defense platforms."

"Aye, Captain," Lieutenant Commander Kaboh answered in the high-pitched tones of a Kaithian—one of the few that were aboard the *Vesta*. Most of Kaboh's species preferred to remain close together, where the benefits of their psychic Consensus was multiplied. But under the direction of the Interstellar Union, the Fleet had assigned Kaboh to serve in Husher's CIC, and Husher was pretty sure he knew why.

"The Gok carrier has doubled its acceleration, Captain," the sensor operator reported, from two consoles to Husher's right. "Her main gun is aligned with our forward starboard engine."

Husher's fingers tightened around the cold steel of his chair's armrests. Peering at the CIC's main display, he raised his right hand to a sturdy white switch positioned on the side of his console, flicking from a tactical representation of the two warships to the view from an exterior visual sensor. It showed mostly empty space at the moment; the Gok ship nothing more than a distant gleam.

Flicking the ivory switch once again, Husher changed the display back to a tactical overview. That likely wouldn't be what the other officers saw on the display. When his Coms officer looked at the main display, she likely saw a data readout on the warship's communications array, or maybe reports from subordinates in her department as they worked together to hail the Gok ship. The sensor operator would likely be managing multiple streams of information provided by various sensor types—RADAR, LIDAR, visual, and so on.

Of course, Chief Benno Tremaine, his Tactical officer, probably did have the tactical display up, alongside multiple targeting calculations. Husher had long ago drilled into the man's head that he should always be ready with multiple firing solutions whenever a nearby ship had even the slimmest chance of becoming violent. It was far more efficient to modify an existing firing solution than to whip up one from scratch.

Without Oculenses, it wouldn't have been possible for each officer to see something different on the main display—the invention had certainly been a boon for CIC operations. The public had found plenty of other uses for Oculenses, of course, but Husher didn't consider all of those to be quite as beneficial.

As captain, he could tap into what any of his CIC's officers were looking at while they were on duty. He did so now, switching to his sensor operator's overlay. "Winterton, collaborate with Nav to provide me with an estimate of when the carrier will enter an optimal range for—"

"Captain, the carrier just launched two squadrons of third-generation Slags!"

Husher's head whipped toward his Tactical officer. Normally, his sensor operator would have delivered that information, but Winterton had been looking away from his readout, at Husher.

"Have any of them started firing?" Husher asked. Slags were the Gok's idea of space fighters, so-named for their close resemblance to melted hunks of metal. If they'd begun to attack, then so could Husher. Scrambling Slags at all seemed like a clearly hostile act to him, but he knew the politicians would say differently.

"Negative."

With the *Vesta*'s present course locked in, Kaboh didn't have much to do. His muscular head-tail shifted against his chair's back as he turned toward Husher, looking totally relaxed. "Captain, I would remind you that the presiding ROEs prohibit—"

"I'm familiar with the ROEs," Husher snapped. "Helm, punch the engines up to eighty percent."

"The Slags will overtake us at this rate, Captain," Winterton said.

"They'll overtake us no matter what we do," Husher muttered. His ship's top speed was—well, it was superluminal, thanks to the warp tech that had come online fleet-wide during the last five years. But her sheer mass meant that accelerating to any meaningful velocity took time, even if he were to have his Helm officer bring the engines up to full power.

Slowly, he shook his head, his heart pounding an increasing cadence in his ears. The *Vesta* truly was a wonder—much bigger and far more powerful than anything ever fielded before her. But her capabilities were nearly wasted under the limitations the interspecies government had placed on military action. Husher had been expecting a situation like the one developing right now for a long time. It was just his luck that it was happening to him—and at a time when the battle group that normally accompanied his ship was already halfway to the darkgate into the next system.

"Ready point defense systems, Tactical," Husher growled, eyeing Kaboh as he finished. "Unless you're going to tell me the ROEs forbid that, now?"

"No more than they forbid readying firing solutions for ships that never end up attacking us, Captain," the Kaithian said, his tone conspicuously neutral.

Husher caught himself grinding his teeth at the implied dig, and he forced himself to stop. Modern military doctrine gave subordinates far more leeway when criticizing their superiors than was once considered proper. The thinking was that encouraging debate would reduce mistakes made by the CO and others in command positions.

Husher wasn't so sure about that, but he did know that the freer dialog did real harm to discipline and the chain of command.

It doesn't help that Kaboh's real job is to spy on me for the IU, Husher reflected.

"Still no response from the Gok commander," the Coms officer said, and the sensor operator spoke on the heels of that: "Enemy—uh, Gok Slags are drawing even with us, Captain." Winterton blushed as Kaboh's widened eyes fell on him. No doubt the Kaithian was outraged at the sensor operator for 'prematurely' classifying the aggressively maneuvering ships as enemies.

Fortunately for the young ensign—though unfortunate for the *Vesta*—his slip-up was vindicated almost immediately. "The carrier just fired two guided missiles!" he said.

Good enough for me. "Tactical, tell Commander Ayam to scramble Pythons, prioritizing enemy Slags as targets," Husher rattled off, his speech as rapid and clipped as machine gun fire. "I don't want those missiles getting anywhere near my hull—neutralize them with a pair of Gorgons." With their advanced stealth capabilities, Gorgon missiles would likely be perfect, since the Gok missiles' sensors weren't sophisticated enough to detect the threat in time to adjust course. Gorgons were propelled by cold-gas thrusters, and they were covered in the darkest material ever made, which absorbed all but one-hundredth of one percent of the light it encountered.

"The carrier's continuing to accelerate, Captain," the sensor operator said. "I think they're aiming to ram us."

Husher's gaze snapped to the tactical display. *I can't believe it.* Even during the Gok Wars, only two of the Gok's warships had ever attempted a kamikaze run. *This really isn't my day, is it?* "Nav, evasive maneuvers, now!" he barked.

"Aye, Captain," Kaboh said, tiny blue-white fingers flying across his console.

But as the *Vesta* listed to port, its starboard thrusters firing, the Gok warship turned as well, its main gun tracking the supercarrier's trajectory.

It was a feint. "Helm, engines all ahead!" he yelled.

"Yes, sir," the Helm officer said, but it was too late. The *Vesta* had no time to overcome the inertia from her recent reverse thrust, and while her engines were powerful, the Gok's trickery paid off. Kinetic impactors tore into the supercarrier's starboard side near the stern, sending violent tremors through her entire frame and rocking Husher in his seat.

He tried to give another order, but his throat had closed up, and his ears began to ring shrilly. Dark spots danced before his eyes, and suddenly a memory overtook him, so vividly that he might have been watching a vid:

A white clapboard house, standing proud in the suburbs. Lights on in both the living room and upstairs washroom, piercing the deepening dusk.

Then: a fiery gash across the night sky. A deafening explosion. Fire that blossomed until it engulfed the entire house.

"Captain?" It was Fesky, who'd risen from the XO's Chair and was standing over him, shaking him. "Captain!"

"Hit them," he managed to gasp. "Hit them with everything we've got."

CHAPTER 2

Cybele

Husher and Fesky walked in silence as they neared the hatch where the crew section of the *Vesta* ended, their muffled footfalls the only sound other than the rustling of the Winger's feathers.

"Are you sure you're all right?" Fesky asked, shattering the quiet. "Back in the CIC...I wasn't sure you'd make it through the engagement. What happened?"

"I'm not sure, exactly. But we won, Fesky. That's what matters. We took out the Gok carrier before it could do the same to us."

"Don't you think you should see Doctor Bancroft?"

He shrugged. "I have a checkup soon. I'll mention what happened to her then."

Fesky sighed, shaking her head a little. "I can come with you to this meeting, you know. You don't have to go alone."

A wry smile played across Husher's lips. "No thanks, Fesky. I'm not eager to leave the CIC to Kaboh for longer than I already have. I'm worried he'll go looking for another Gok warship, so he can offer them the *Vesta* on a platter. I'm fine, and at a time like this, I want you in the command seat."

The Gok had always been close allies of the Ixa, and Husher didn't want to give voice to his worst fear, even though it was probably on Fesky's mind, too: that the Gok attack might have something to do with the return of the AIs who'd created the Ixa.

"Understood," the Winger said, reaching up to straighten his uniform's lapel using the flat of her thickest talon. "This isn't ironed properly, by the way."

"I'm sure it isn't. With the number of reports I fill out every day, it's a wonder I get a chance to eat."

"You could easily have someone iron it for you."

"A captain should iron his own uniform," he said, turning toward the hatch and punching his access code into the terminal.

"But you clearly aren't doing it properly, human!" Fesky called after him as he strode through the hatch. He didn't turn back, not wanting her to witness the return of his smile.

Husher exited the corridor into a vast desert that stretched from horizon to horizon, dotted with cacti and rocks and not much else. Where the desert would have met the sky, it met the base of snowcapped mountains instead. By all appearances, he stood in the center of an enormous valley.

When he turned to ensure the hatch had closed automatically, he saw that it had—a disembodied metal barrier, stark against the gleaming white of the barren wilderness. An access panel hung in midair beside it. Nodding to himself, Husher turned and continued on his way.

Other than the sand, which actually did exist, the desert was an illusion conjured by his Oculenses, and it wasn't nearly as vast as it seemed. It wasn't anywhere as hot as a desert would be, either, though this section's heating coils were located here, so it was warmer than elsewhere.

The Oculenses had conjured the mountains, too, as well as the lush plain he strode toward. As for the gleaming city straddling that plain...that was mostly real. Mostly. Its name was Cybele.

Not for the first time in the last thirteen years, Husher wondered how things had come to this—how he'd come to have fifty thousand civilians living on his warship.

You know how, he told himself, and that was true. Even so, he still couldn't quite believe it.

In a time with so much talk of cutting the military, the idea of capital starships carrying actual capitals had seemed like the only way to avoid the cuts, even to Husher. They'd represented a way to expand military might that would be palatable even to the new Interstellar Union, who'd been bent on radical downsizing.

Husher himself had been among the most emphatic to make the case: when the tech underlying the micronet's instant communication system had been found to endanger the fabric of the universe, galactic society had needed something to bind it together. And so the new supercarriers would serve more than just a defensive function as they patrolled the galaxy with their vast arsenals. Those same arsenals would also keep safe the cities aboard them, and the cities would in turn allow the giant starships to justify their own expense by turning them into roving economic engines.

The galaxy-wide exchange of news, ideas, and goods that the nomadic cities enabled had singlehandedly saved the military. But the cities' existence also brought intense scrutiny to the actions of those commanding the warships carrying them. When engaging in battle had come to mean endangering thousands of galactic citizens, government oversight had intensified, and the ROEs became paralyzing.

A tiny figure standing in the sand up ahead caught Husher's eye, and he neared it faster than he should have—such was the nature of the illusory desert, which had a way of distorting distance. At first he thought it was a real girl, who'd wandered out here alone. But as he drew closer, he saw that she was just as nonexistent as the desert itself.

Nevertheless, she frowned in his direction, though she remained completely motionless. He stopped for a moment, staring back. "I'm so sorry," he said to her, before moving on. When he glanced back two minutes later, she was gone.

The Oculenses were one of the few technological gifts the Kaithe had been willing to bestow upon the galaxy's other species, and the things had a limited ability to detect and interpret brain waves. It was an attempt at a noninvasive brain-computer interface, and usually it worked like it was supposed to. Other times, it picked up on threads from your subconscious and manifested them before your eyes. That wasn't a pleasant experience, typically.

The Kaithe's technological stinginess wasn't due to a lack of proficiency. During their isolationist days, the diminutive aliens had often been called "the children," but that name had fallen into disuse after their immense physical strength became known. There was also the revelation that they had created humanity millions of years ago, with the intention of using humans as weapons of war. During the eons since, they'd come to regret what they'd done, and now they were staunch pacifists, flatly refusing to contribute any tech that would bolster military capability.

The Kaithe had, however, been perfectly willing to confer the ability to efficiently synthesize atmosphere in space, so that it didn't have to be rocketed up from a planet at great cost. That had been the same advancement that had resulted in thousands of civilians living in the bowels of Vin Husher's warship.

Of course, the citizens of Cybele didn't characterize it quite that way. They referred to this part of the ship as the Womb, and on days they were feeling particularly grandiose, they called it the Womb of Civilization.

The desert sand transitioned smoothly into rolling, green plains overhung by a cloudless, sapphire sky. Like the desert's sand, the grass of the plains was really there, as well as the soil it grew from—poured by the ton over the cold steel of the deck. Considering it existed inside a starship, this compartment was incredibly spacious, but the Oculenses made it look far, far bigger than it actually was. In reality, most of the city's inhabitants occupied living quarters that were quite cramped. At fifty thousand people, Husher considered the city inside his ship to be extremely overpopulated.

He reached the outskirts of Cybele, first passing protein synthesis and hydroponics facilities, where most of the ship's food was produced. That included the food for his crew, which certainly cut down on the number of supply stops he had to make.

This place does have its uses, he admitted.

Next, he passed row after row of cubic residences, all clean and tidy. At least, their Oculens overlays were clean and tidy. Husher knew that underneath those overlays, most of Cybele's structures were drab and covered in dust. Persistent illusions were a great help when it came to ignoring the need for regular cleaning.

Everyone was free to take out their Oculenses, of course, but they rarely did. When someone installed an overlay—whether for their house or their body—everyone's Oculenses forced them to see only that. There wasn't an option to deactivate someone else's overlay, even temporarily. Yes, you could leave your house without your Oculenses in, but that was now considered taboo, and anyway, there was a strong correlation between taking out your Oculenses and depression. That correlation was strongest in cities on capital starships like the *Vesta*, but it was fairly strong on planetary colonies, too.

As a high-ranking military officer, Husher *did* have the rare ability to turn off any overlay, for security reasons. But he barely ever took advantage of that 'privilege,' since he also found it depressing to look at Cybele without its makeup on.

Before long he reached Cybele City Hall; a great dot of a building made up of nested, concentric circles. Curiously, it didn't occupy the city's center, but a spot just off it.

The real center of the city was reserved for Cybele University. According to Husher's Oculenses, the campus' snowy towers reared against the sky; sturdy obelisks streaming bright banners of many hues. The towers kept a watchful eye on all who lived in the city—according to the overlay, anyway. In reality, Husher knew the university was made up of drab buildings, none of which exceeded three stories. Cracks and vines ran up the beige walls in equal measure, and just a few meters over the roof, instead of sky, a gray, metal ceiling loomed.

He entered city hall, passing between identical burgundy plaques proclaiming the building's function. As he made his way toward the council chambers at the center, he was required to provide his ID code at three different checkpoints, despite that everyone on board the *Vesta* knew who he was.

Of course, for all they know, my appearance could be just another overlay. That thought almost made him chuckle. He doubted many citizens of Cybele were inclined to dress themselves up as him.

"Welcome, Captain Husher," Mayor Dylan Chancey said in his usual warm tones from where he sat in his short-walled enclosure. It wasn't immediately obvious Chancey was mayor just by looking at his seat—it resembled every other seat ringing the circular council chamber.

"You know all the councilors, of course," Chancey continued, "but we also have Maeve Aldaine with us, a Sociology undergrad from Cybele University. As a supplement to her studies, she expressed an interest in observing this meeting. I hope you don't mind her being here." The mayor gestured toward the young woman sitting beside him, whose bright red hair hung halfway down her head. She looked around the same age his daughter would have been.

"That's fine," Husher said, nodding toward the young woman before returning his gaze to Chancey. The man never did much with his overlay, other than ensuring it concealed most of his gray hairs. He had a chiseled jaw naturally, as well as piercing eyes so brown they were almost black. Those eyes belied his mostly conciliatory demeanor.

The woman who spoke next, on the other hand, made ample use of her overlay. "We were starting to wonder whether you'd show up, Captain," Penelope Snyder said, leaning toward Husher. Her belly top and silk pants would have put a peacock to shame, and a bright, unnatural blue shone through the black feathered mask she wore at all times. Gleaming waves of midnight hair spilled down her face to frame her perfect complexion.

Penelope Snyder was the president of Cybele University. Underneath her carefully assembled mirage, Husher knew that she carried at least forty pounds more than the overlay suggested, and also that she looked much closer to seventy than twenty. But with the magic of Oculenses, she could continue looking like this until the day she died.

"I had an unusual amount of desk work to complete, today," Husher said as he settled himself into the only empty chair. With that, he met Mayor Chancey's gaze.

The man nodded. "Yes, I expect you did. Today could come to mark either the end of a long peace or a historical anomaly. But let's waste no more time in beginning. Today's meeting won't follow the typical format, since the event that necessitated it certainly wasn't typical. We'll see to our more usual tasks at the next council meeting, so that we can keep Captain Husher away from his duties as briefly as possible."

Husher nodded, folding his hands over his right thigh. "That's appreciated, Mayor Chancey. Though I'm not exactly clear on the necessity for today's meeting."

Chancey looked around at the nine councilors—three humans, four Wingers, a Kaithian, and a Tumbran—before his gaze settled on Snyder. "Would you care to explain our concerns to the captain, Penelope?"

"With pleasure," the university president said, smiling sweetly at Husher. "And I will try to stick to the mayor's prescription for brevity, though as an academic I *do* struggle with that from time to time." The remark brought a round of tittering from the other councilors. "To put it quite simply, Captain, we worry about whether you might be...well, *prejudiced* seems like a harsh word for this particular context. Biased, let's say. We're concerned it's likely you carry an unconscious bias against the Gok."

Husher shook his head, his eyes narrowing slightly as he studied Snyder's face—at least, the digital fantasy she called her face. "I'm not sure I understand," he said. "I took pains to ensure my actions followed the ROEs set out by the Interstellar Union."

"That's true," Snyder said, nodding, her raven feathers gently waving. "Technically."

"Technically?"

The mayor interjected. "What Penelope means to say, Captain, is that while your actions did satisfy the prevailing Rules of Engagement, they satisfied them in letter more than they did in spirit."

"I'm still not following," Husher said, trying not to growl. "If I can be frank, I already feel like the ROEs permitted the Gok warship to maneuver close enough to pose a significant danger to this ship."

"Ridiculous," Snyder said, drawing out the last syllable. "I'm sorry, Captain, but given the firepower you have at your disposal, that carrier was a gnat compared to you. Listen, here's our issue with what you did: you could have easily given the order to *disable* the Gok ship rather than destroy it outright."

"Ms. Snyder, if we're about to go to war with the Gok—"

"But we have absolutely no evidence that a war is actually brewing, Captain. That carrier could have just as easily been acting independently from the Gok government. But thanks to your actions, we don't know. The handful of Gok pilots you took prisoner certainly haven't told us. They may not even be privy to what their captain's objective was."

Husher resisted the urge to shift in his seat. *Did I act irrationally?* He'd given the order to obliterate the Gok warship while coming out of whatever episode he'd suffered. It had seemed like the right call, but now Snyder and the other councilors were causing him to doubt his own judgment.

Don't be an idiot, he told himself. "It's my job to do battle with vessels that attack us," he said at last. "Often, that leads to destroying them. That's the reality of war, and if we're about to start a war with the Gok, then our position will be strengthened with one less carrier to—"

"*Captain,*" Snyder said, her voice climbing in pitch. "I would remind you of our mandate to act as an extension of the Interstellar Union in overseeing, regulating, and deploying the Integrated Galactic Fleet. This is *exactly* why shipboard cities are so often called the Wombs of Civilization. It's our job to keep galactic civilization intact, by innovating and sharing our successes with the rest of the galaxy for implementation everywhere. Despite what you might think, it isn't warfare that we're at the forefront of, here. No, Captain, we're on the forefront of *progress.*"

Husher studied Snyder's face, shaking his head a little. It was hard to know how to respond to her, especially since he truly did think her intentions were good. Snyder seemed to think she was doing well by nonhuman species, who she considered in need of her help.

Besides that, Husher sensed that Snyder was deeply insecure—her elaborate overlay spoke to that. Fighting for causes likely made her feel like a good, worthy person. But in Husher's view, her tactics were hurting more than they was helping.

He sighed. "Why was I called here today?"

The mayor cleared his throat. “We’d like you to undergo Implicit Association and Bias Testing, to investigate whether our fear about your attitude toward the Gok is warranted.” Chancey lowered his voice. “There’s a decent chance it might be, Captain, especially considering the unfortunate loss you suffered in association with the Gok.”

Husher felt his eyes widen. *Suffered in association with...?* The detached, clinical phrasing came nowhere close to describing what Gok had done to his family.

Abruptly, he stood. “I won’t take this test. The suggestion that I’m biased against the Gok is crazy, and besides, the fact you’ve accused *me* of bias, merely for doing my job, will make it harder to fight actual examples of bias when they come up.”

With that, Husher left the council chamber.

CHAPTER 3

Military Applications

Cybele's artificial day was darkening, with the vast compartment's overhead lighting gradually dimming. Husher's Oculenses matched that reality, and as he neared Ochrim's house, stars began appearing in the simulated sky, one by one.

Ochrim hadn't done a lot with his home's overlay, but other than that, there wasn't much to distinguish it from any other house in Cybele. Nothing to indicate that he was a mass murderer, certainly, or that he'd played a major part in shaping both Galactic Wars.

Husher rang the bell, and the Ixan let him in a few seconds later. "Can I supply you with a beverage, Captain?" Ochrim asked as Husher lowered himself into the alien's favorite chair.

"Beer's fine," Husher grunted. *I could certainly use it, after that meeting.*

The alien returned holding two sweating bottles, and Husher accepted his with a nod.

"It always fascinates me to contemplate that humans and Ixa metabolize alcohol at similar rates," Ochrim said, still standing.

"I don't know what you're talking about," Husher said. "I'd drink you under the table before I even started to feel it."

"Of course, Captain."

"Why don't you have a seat?"

"Because I don't expect you visited merely to drink beer."

"I came because your message said you have something for me." Husher tipped the beer's neck toward the couch across the room. "I need to sit for a few minutes."

"Very well." Ochrim settled himself onto the couch.

"I just came from city hall."

"Ah."

Another long sip from his beer, and Husher exhaled, long and slow. "After we won the Second Galactic War, I tried so hard to convince the new government to start developing the tech to search outside the galaxy for your species' creators, so we could deal with them before they dealt with us. But the government wanted nothing to do with it. And here we are."

"What happened at city hall?"

"They want me to take some test that's supposed to find out whether I'm biased against Gok."

The lighter patches around Ochrim's eyes broadened. "Would that happen to be the Implicit Association and Bias Test?"

"Yeah. That's the one."

"Ah. That procedure is riddled with methodological issues. A form of it was determined to be almost completely useless centuries ago, and not much about it has changed."

"Hmm. Well, I refused to take it. I feel like agreeing to it would amount to admitting I could be biased, and I'm insulted by the very suggestion." Refusing to take the test was risky, Husher knew. In the last year alone, a capital starship captain had been removed from duty for refusing to do what her city council had required of her. He took another sip of beer, then he asked, "What are the issues with the test?"

"It's based on your response times, but one of the major problems is that it confuses the novelty response with bias. If you aren't as familiar with other species as you are with your own—which is usually the case, sadly—then the test will almost certainly conclude that you are biased."

"Wonderful," Husher said.

"After you failed it, they would probably have recommend that you undergo Awareness Training, to purge you of your presumed bias. The training's intended to make you aware of your biases, and to help you overcome them. But in reality, Awareness Training has been found to achieve the opposite of its stated intent: studies show it *increases* bias." Shaking his head, Ochrim said, "I have plenty of personal experience that shows bias still exists between the species. The problem is real. But the proposed solutions aren't really solutions."

"Why are they using procedures proven not to work?"

Ochrim shrugged. "I'm sure there are several reasons. For one, these measures are concrete and relatively easy to implement. For a politician who's only thinking about the next election, it's much simpler to have everyone undergo Awareness Training than to implement the type of solution that would bring actual, long-term results."

"Like what?"

"Again, I can only tell you what the research shows. Addressing galactic poverty is one thing that would benefit all species—Gok, Wingers, Tumbra, humans, and even Kaithe. All have beings who are downtrodden. Studies have also demonstrated that a being's level of bias correlates strongly with a lack of exposure to members of other species. By finding a way to increase interaction between the species..."

"Yeah," Husher said before emptying the rest of his beer and placing the empty bottle on an end table. He stood. "I want to see what you've discovered."

Ochrim also stood, though he made no other move. "I have to admit, Captain, that I'm becoming somewhat concerned about our activities."

"Why?"

"Because the farther I progress with my work, the closer we get to tangible military advancements. Those aren't viewed favorably in the current political climate, and I've gotten in significant...trouble...for contributing to them in the past."

Eyeing the Ixan with raised eyebrows, Husher said, "I'm sorry, Ochrim, but are you under the impression that not sharing your findings with me is even an option?"

"I am," Ochrim said holding up claw-tipped fingers to forestall Husher's next remark. "It's an option with consequences, but an option nevertheless. The question is whether the consequences of telling you what I've discovered are likely to outweigh those of withholding my findings."

"Right. Let me refresh you on the logic of your situation, Ochrim: this ship is the only place you'll ever get to live in anything approaching peace. No other captain would even consider letting you step foot on their ship, and as you know from experience, planetary colonies don't want you either."

The alien lowered his gaze. "You're right, of course."

"I'm glad you recognize it. So let's hear no more talk of refraining from sharing your findings with me, hmm?"

"Of course."

"Good answer."

Ochrim's jail sentence for his war crimes had ended just a few months before, and though he and Husher were mostly cordial with each other, their relationship clearly still had a few wrinkles that needed ironing out. The alien might have ended up spending the rest of his life in jail, except that in addition to killing hundreds of thousands of humans, he'd also been the reason humanity had survived the Second Galactic War at all. Ochrim had been the one to finally convince the Kaithe to join the fight.

"Lead on," Husher said.

Ochrim left the living room, passed through the kitchen, and turned left down a short hallway. Husher followed, pausing only to grab another couple beers on his way through.

"Do you ever miss your people, Ochrim?" Husher asked as they made their way through the hall. He idly fingered a picture frame as he passed—it bordered an artistic rendering of some nebula.

"You mean, do I miss the species that almost exterminated yours, Captain? Seems like something of a loaded question."

"It's not."

As they entered a small, rectangular room at the back of the house, Ochrim sighed. "I was always quite different from the rest of the Ixa. Especially my father, and my brother."

"I wasn't asking about your family."

"I miss...I miss being convinced that I knew what was best for the galaxy. Though false, that level of moral clarity was soothing."

"You're still dodging the question, but whatever. By the way," Husher said, pointing at the floor. "This. This is what's best for the galaxy."

"I hope you're right." With that, Ochrim knelt, lifting a cream-colored floor tile to reveal a touch interface. Tapping it made a section of the floor lower and slide out of sight to Husher's left. Below, a dimly lit ladder extended down until it disappeared from sight.

"After you," Husher said, and the Ixan complied, settling his right foot on one of the upper rungs, then lowering himself to the next.

Husher loosened his belt a notch, tucked the beers into it, and began the climb down as well. His joints creaked as he descended.

Before long, Ochrim started wheezing slightly. *He's getting pretty old, even for an Ixan.*

Ochrim's history was nothing if not complicated. During the First Galactic War, he'd given humanity dark tech, seemingly betraying his own species and allowing humans to dominate the galaxy for the next twenty years. Dark tech was enabled by a rare mineral humanity had named Ocharium, after Ochrim, and it had allowed them to create galaxy-spanning wormholes that could be modified to destroy anything they didn't want passing through them—like enemy ordnance, for example.

But the gift of dark tech had been part of a plan formulated by a far-seeing, superintelligent AI named Baxa bent on dominating the Milky Way. Baxa had created the Ixa, and he'd been around for several millennia, but he'd also spent some time as a biological Ixan before uploading his consciousness once again. During his time as a flesh-and-blood Ixan, he'd sired two sons: Teth and Ochrim.

Humanity came to completely rely on dark tech, leaving them totally vulnerable when Ochrim used a master control of his own design to subvert each ship's wormhole generator so that any wormhole it produced would vaporize all organic matter that passed through it. In one fell swoop, the United Human Fleet had lost almost half its crews—hundreds of thousands of service members killed within a few seconds of each other.

If Ochrim was to be believed, his father had convinced him that humanity's downfall was the best of two horrible options: the other involved humans eventually destroying the universe itself. Except, in addition to humankind's destruction, the future that Baxa envisioned also included enslaving every living Ixan. When he'd learned that, Ochrim had concluded that his father wasn't trustworthy after all, and he switched to humanity's side, abandoning his father as well as his brother, Teth, who'd commanded the Ixan fleet.

Whatever the case, Ochrim was clearly a genius, which was why Husher was willing to have him aboard the *Vesta*. The way he saw it, they needed Ochrim, to help prepare for what was coming. The AI that had created and manipulated the Ixa had been just one of many such AIs, and though the Ixa had died along with it—all but Ochrim—Husher was sure superintelligence would come to finish the job that Baxa had started. He'd long considered it his duty to do whatever he could to prepare the galaxy for the AIs' return. Since the Interstellar Union seemed determined to stunt military advancements, it fell to him to do whatever he could to foster them.

They reached the bottom of the ladder, which touched down in the middle of Ochrim's hidden lab. The ladder was the only way to enter or leave this room—for Ochrim, anyway. One of the walls could be opened, for the purposes of bringing in or removing equipment, but Husher didn't allow Ochrim control over that.

Husher had had this lab constructed during a planetary stopover, before Ochrim had even arrived aboard the *Vesta*. He'd hired outside contractors to do it, to keep it a secret from those who lived and worked on the supercarrier.

Once he'd arrived, the Ixan already had an experiment ready to go, but it took Husher a while to procure the necessary equipment for him. He'd managed it, though, calling in a favor owed him by a Cybele University physics researcher, and he'd obtained the last piece the Ixan needed just three weeks ago.

Ochrim walked to a sturdy black tabletop and leaned back against it, studying Husher with weary eyes under the dim halogens. The Ixan's age showed in the whitening of his scales around those eyes, as well as wherever they stretched across the many bone protrusions typical of Ixan faces. "You didn't ask me much about the experiment I intended to conduct."

"I asked whether it would blow up my ship. That seemed like the most important question to me." Husher passed the Ixan one of the beers from behind his belt, and Ochrim accepted it gingerly.

"Fair enough, I suppose," the alien said, opening his beverage. "Either way, to understand my findings, I'll need to run through the experiment with you first."

"Try to keep it brief. My next watch starts soon, and Fesky will complain if I'm late to the CIC."

"Very well. The experiment was a success, and also a historic achievement, I might add."

"Great. But I'm interested in what it'll do for my combat effectiveness, not what it would do for your stature as a scientist if you weren't excommunicated from the scientific community."

"We're getting to that, Captain. The experiment involved firing a photon at a polarization filter, calibrated so that there was a fifty-fifty chance it would pass through. I also programmed a com to switch on a microwave emitter only if it detected the photon passing through the filter. Under the many-worlds interpretation of quantum physics, you see, two distinct parallel universes form after every quantum mechanical measurement, and so according to the theory, the moment the com detected whether the photon passed through, there were two coms, two Ochrims, and two starship laboratories."

"Two universes," Husher said.

"Yes. There's a lot of evidence to support the many-worlds theory, but none to prove it. Until now. I've successfully confirmed the many-worlds interpretation, Captain, by overcoming the quantum decoherence that keeps the universes separate."

"How?"

"Before even firing the photon, I isolated part of the experimental apparatus so that it did not immediately decohere along with the rest of the system. The isolated part was comprised of an ion inside a Penning trap, which was excited using the microwave emitter only if the photon was detected passing through the filter. Since, under these conditions, the isolated ion takes seconds longer to decohere, there's enough time to change its state using the emitter. Once it's excited by an Ochrim in one of the universes—Ochrim One, let's say—Ochrim Two measures the ion and finds that it's excited, even though in his universe, the microwave emitter was never turned on."

"Okay, so Ochrim Two knows about Ochrim One, but doesn't that leave Ochrim One still in the dark?"

"It would, if I hadn't performed the experiment many times. And in roughly half of the trials, it was I that detected the existence of my parallel twin." A thin smile stretched across Ochrim's face—a rare occurrence, these days.

"That's incredible, Ochrim. But I'm not sensing military applications."

"We're still at the very beginning. While monumental, I did not spend two decades in prison planning only to detect parallel universes."

"Out with it, then. What's your end goal?"

"Captain, I believe it may be possible to manipulate the quantum decoherence process such that we will not only communicate with parallel universes, but travel to them as well. Can you see the military applications in *that?*"

A thrill forked through Husher's stomach. "I think I'm starting to, Ochrim. Tell me what you need next."

CHAPTER 4

PTSD

It felt good to be back in the *Vesta*'s crew corridor after spending so much time in Cybele recently. In many ways, Husher's supercarrier resembled the *Providence*, which she'd been modeled after. He'd served on the *Providence*, under Captain Keyes, and he'd first met Fesky there, too.

Like Keyes's ship, the *Vesta*'s crew corridors were just wide enough to allow for the efficient flow of traffic, and no wider. Gray, white, and black dominated the decor, such as it was—ornamentation was sparse. Husher liked it that way, and so had Keyes. He wondered for a moment what his old captain might have said about civilian cities on warships.

Three hours before his next watch, a regular checkup brought him to the office of the ship's doctor, Lindsay Bancroft.

"Mostly everything looks good," she said, staring at a blank wall where her Oculenses were no doubt displaying the results from the tests she'd performed. A lot of people kept at least one wall clear in their office, so that they didn't have to stare into space in order to view whatever their Oculenses showed them.

Some did do the "staring into space" thing, but many found that awkward.

"Mostly everything?" Husher said.

"Well, your blood pressure's high, which is unusual if you've been following the diet I recommended to you a couple months ago. I know you spend time in the gym regularly, so I'm sure lack of exercise isn't the cause."

She peered at him, as though expecting him to volunteer some revelation. Returning her stare somewhat uncomfortably, he blinked, wishing he could come up with something funny to say. He struggled with that, lately.

"How's your mental health, Captain Husher?"

"My...mental health? It's, well—"

"I heard about the episode during the Gok engagement. Reports say you entered some sort of trance."

He squinted. "Who told you that?"

"Scuttlebutt. Surely you're familiar with how fast word travels, after serving aboard starships for so long."

"It was Fesky, wasn't it? She's constantly fussing over me."

"How's your sleep, Captain?" Doctor Bancroft asked, and he didn't miss the way she answered his question with one of her own.

It was definitely Fesky. "I'm sleeping all right, I guess."

"You look tired, to me. There are dark patches under your eyes. Have you been having more nightmares?"

He sighed. "They've been getting more vivid. More intense."

"They've been robbing your sleep."

He nodded.

"The episode in the CIC...was that experience similar to your nightmares?"

"Yes."

"And have you been feeling anxious?"

"Yeah. That's pretty common since...since what happened. Lately, though, my temper's pretty out of control, too." Husher cleared his throat. "If you have any ideas for what I might do about any of this, I'd be grateful, Doctor. I think it's affecting my ability to do my job, and I can't have that."

Bancroft's mouth quirked to one side. "I think the first step is to start being a little more forgiving with yourself. Losing your daughter was devastating enough, but the way you lost her...honestly, I'm amazed that you've functioned as well as you have for this long."

Husher pressed his lips together, trying not to focus on the little knot of tension that, years ago, had taken up permanent residence at the base of his throat.

His memory of losing Iris was crisp and clear enough that it might have happened an hour ago, instead of seventeen years. Sera, his wife at the time, had been at some charity event—the specific charity was one of the few details that had faded over the years—and she'd hired a babysitter to be with their three-year-old.

As luck had it, Husher had been getting back from a months-long deployment that very night, but he wasn't due to get back until eleven. Hence, the babysitter.

Husher knew how it had killed Sera to have to leave Iris with a sitter, and she'd rarely ever done it. More than once, he'd accused her of being a helicopter parent—jokingly, but only half-jokingly. His ex-wife hadn't wanted to expose their daughter to even the lowest levels of danger. Sera had baby-proofed their house months before she gave birth, and at three, Iris's play dates with other kids her age were closely monitored by her mother, who didn't get in much socializing with the other mothers.

Husher had made fun of her for that, but she'd been right, damn him. About all of it. Because as his self-driving taxi had pulled in front of his home that night, a precision-targeted kinetic orbital strike hit his house, and he'd watched in horror as an inferno consumed the structure he'd been seconds from entering.

Husher had been alone in the taxi, and he flung the door open, rushing to the front lawn before sinking to his knees, feeling thoroughly helpless. Though he knew both his daughter and her babysitter were both already dead, he took out his com and dialed the police.

It was no use. Robot-assisted firefighters efficiently extinguished the blaze thirty minutes later, but the house was obliterated, leaving no trace of either Iris or Candace, the sitter.

A couple hours later, authorities caught a Gok Slag attempting to sneak out of the Petrichor System using stealth systems that were barely functional copies of Winger tech. When they found the type of tungsten rods used in kinetic orbital strikes—strictly illegal under galactic law since the First Galactic War—they knew they had their culprit.

Husher's marriage with Sera Caine had disintegrated rapidly in the months that followed. She never said it, but Husher was convinced that a big part of her blamed him for their daughter's death. He'd been responsible for killing tens of thousands of Gok during the vicious conflict that had come hard on the heels of the Second Galactic War, and the attack on his house was a pretty clear act of vengeance.

Husher didn't disagree with Sera's thinking. He blamed himself, too.

"Captain," Doctor Bancroft said, yanking him back to the present, "it's my assessment that you've been suffering from undiagnosed PTSD in the years since your daughter's death, and lately it's come to the fore in a major way. There are a number of reasons that might be—for example, the fact that as we age, short-term memory begins to decline, often rendering longer-term memories more vivid and real. I strongly recommend we explore treatment options immediately."

Nodding, Husher said, "Okay. What are our options?"

"There are two dominant treatments in the current literature. Drugs represent one option—SSRIs, specifically. Antidepressants and the like, which can also be quite effective in treating anxiety."

"What's the other option?"

"Prolonged Exposure Therapy, using virtual reality. Essentially, it involves gradual, increasing exposure to stimuli similar to that which triggered the disorder in the first place."

"I'd rather not risk the drugs. I'm worried they'd impair my ability to do my job even more than the nightmares already are."

That brought a slight shrug from Bancroft. "The only real way to determine that would be to try them out."

"I can't afford to risk it, Doctor. Not with a possible conflict with the Gok brewing. Let's try the exposure therapy."

"Very well," Bancroft said, leaning sideways to tap a note into a datapad. "I'll schedule your first session for two days' time."

CHAPTER 5

Anything Anomalous

"Winterton," Husher said, and the sensor operator twisted in his seat to face him. "You've been keeping an eye on the readouts from our active sensor sweeps?"

"Yes, sir," he said, turning from his study of the display at the front of the CIC.

"Anything to report?"

"Negative, Captain."

"I want to be notified the moment you see anything anomalous. I don't care how mundane you think it might be, if it catches your attention, I'm to be notified immediately, even if I'm not in the CIC at the time. Make a note for your second- and third-watch counterparts to do the same."

"I will, sir."

Husher nodded, drumming his fingers on the command seat's armrest, though he quickly stopped himself. *I shouldn't make my boredom so evident to the crew. Next, they'll all be fidgeting.*

When the Gok carrier had attacked the *Vesta*, the supercarrier had been fresh from orbit over Zakros, where she'd been parked for a week. Had his ship not been waylaid, Husher would have ordered her on to the Caprice System, the next stop along their patrol route. There, they would have orbited the system's three colonies for a week each, doing exactly as they'd done over Zakros.

Instead, he ordered a return to her previous orbit. If a second threat reared its head, Zakros' orbital defense platforms should help him make quick work of it. In the meantime, he ordered the Gok prisoners left over from the battle transferred to a planetside prison.

In total, the peacetime patrols fielded by the Integrated Galactic Fleet consisted of eight capital starships and their accompanying battle groups. But since the advent of cities aboard those capital starships, the purpose of patrol was no longer limited to defense. Instead, the rounds they made throughout the galaxy were viewed as an important engine for economic growth and stability.

To a well-established colony of billions, the appearance of a new city in their skies represented a modest yet valuable source of trade in both services and commodities from other systems. An employer unable to fill a position from among planetary populations might hire a graduate of a starship-based university, or people seeking work might rent a room or apartment aboard a starship city, in hopes of finding a job at one of the stops, if not in the city itself.

To a more recently established planetary colony, however, a visit from a capital starship represented significant economic stimulus.

Life aboard a starship city was the new life of glamor in the galactic consciousness, though while the citizens tended to be wealthier than most, Husher wasn't sure he completely agreed. That said, it wasn't his job to agree. It was his job to carry Cybele around the galaxy, which often made him feel more like a glorified cruise ship captain than the commander of the biggest warship the galaxy had ever known. Such was the screwed-up situation that had developed since the Gok Wars.

What worries me is that I'm pretty sure it's still developing.

Whatever the case, their stops in the Caprice System would now be delayed while he awaited orders from IGF Command. Communication between star systems occurred exclusively via com drone. Once, humanity had had instantaneous communication via the dark tech-enabled micronet, but dark tech had been almost completely discontinued after the discovery that its use was gradually tearing apart the fabric of the universe.

That had been a near thing. Majorana fermion-infused starship decks were the one case where dark tech was still used, since no one had discovered a better way to simulate gravity other than to inject everyone and everything with Ocharium nanites, which interacted with the fermion matrix to provide an experience virtually identical to one G. However many Gs one wanted, actually. It depended on the number of nanites injected.

Luckily, after cutting out every other instance of dark tech, use of the Majorana fermions in starship decks had been found to have a negligible effect on the universe, and so they alone had been kept.

The CIC hatch, located to the left of the main display, opened to admit Fesky. She came to attention just inside, saluting.

"At ease, Commander. May I ask why you're here? Your watch doesn't start for another four hours."

"I wanted to request a private audience with you, Captain."

"You couldn't request it over com?"

"I was nearby, so I decided to come here myself."

Slowly, Husher nodded. It occurred to him that this was likely Fesky's way of letting him know that whatever she wanted, it was important. He might have brushed off a com message, but for her to show up in person...

Of course, she could have let me know over com why it's so important that we speak. Unless she was worried about their conversations being monitored, or reviewed at some point in the future. That was always a possibility, with the increasing levels of oversight from the Interstellar Union.

Husher rose from the command seat. "Kaboh, you have the CIC."

"Aye, Captain," the Kaithian said.

"My office?" Husher asked Fesky as the CIC hatch hissed closed behind them.

She nodded, saying nothing, and they walked in silence to his office, located a short distance away.

The chamber was sparsely decorated, though it was nowhere near as Spartan as Captain Keyes's had been, back on the *Provi-*

dence. Two pairs of identically sized photos faced each other from the walls on either end of Husher's desk. A photo of the *Vesta*, captured in all her glory on the day of her christening, hung opposite one of the *Providence*, taken from a research station after the supercarrier's first successful mission in the Bastion Sector. It showed the *Providence* in orbit, with Thessaly's moon behind her, and Thessaly below.

Husher hadn't been serving on the *Providence* the day that photo was taken, but the image was the best he could find. Hanging beside it was a photo of the old supercarrier's entire Air Group, standing in front of a row of Condor starfighters. The image featured both Husher and Fesky prominently. *I miss my Condor.* There were a few of the old fighters sitting by themselves down on Hangar Bay Theta, and a couple times, when Husher had needed time alone to think, he'd gone down there to tinker with them, knowing he wasn't likely to run into anyone in the largely unused hangar bay.

Next to the *Vesta*'s likeness hung a photo of Husher and Captain Keyes standing beside each other in full uniform, in front of the Human Commonwealth flag. That photo had been taken in orbit over Mars during a lull that had preceded all-out war with the Ixa.

Two captains connected across time, Husher thought as he glimpsed that photo.

"You miss him," Fesky said as she settled into the chair in front of his desk without having to be asked. Their friendship was such that they dropped military formalities whenever they were in private.

"Don't you?"

"With all my heart."

Husher's shoulders slumped a little. "He was a better captain then I'll ever be, Madcap," he said, using Fesky's callsign from their Condor-piloting days. "He never would have let things get this bad."

"You've had to deal with pressures he never did."

"I don't know about that, exactly."

Fesky clacked her beak, and her head twitched, as it often did. Every Winger looked distinct, but to Husher, Fesky had always most resembled a falcon. Her mood could be read pretty accurately by the stiffness of her feathers, and right now, he could see that she was agitated. "One man alone can't hold back the tides of change, Husher."

"Why did you ask to speak with me? I can tell something's bothering you."

It took a few seconds for Fesky to answer. "There's been a group of protesters hanging out in the desert near the hatch," she said. "They've been waiting for crewmembers to pass by on their way to the city. When one appears, they start chanting, and sometimes they even follow them to the city, drawing attention to them. One petty officer told me she was so embarrassed that she doesn't plan to go back anytime soon."

Husher could feel his cheeks heating up, and he remembered his discussion with Doctor Bancroft, about his temper. *I have to make it to our first treatment session without blowing up.* "What's their problem?" he ground out, managing to keep his voice level.

"Apparently, they see your refusal to take the Implicit Association and Bias Test as a symptom of problematic attitudes among the crew. They want you and every human crewmember to undergo Awareness Training."

Husher rose from his chair, and so did Fesky. He walked around the desk to join her.

"I'm going right now to talk some sense into them."

"All right. I'll have Major Gamble put together a marine escort."

"No, you will not. I'm not going to start towing around bodyguards on my own ship."

"Husher..."

"It's not open to debate, Fesky."

"Well, you should at least polish your boots before you go."

Glancing down at them, he said, "They're fine," and he marched out into the corridor.

CHAPTER 6

Owning the Floor

Husher emerged from the hatch to find a couple dozen demonstrators with digital protest signs, which they'd incorporated into their Oculens overlays. *The modern protester doesn't need to bother with making a physical sign, or with holding it up.*

When he first emerged, the demonstrators weren't doing a lot of demonstrating, but they soon noticed him. They rallied around him in a semicircle and instructed their Oculenses to waggle their signs at him vigorously.

When they opened their mouths, no doubt to deploy a chant of some sort, Husher spoke up in an attempt to initiate a dialog instead.

"What are you trying to accomplish by yelling at off-duty service members?" he asked, struggling to keep his tone neutral.

"We're making your walk into town as uncomfortable as your actions make members of marginalized groups," said one of the protesters, who he recognized as Maeve Aldaine, the undergrad who'd sat in on the city council meeting.

Looking around at the group of protesters, Husher saw they were mostly human, though there were a handful of Wingers as well as two Tumbra. He'd spent enough time around both alien species to know these were almost certainly as young as Aldaine and the other humans—so, probably all Cybele U students.

"What actions are you referring to?" Husher said, amazed at his ability to keep his tone mostly level. *That session with Doctor Bancroft can't come fast enough.*

"You refused to take the Implicit Association and Bias Test, which only told us what we already knew: you don't take this seriously *at all.*"

Husher inhaled slowly. "What does that have to do with my crew?"

Aldaine planted both hands on her hips, her sign floating freely above her head. "It's not hard to tell your attitude is an indication of deep-rooted problems that run through your entire crew, which is made up of mostly humans. I can only imagine the psychological toll your attitudes must have on the Wingers, Gok, and Kaithe among the crew of the *Vesta.*"

"Wait," Husher said. "I thought this had to do with just the Gok. Why are you bringing other species into it?" *And why didn't you mention the Tumbra?* Husher had over three hundred Tumbran crewmembers, mostly in Engineering and Coms.

"Because it's clear that your treatment of the Gok isn't an isolated incident. The fact—"

"My *treatment?*" Husher said, his voice rising sharply. "We've been at war with the Gok, multiple times. It was my job to fight them!" Again, he fought to calm himself. "Ms. Aldaine, I'm not denying that we have a problem when it comes to—"

"*Excuse me!*" Aldaine yelled, marching forward until she stood three feet from him. "You've done enough talking. Now's your time to listen."

Brows drawing down, Husher studied the young woman, marveling. "Ms. Aldaine, do I need to remind you that I *captain* this—"

"Humanity is finished owning the floor!" Aldaine said, voice ringing over the crowd as she spread her arms and walked backward to join her fellow protesters in a line. They linked with each other, arm in arm. "Now's your time to *shut up* and *listen* to marginalized species and their allies. It's past time. Your hiring practices say you favor humanity over the other species, and your other actions scream it."

Husher opened his mouth to respond to that, but the protesters began a chant they'd clearly rehearsed, led by Aldaine:

"Say it loud, say it clear, humans are done talking here! Say it loud, say it clear, time for them to open ears!"

A strange mixture of bafflement, anger, and anxiety made its home in Husher's chest. His hands balled into fists as he waited for them to stop shouting, but it soon became clear they had no intention of stopping, until either he left or they keeled over from exhaustion.

He didn't have time to wait for that to happen. He spun on his heels, slammed the hatch's access panel with his palm, and strode through, double-checking to make sure it was secured before marching deeper into the crew section.

Back in his cabin, he leaned against the mirror, gripping both sides of it and studying his own lined face. *Am I biased against the Gok? Did I use what happened to me to justify destroying that ship?* He didn't think so—he'd often reminded himself that the Gok who'd killed his daughter weren't representative of their entire species—but now he was filled with doubt.

He'd always cared deeply about doing the right thing according to his principles. According to what was best for the galaxy. Always, he'd believed that meant preparing for war.

But lately, he felt like he was losing focus.

CHAPTER 7

The Quince Engagement

For most messages, Husher had configured his com not to vibrate or make a sound, but for messages designated "Priority," it beeped harshly until he checked it.

That happened now, three hours into a sleep that, so far, had been blissfully dreamless.

The message was from Ensign Fields, the Coms officer currently on watch in the CIC. "Captain, I've just received word that Admiral Connor Iver has transitioned into the system through the Feverfew-Caprice darkgate and intends to meet with you aboard the *Vesta*. Accounting for transmission lag, we can expect his arrival within four hours."

The moment Husher finished the message, he dashed across the chamber and into the cramped head, to splash cold water on his face. Pausing with fingertips on his upper cheeks, he studied the lined face that peered back at him from the glass.

Readying to receive an admiral would require no small amount of preparations, and before anything else, he used his com to send orders to several different departments. Then, while his ship was no doubt jumping to an even livelier state than usual in the corridors and chambers outside, he opened his wardrobe, swept aside the clothing hanging there, and folded down the ironing board from the back, extending its single leg to stabilize it against the deck.

Fesky's usual admonishments about his uniform rang in his ears as he carefully creased his pants. "I'll show her," he muttered as he dug his black polish out from the back of the wardrobe and gave the boots some elbow grease.

Forty minutes later, he was finished, admiring himself in the mirror. "Still got it," he told himself, straightening his midnight overcoat. Although, it shocked him, sometimes—to see the lightly creased face surrounding his bright blue eyes. His hair was now iron-gray, a shade that almost matched the *Vesta*'s hull.

As he stepped into the corridor outside, his XO happened to be rushing by, feathers rustling as she stalked forward on talons that clicked against the gray metal of the deck. When she saw him, she turned, eyeing him from top to bottom.

"Notice anything?" he said, unable to suppress the grin that curled the corners of his mouth.

"I do," Fesky said. "You forgot your medals."

His smile drooped.

"This is an admiral of the fleet you're meeting with, Captain, not your dogsitter's second cousin."

"I don't own a dog," Husher grumbled as he opened the hatch to his quarters and went in to pin the medals above his overcoat's left breast pocket.

When he reemerged, Fesky was still waiting, and they strode down the corridor together, toward whatever last-minute business awaited them before the admiral's arrival.

"I haven't spoken with you since you confronted the protesters," the Winger said. "How did it go?"

"Not well."

"I gathered that. Based on the growing agitation on the narrownet, anyway."

Husher tried not to sigh. They marched on toward the conference room, to ensure everything was ready for the admiral's arrival.

To Husher, it seemed like no time at all before his officers were gathered around the conference table, all seated and chatting softly amongst themselves while they waited for Iver.

The hatch hissed open, and everyone in the room rose to attention, turning toward the entering admiral and saluting as one.

"At ease," Iver said after returning their salute for a couple of seconds, and everyone sat. The admiral joined them, sitting at the end of the table opposite Husher. Iver wore a thick mustache that, at his age, had either been dyed black or made to look that way using an overlay. Given the general tendency among military personnel to avoid overlay use to alter their own appearances, Husher would have put his money on dye.

"Welcome to the *Vesta,* Admiral Iver," Husher said. "It's an honor to have you with us."

"It's an honor to be here," Iver said, his tone almost raucous in its forced joviality, "though I wish more pleasant circumstances had led to my arrival."

"I'm guessing you're referring to the engagement with the Gok carrier that we underwent in this system several days ago."

With a curt nod, Iver said, "That, as well as an engagement that happened around the same time, in the Quince System. The galactic government received word of both engagements almost simultaneously. The Quince engagement involved the *Ceres,* and her crew faced a much bigger Gok force."

"Was the *Ceres'* battle group accompanying her?" Husher asked, wincing. The *Ceres* was another supercarrier, and one of the eight capital starships that formed the backbone of the Integrated Galactic Fleet.

"It was, though the Gok still managed to...well, I'll show you. Orient yourselves, everyone—I'm about to take over your Oculenses. Anyone have any particular objections to that?" No one spoke. "Very well."

Suddenly, Husher found himself in space, perched on the starboard hull of the *Ceres.* He surmised that he was about to witness the Quince System engagement from the perspective of one of the supercarrier's visual sensors.

Indeed, light flickered twice in the star-speckled dark, followed by fire that flowered then shriveled just as quickly, choked by the vacuum of space.

"That was the *Constellation* getting blown apart," came Iver's voice, cutting through the void. "A good ship. It was a destroyer named for the one that the Tumbran, Piper, boarded at the end of the Second Galactic War. The one he used to trigger the wormhole collapse that wiped out the Ixan fleet."

Husher shook his head, which caused his view of the battle to jostle back and forth. Before this, it had been seventeen years since the last time they'd lost a vessel in combat. *Seventeen years of peace. More than I would have expected, but not nearly enough. It's never enough.*

The *Agron* was next to go, followed by the *Pronax*. After that, the Gok battle group assembled themselves into a loose formation, swooping toward the *Ceres* and concentrating their fire on her starboard hull.

Husher winced away from the missiles that screamed through the blackness toward him, and when they battered the high-yield steel hull all around him, he yelled, his heart hammering in his chest.

Abruptly, the Gok vanished, and so did the stars, and the explosions. Husher was no longer a visual sensor on the hull of a supercarrier, but Vin Husher, who captained a supercarrier of his own.

Everyone sitting around the conference table was staring at him, with expressions ranging from confusion to concern.

For his part, Admiral Iver looked slightly annoyed. "Captain?" he said, his head tilted to one side. "Are you all right?"

"I...sorry. Yes, I'm fine."

"I can hardly think this is your first time viewing a panoramic recording of a military engagement."

"It's not. It's far from my first, Admiral."

"Were you playing some sort of joke on us, then?" Iver's eyed narrowed.

"No, sir. I'm honestly not sure what came over me."

"Are we clear to proceed, then?"

"Yes, sir."

Iver resumed the recording, during which the *Ceres* took significant damage before bringing its considerable arsenal to bear in wiping out four Gok ships, causing the remaining three to scatter, which was very unusual for them. Husher had often wondered whether the Gok even considered retreat an option, and yet here they were, fleeing before the *Ceres*' might.

He managed to get through the rest of the footage without any more visible or audible reactions, though blood rushed through his ears, and sweat oozed from his pores, dampening his uniform in several places.

Isn't this exactly the sort of thing Doctor Bancroft plans to expose me to? Probably it was, but instead of a controlled therapy environment, he'd been thrust into it without warning.

Of course, as the admiral had pointed out, such viewings were standard, and they'd never given Husher much trouble before. That said, recording technology had improved by leaps and bounds since the last military engagements had been documented, and maybe that explained the difference in his reaction.

"Galactic Congress is extremely reluctant to issue a declaration of war," Iver said once the recording had ended, his gaze lingering on Husher. "If it can be avoided, they'd rather not throw away a peace that's lasted almost two decades, and I can't say I disagree with them." Iver coughed into a balled hand, then continued. "You're currently the capital starship closest to the Gok seat of power, and records show that you have in Cybele at least two galaxy-class diplomats—the Kaithian, Shobi, as well as the Winger named Bryson. Can you verify their presence, Captain?"

"I'll see that it's verified within the hour."

"Very good. Your mission is to transport those diplomats to the Gok home system, to see whether they can't uncover what's causing the Gok to become so agitated. Their primary objective will be to renew the peace we've enjoyed since the Gok Wars, but if they're able to entice the Gok to join the Interstellar Union, they'll have considerable latitude to do so. The chances for accomplishing that are projected to be higher than they have been—the Gok government has been getting better on respecting sentient rights, lately, and their government seems to grow less regressive with every passing year. Is everything I just said understood?"

Husher joined the chorus of "Yes, Admiral," but he had to stop himself from shaking his head. *The Gok attack us twice, and the Union's still trying to stay friends.*

In one sense, he supposed it was a noble sentiment—they had lived in peace for this long, so maybe regaining that peace was possible. But it did make him worry about what the Union's reaction would be when the Ixa's creators returned. There would be no chance of quarter, then.

CHAPTER 8

Feeling Unsafe

Husher crouched inside a sniper hide they'd fashioned from the fourth story of an apartment building on the outskirts of Larissa, the capital of Thessaly. He hadn't gone to sniper school, so it was his job to watch the sniper's back by looking through the other windows for insurgents and keeping an eye on the apartment door.

The hide his task unit's best sniper, Rogers, had put together consisted of two mattresses stacked on top of a folded-out futon, atop which Rogers lay, eyeing the streets below through his scope. Even here in what the locals termed Larissa's outskirts, the buildings below were so tightly packed that it wasn't possible to cover the streets for more than a few blocks.

"I have a military-aged male who appears to be moving tactically toward our location," Rogers whispered into his com. Husher couldn't hear what the reply was, but the sniper didn't fire, so he guessed that it wasn't a go-ahead.

An RPG hit the building they were in, obliterating the wall between two windows and sending shrapnel tearing through the apartment. Miraculously, Husher was untouched, but through the smoke and debris he could see that Rogers had been tossed against the wall and looked to be unconscious.

Keeping an eye on the outside, he scrambled across the plaster-littered apartment toward Rogers, shaking the sniper once he reached him. Blood trickled down the side of Rogers's face, and he didn't react. Husher heaved the slight man up, slinging him over his shoulder, and started toward the apartment door.

Another RPG hit—this one made its way to an interior wall, right next to Husher. The explosion threw him to the floor, and he dropped Rogers. Looking down at himself, he saw that his own leg was missing below the knee. He screamed.

The Larissa apartment dissolved to reveal Doctor Bancroft's office, as well as Bancroft herself, who wore an expression of professional concern.

"Here," she said, retrieving an unopened bottle of water from the mini-fridge built into her desk.

"Thanks."

"It'll get better as you're exposed to more stimuli."

"Yeah." He picked up a cloth sitting on a metal table nearby and used it to wipe his brow. "Although, that didn't feel much better than yesterday."

Bancroft's eyebrows climbed toward her hairline. "Yesterday?"

Nodding, Husher explained the type of footage Admiral Iver had shown them, without getting into the particulars of the engagement.

"So you started your therapy without me," Bancroft said with a prim smile, and Husher forced a chuckle, figuring it was her idea of a joke.

"I guess so," he said. "It's a bit strange to me, though. Both simulations that triggered this reaction were of military engagements. But the day my daughter died...that wasn't an engagement."

"Well..." Bancroft said softly, "It *was* a military action, arguably. And the basic stimuli—explosions, fire—are the same."

"I guess you're right."

"Are you okay to continue pursuing this line of treatment, or would you prefer to try the SSRIs?"

"Let's keep trying this." *It's way too early to switch now,* he reflected. *Especially given the effects the drugs might have on my performance.* "Next simulation?"

"Captain, before we continue, there's a concern I wanted to raise with you."

"Oh?"

"I'm not sure how else to say this. I've gotten...reports from some crewmembers who say they're feeling unsafe aboard the *Vesta.*"

"Unsafe," Husher said, and sniffed. "I mean, this is a military vessel, but for now we've been sent on a diplomatic mission. Yes, we'll be negotiating with a power that attacked us twice in the last week, but I'd argue that this is around as safe as it gets aboard a warship."

"Their feelings don't have anything to do with a particular mission."

"I see," Husher said, pausing to study Bancroft's face. 'I'm afraid I'm at a loss, Doctor. What's causing them to feel unsafe?"

"They say it's the general atmosphere in the crew section of the *Vesta*. Your refusal to undergo Awareness Training, and the fact that most of your human crew hasn't undergone the training either...it speaks to attitudes that aren't perceived as particularly friendly by members of nonhuman species."

This time, Husher paused for much longer. At last, he said, "How many of these reports have you received?"

"I'm afraid it would be a breach of doctor-patient confidentiality to tell you. The only circumstance under which I'd be required to break that confidentiality would be if a crewmember's diagnosis rendered them unfit for service, and that isn't the case, here."

Nodding slowly, Husher said, "I promise you that I'll give careful thought to what you've told me, but I think you should know that Awareness Training has been proven to only worsen—"

His com beeped stridently from his hip, and he snatched it from his holster to read the displayed message.

It was from Mayor Chancey: "Captain Husher, your presence is requested in the main city council chamber at once. Cheers, Dylan Chancey."

Husher's fingers tightened around the device, and he forced himself to relax his grip. His eyes met Bancroft's. "I'm sorry, Doctor, it looks like I'll have to cut our session short."

CHAPTER 9

Scapegoated for Wrongs

"We're here, Captain Husher," Chancey said as the last councilor filed in, "to require every human in your crew to undergo Awareness Training as soon as reasonably possible. That includes you."

Husher narrowed his eyes. "Wait, is the council just pasting protester demands straight into the agenda, now?"

"Those *demands* arise from legitimate concerns," Penelope Snyder said from across the room. As usual, she wore an ostentatious garment that exposed a midriff toned by digital artifice. "The fact that you refused to take the Implicit Association and Bias Test only tells us what we already knew: you are prejudiced against the Gok, Captain. We would have prescribed Awareness Training for *you* regardless, but we agree with the demonstrators that extending the training to your human crew is the logical next step. As you've been the one in command of the *Vesta* since it was first commissioned, I find patently absurd the suggestion that the environment in her crew section *isn't* toxic."

"And I find it toxic that you're singling out the human part of my crew for this training," Husher answered, his words clipped. "The implication seems to be that only human beings can possibly be biased against other species, which in itself is an incredibly biased assumption."

"You shouldn't draw conclusions based on how things seem to *you,*" Snyder said. "Very little will become clear if we rely on *your* perceptions. Your accusation that we're biased only further demonstrates how misguided and ignorant you are, Captain Husher. With almost every word you say, you deny the experiences of oppressed beings like the Wingers, the Gok, and the Kaithe."

"What about the Tumbra?"

"Excuse me?"

"I've noticed something about these conversations surrounding bias. The Tumbra are almost always left out. Why?"

That seemed to give Snyder pause for a moment, and she exchanged glances with the mayor, who cleared his throat. "I think we can all agree the Tumbra have done quite well for themselves, haven't they?" he said, offering Husher an ingratiating smile.

As he was doing so often lately, Husher squinted in confusion. "Fascinating," he muttered.

With that, Snyder managed to get back on track. "As I was saying, Captain, to suggest that a species such as the Wingers should have to undergo Awareness Training is so wrongheaded I'm not sure where to start. It denies the advantages humans have enjoyed, stemming mostly from their twenty-year domination of the galaxy. Do you not remember the savage attacks the United Human Fleet inflicted on the Wingers, killing tens of thousands? Do you so soon forget the way they were scapegoated for wrongs that belonged at the feet of human corporations?"

"I'm not claiming the Wingers haven't suffered," Husher said. "I'm not even denying that some humans have had advantages, though there are plenty of humans who are struggling, too. What I'm trying to say—"

"How do you explain that the vast majority of your crewmembers are humans?" Snyder cut in.

"Are you actually going to let me answer, or do you plan to continue talking over me?"

"Go ahead."

Husher shook his head. "The reason I have more human crewmembers than beings from other species can easily be explained. Other than the Ixa and the Gok, the UHF has always dwarfed other species' militaries. As a result, when we integrated our fleets, the majority of candidates to fill a given position were always human. More humans have experience in the military than do members of other species, that's just a—"

"Let me see if I understand you," Snyder said, her tone much softer and sweeter than before, despite that she'd cut him off again. "Are you saying humans are more qualified than other beings?"

"I'm saying that there are more humans qualified to fill military positions than there are similarly qualified beings from any other species."

Snyder peered around at the other councilors, wearing a knowing smirk, as though Husher had just proven her point for her.

Taking her silence as an opportunity to speak, Husher said, "I think it has some bearing on this discussion that studies have found that Awareness Training doesn't actually work. In fact, it's been shown to increase bias."

That caused Snyder's gaze to snap back to his face, and the other councilors turned to study him as well. "Can you cite the studies that claim to demonstrate that?" Snyder asked.

Husher paused. "Not off-hand." He was sure they existed, though—he'd never known Ochrim to be wrong about anything science-related.

"Well, then. Feel free to submit these studies to the council at your leisure, so that we can review their methodology and determine whether the researchers themselves were prejudiced against other species."

Blinking, Husher tried to grasp at the words he might use to answer Snyder's argument, which struck him as circular, though his blurring vision and ringing ears were making it difficult to articulate why.

At last, Chancey spoke. "Captain, there's something I should probably have made clear to you from the beginning of this meeting. It pains me to say this, but if you don't comply with our requirement that both you and your human crewmembers undergo Awareness Training, you will be removed from command of the *Vesta*. Admiral Iver himself signed off on that action before he left the ship."

Suddenly, Husher felt light-headed. “The admiral…?”

“I’m afraid so,” Chancey said, nodding. “There’s a growing sentiment—not only among this council but also the admiralty as well as the Galactic Congress and Senate—that your methods have become outdated for these modern times. Personally, I want you to prove us wrong, I really do. But that starts with agreeing to undergo this training, and agreeing to require your human crewmembers to do so as well.”

All around the circular council chamber, Cybele’s city councilors were staring at him, waiting to see what his answer would be.

There was only one answer he could give. Husher considered it vital to the survival of the galaxy that he remain in the command seat of the *Vesta*, though he knew the council couldn’t see that. There was a lot more at stake here than Awareness Training, or his pride, or the fact that he felt he was being grossly misrepresented.

They’ve painted me into a corner.

“Very well,” he breathed. “I’ll do it.”

CHAPTER 10

As Carbon Steel

Eating her stew as quietly as she could manage, Fesky tried her best not to look like she was listening to the conversations of the enlisted crewmembers around her. At the next table, a group from Engineering was playing Poker. "Ante up, Sammy," one of them said. "You gotta pay to play."

Ante up, Fesky thought. She dined in the crew's mess about as much as she did in the officer's. That was one of the many things she'd learned from Captain—later Admiral—Keyes: eat with the crew often, where you can pick up on their moods and show them you don't think you're any better than they are. Too many officers let their rank go to their heads, treating enlisted service members like unwashed masses while doing their best to keep themselves separate whenever possible.

Not Keyes. He'd shared in his crew's burdens, joined in their celebrations, and mourned every loss alongside them. Everyone on the *Providence* had been part of one big extended family, under Captain Keyes.

Fesky knew that Husher also considered it important to eat with the crew, in principle, at least. In practice, he was often so swamped that there was only time to sneak in short meals at his desk around an ever-growing workload.

A capital starship captain can't focus only on military matters, anymore. Every decision must also be viewed through the lens of appeasing the thousands of civilians scrutinizing everything he does.

It often seemed an impossible balance to Fesky, and maybe it was. Either way, she frequently passed on to Husher what she overheard in the crew's mess, where she tried to make herself as inconspicuous as possible.

When she came here, she was often reminded of her dearest friend, Ek, who she hadn't seen in two decades. Ek was a Fin, who had evolved on Fesky's homeworld—in fact, their species had grown up together. Like most Fins, Ek was incredibly perceptive. If she'd still been here, Fesky probably wouldn't have needed to come to the mess to gauge the crew's mood. She could have just asked Ek. *The* Vesta *could really use Ek's perceptiveness, about now.*

Other than Ek, the Fins had all been killed twenty years ago during a Gok attack on Spire, the homeworld the aquatic species had shared with the Wingers. Ek had survived because she was highly unusual among Fins. Her species was one that could only breathe underwater, yet she'd had a breather made, as well as a set of prosthetic legs, which had allowed her to travel the galaxy. They'd also allowed her to escape Spire just before its destruction.

Gathering intel from the crew's mess wasn't easy. Whenever she entered the mess, someone always noticed, calling everyone to attention. But if she made it there early enough, then other crewmembers would come later, and if they sat nearby, failing to look too closely at her, and assuming she was just another Winger crewmember...

...if they did that, she could pick up some fairly valuable information.

Just such a group of marines took the table behind her now—three humans, two Wingers, and a Gok. The Gok was none other than Tort, who'd helped Husher take down Baxa during the mission that had ended the Second Galactic War.

"Did you see the bullshit posted on the Board today?' said one of the human marines, whose voice Fesky recognized as belonging to Corporal Toby Yung.

The Board was a digital bulletin board that could be accessed using Oculenses from anywhere in the crew section. The captain and other high-ranking officers used it to get non-priority messages to the crew. Fesky hadn't read it recently, so she was interested to hear this, too.

"Have not checked," Tort rumbled in his gravelly tones.

"It's bullshit," Yung repeated. "The captain announced that all human crewmembers are now required to undergo Awareness Training."

"Maybe Yung needs Awareness Training," Tort said.

"Are you serious?"

"Yes. Yung not *aware* of fellow marines trying to eat." The big alien slammed his fist down on the table, rattling cutlery and making trays and dishes jump.

Everyone at the table behind Fesky fell silent for a moment. Then, they burst into gales of laughter.

Yung didn't join in. "Very funny, but I'm being serious."

"Why do *we* have to take it?" asked another marine—Lance Corporal Cassie Roux, unless Fesky missed her guess. "What did *we* do wrong? I mean, I know I like to rough up Tort here every now and then..."

That brought a few more chuckles, but Yung spoke over them. "Damned if I know," he said. "All I can say is, most of the aliens I know in this crew are tough as carbon steel. They don't need some elitist parasites trying to coddle and protect them. If someone disrespects Tort, he'll just kill 'em, for example."

"It's true, though," Roux said. "We've all been working together for years. Maybe people over in Cybele need politicians to tell them how to get along, but we sure as hell don't."

"I'll tell you one thing," Yung said. "The captain's completely lost it. He's so busy kowtowing to the parasites over in Cybele, he's forgotten what it means to command a warship."

Before she knew what she was doing, Fesky rose to her seat, whirling around to tower over the marines sitting at the other table—well, all except Tort, who stared at her with tiny red eyes that blinked slowly beneath his green forehead ridge.

When they saw who she was, they all leapt to attention, saluting, and Fesky returned the salute, staring each of them down as she did.

"I'm not familiar with the captain's directive," she said, "because I haven't had a chance to check the Board today. But I'm sure that whatever Captain Husher's decided, he did it not only with this ship's best interests in mind, but with the Fleet's too, as well as the entire Interstellar Union. I know that because I've served with him for over twenty years, and that's how Captain Husher conducts himself. Unless you question my judgment, too?"

"No, ma'am," the marines answered in unison. According to the surprise that lingered on their faces, they still hadn't recovered from the realization she'd overheard their entire conversation.

"At ease," she told them, then walked out of the mess, leaving her lunch half-eaten and silently cursing herself.

Before those marines had another conversation like that one, they'd be on the lookout for Fesky, and they'd probably tell others what had happened, too. Meaning she'd just rendered a valuable source of intel about the crew less so.

Why did I have to butt in? She knew why, of course: her shock and anger from hearing her friend badmouthed by his marines had caused her to act rashly. Knowing the reason didn't make it rankle any less, though.

Under other circumstances, she would have brought disciplinary measures to bear. But something had stopped her. *Why didn't I discipline them?*

By the time she reached the corridor outside the crew's mess, she'd figured it out.

The reason she hadn't disciplined the marines was because she also had her doubts about Husher's choices, lately.

CHAPTER 11

Vanguard

Husher worked best in his office, where he could be alone for the most part. Often, he ended up eating in here, too. He kept a stash of nutrient bars in his desk drawer, and he opened the drawer now, with the intention of snacking on one as he reviewed his primary Nav officer's proposed route to the Gok home system.

He didn't expect the route to contain many surprises. It would almost certainly involve the use of darkgates, which were still the main way to get around the galaxy. Luckily, the route shouldn't involve passing through any systems colonized since the Second Galactic War. No new darkgates had been built since the discovery that dark tech endangered the universe, so most newly colonized systems could only be accessed via warp drive, which took a lot longer.

As he rooted around in the drawer, his hand became tangled in a leather thong, and he raised it out to disentangle himself. The thong was attached to a small wooden crucifix, which had been the only thing Captain Keyes had left him in his will.

Husher hadn't expected Keyes to have made any arrangements to leave him anything, and he definitely didn't know why he'd left him the little cross. He hadn't even known Keyes was religious—the man had never discussed God or faith. The crucifix must have been important to him, though, considering he'd not only made the arrangements to bequeath it but had also stored it off-ship, allowing it to escape the eventual destruction of the *Providence*.

Despite his confusion, Husher had kept the gift. It was all he had left of his mentor.

Before he could get to reviewing his Nav officer's work, his com lit up where it lay on the desk, inches from his right hand. It was a message from Mayor Chancey: "Captain. Got a minute?"

After staring at the display for a couple seconds, Husher messaged back: "Sure."

Next, his Oculenses displayed a translucent alert about an incoming call from Dylan Chancey. He accepted, and the mayor appeared before his desk, sitting in an overstuffed leather armchair that erased from view the more Spartan chair that was actually there.

This was accomplished using sensors embedded in the wall of the mayor's residence—similarly positioned sensors would now be transmitting Husher's likeness to the mayor. Although, to Chancey, it would seem like he was actually sitting inside Husher's office. The recipient of a call always played virtual "host" in this way.

"Yes?" Husher said.

“Captain, I’d like to offer my sincere apologies for the tone of the council meeting yesterday.” Chancey’s voice emerged from speakers built into Husher’s desk.

“Oh?”

“I didn’t intend it to go that way. Penelope can be...enthusiastic. And honestly, I regret having to place this extra burden on your shoulders, on top of everything else.”

“Then why did you vote for it?” Husher said flatly.

“Because I’m beholden to my constituents, and this is what they indicated they wanted.”

“You held a referendum on it?”

The mayor’s mouth quirked, and he raised a hand to rub his broad jaw. “No,” he said after a pause, “but...well, the ones who wanted it were pretty vocal. Listen, if I’m not seen to play ball on issues like this one, then I’m looked at as the bad guy, and that doesn’t help anyone. I have just as much interest in keeping things stable as you do.” Chancey cleared his throat. “I don’t know if I’m making myself clear or not, but...let me try to put this another way. As long as everyone dots their I’s and crosses their T’s when something like this comes up, then all’s well. But when you don’t, people get angry, and the longer you deny them, the louder they get. So it’s easiest to just go along with them in the first place. If you don’t mind me offering you some unasked-for advice, that is.”

Husher folded his hands on the desk. “What if I hold principles that the majority doesn’t view favorably?”

"Hmm. Well, that's not really my wheelhouse. I go where my constituents tell me to, or I don't get their votes next time around."

"I see."

"We're getting a bit off track here. I really did call because I wanted to apologize. Things got pretty ugly yesterday, but I think they're going to be better from here on out. The protesters got what they wanted, so they're happy, and you have my word that I'm going to do my best to make this stuff go away as quickly and quietly as possible. I know you have a job to do, and I want you to know that I consider your job much more important than I consider mine. That probably seems rich coming from me, after what just happened, but it's the truth. I understand how vital your job is, and I'm going to do everything in my power to clear your way so you can do it."

"All right, then," Husher said. "Anything else?"

"Not at the moment. Thanks for taking the time to speak with me, Captain."

"Any time, Mayor Chancey." *It's apparently part of my job, now, anyway.* Husher terminated the call, wondering why the mayor had bothered to try clearing the air. Maybe the man really did feel bad.

That done, he left his office and headed for the CIC. He wanted to be there when they transitioned out of the Feverfew System, and he planned to schedule his watches so that he'd have the CIC for as many of the necessary transitions as possible. Even though his mission was diplomatic in nature, that didn't mean he trusted the Gok not to spring an ambush at the slightest opportunity.

The *Vesta*'s battle group had rejoined her in the small hours of the morning, and as Husher settled into the command seat, he ordered his Coms officer to distribute orders to the other captains to form up behind her.

"Yes, sir," Ensign Fry said.

Technically, the other captains had autonomy over their respective ships, though Husher could also direct them as he saw fit. Ultimately, the battle group went where the admiralty told it to go, and adhered to whatever ROEs the admiralty laid out. But in certain situations, Husher performed the function of admiral without holding the actual rank. *Just another role to round out my endless list of duties.*

"Captain," Ensign Fry said, "we've just received a priority transmission from a com drone that recently entered the system. It's audio and video, addressed to you. Should I play it here or would you prefer to take it in your office?"

"Play it here, and give everyone access."

Admiral Iver appeared on the main display, and as per Husher's order, everyone's Oculenses would have access to his likeness as he spoke. "Captain Husher, hopefully this message reaches you before you leave the Feverfew system, since time has suddenly become precious. We've just received a distress call from the governor of Tyros in the Wintercress System, which at the time of Governor Jomo's transmission was under attack by a vessel of unknown origin.

"On the heels of this message, I've ordered the com drone carrying it to transmit to you all the sensor data collected by the Wintercress System's sensor web. Your new orders are as follows: the *Vesta* is to make all reasonable haste toward Wintercress and answer this new threat. Before you do, please hand off the diplomats I've already designated, Shobi and Bryson, to your battle group ships. Those ships are to proceed to the Gok homeworld and continue their diplomatic mission. I have full confidence that you will have the situation in Wintercress well in hand. While the attacking vessel's origins are unknown, it is only one ship—a destroyer, from the looks of it. It did manage to neutralize two IGF ships on patrol in the system, the *Stentor* and the *Orion*, but I highly doubt it will be any match for the *Vesta*. Iver out."

The main wall display returned to whatever each CIC officer had been viewing prior to the recording—for Husher, data on the main engines, on which he'd had Engineering perform a full inspection before getting underway to the Gok home system.

"The promised data package just arrived, Captain," Ensign Fry said. "Should I—?"

"Put it on the display." There was no need to conceal from the crew anything about what they would be facing in Wintercress.

The destroyer that appeared had a hull the color of a storm cloud, rendering visual sensors somewhat less effective in picking it out from the inky blackness of space. *Not so bad for visuals as the jet-black Ixan vessels we saw during the Second Galactic War.*

In every other way, however, the enemy ship cut a menacing figure. Despite Iver's abundance of confidence, the ship was nearly half the size of the *Vesta*, according to the readouts that accompanied the image. Its form was that of a flat, elongated diamond, and it bristled with what Husher felt sure was weaponry, though each gun's dimensions differed dramatically from anything fielded by the IGF.

Could this be it? Husher asked himself. *What I've been bracing for all these years?*

He wanted it to be, he realized. For multiple reasons—such as the interminable waiting, which was slowly driving him insane. Or the fact that, if this ship didn't represent the vanguard of the AIs' attack fleet, then it belonged to a different threat altogether, while the danger posed by the AIs still loomed.

A third factor: Husher didn't know how much longer he could keep at bay the twin advances of pacifism and bureaucracy, which threatened to choke out their military effectiveness altogether. The former was a noble impulse, Husher recognized that, but a noble death at the hands of a merciless attacker was still death.

He heaved a sigh that sounded a lot like relief, drawing some curious looks from a couple of his CIC officers.

This was what he was made to do. It was what he'd trained to do, and also what he'd been preparing for, for the better part of his life. Maybe all his life.

CHAPTER 12

Debris Cloud

"Transitioning through the Lilac-Wintercress darkgate now, Captain," Winterton said.

"Acknowledged, Ensign." Husher said. He sat back and waited for more data to come in, wondering how things were in Cybele, right now. Two days into their journey to Wintercress, he'd gone to Penelope Snyder's office to discuss his own Awareness Training, and she'd told him about Nonattendance Day for nonhuman species. It was a day for aliens to stay home, to highlight the vital role they play in society. Husher would have been fine with the idea, except that it happened to coincide with today, the day the *Vesta* was transitioning into a system that had recently been attacked. His alien crewmembers were far *too* vital to give them the day off while a possible engagement was brewing.

"Tyros' planetary net appears to be down, sir," his Coms officer said. "I'm not detecting the usual signal volume—just chatter from a few com drones passing through the system."

"The people of Cybele will be disappointed," Fesky muttered from the XO's chair beside Husher. "Especially if this means they can't download the latest updates for their video games."

Husher suppressed the urge to chuckle, shooting Fesky a reproving look instead. He wanted to clamp down on the joking before it began to compromise the professionalism he expected from his CIC crew. "Any sign of the enemy destroyer, Winterton?"

"I'm detecting a dispersed debris cloud between Tyros and its solar shield—presumably, the debris is what's left of the *Stentor* and the *Orion*. But no sign of the enemy, Captain."

Husher nodded. The solar shield was an enormous loop of conductive wire that was positioned between most major colonies and their suns, meant to deflect large flares. The IU had started installing them after a solar flare had fried the electronic grid of Sestos, ruining its economy and causing untold suffering until relief ships and workers could be dispatched there. There were plans to eventually install solar shields for every colony in the Union.

Husher turned to his Coms officer. "Ensign, continue trying to establish contact with Tyros. Preferably, I'd like to speak to the governor. Kaboh, continue taking us down the system's gravity well at a measured pace, and Winterton, begin active scans of the entire system."

"Aye, sir," all three officers said in rough unison.

As the tense silence lengthened, Husher began to worry what it might mean for the planetary net to be down. Had the enemy vessel sabotaged it and then vacated the system? And had it done anything to harm the civilian population of Tyros before it did?

"Captain, I'm getting something," Fry said at last, two hours into their journey toward the colony. She sounded relieved. "It's a transmission from Governor Jomo."

"If there's video, put it on the display."

The governor, a Tumbran, appeared, fleshy chin-sack wobbling as though she'd just taken a seat. "Captain Husher," the alien said in the impassive tones characteristic of her species. "Thank you for answering our distress call. I am, however, relieved to inform you that the danger seems to have passed. Without warning, after destroying the *Stentor* and the *Orion*, the vessel that attacked us disappeared from our sensors in a most surprising way. It has not returned since."

The Tumbran shifted, glanced to the left, then refocused on the transmission. "Perhaps we should assume that the unknown vessel concluded it could not contend with Tyros' orbital defense platforms, which are fully operational. At any rate, in the spirit of caution, I expect you will want to remain in-system to ensure the hostile vessel does not return. In the meantime, I would like to invite the people of Cybele to conduct trade with us, and I would like to invite you, Captain Husher, to have dinner. Perhaps we can review the footage of the disappearing warship together, and attempt to make some sense of it. I look forward to a real-time conversation with you."

With that, the transmission ended.

Beside him, Fesky twitched. "Did something seem off to you about that message, Captain?"

Husher contemplated the question. "Winterton, I want you to perform a close inspection of the defensive platforms we can see from this side of the planet. Lean on radar, but do what you can with visual sensors at this distance, too. Let me know if you detect any reason to believe they've been disabled."

Twenty minutes later, the sensor operator had his report. "The platforms check out, Captain. There's no sign of damage or malfunction that I can detect."

"Well, we've done our due diligence. Either way, Jomo was right that we'll be staying for a while. And there's no good reason not to allow Cybele to conduct some trade, though anyone who comes aboard should know that they do so at their own risk, and that a military engagement is possible at any time. Even so, in that event, there should be plenty of time to evacuate whoever wants to be elsewhere." Husher glanced at Fesky. "There's also no reason for me to turn down dinner with the governor, so I'm going to go ahead with it."

"Still...I strongly recommend a marine escort, Captain."

Husher considered that for a moment. "It could be interpreted as an insult to our hosts. But all right, Fesky. I'll take your recommendation."

CHAPTER 13

As Though in a Warzone

A shuttle was prepped by the time they reached orbit over Tyros, and as per Fesky's recommendation—which had bordered on insistence—Husher ordered it packed with as many marines as it could hold, which amounted to two full platoons, one to guard the shuttle and one to accompany him to dinner with the governor.

"I'm beginning to feel like a head of state," he remarked to the marine sitting in the crash seat beside him, a corporal named Yung.

"Well, sir, you do command a starship with a city aboard it."

Husher inclined his head slightly. "True enough. Strange times."

Tyros, formerly of the Tumbran Federation, now belonged to the Interstellar Union. To Husher's knowledge, that hadn't made much difference to the colony's composition. It still numbered around a hundred thousand beings, and it still welcomed all comers from other species. There were sizable Winger and even human populations, despite the strained relationship humanity had had with the rest of the galaxy ever since inheriting dark tech. Even during the peak of what Husher readily admitted was human tyranny, humans had felt essentially welcome here. He liked Tyros.

Before the formation of the Interstellar Union, the Tumbra had run what were called Coffee Stations—essentially, space stations where humans *weren't* welcome. Husher didn't like the idea of that, so much, but then, the United Human Fleet had had a strict rule that aliens weren't allowed on their warships, so maybe they were about even on that score.

There weren't any Coffee Stations, anymore. The Tumbra had voluntarily closed them as soon as the IU was formed, in the spirit of unity.

The ride down through the atmosphere was bumpy, though not nearly as bad as some reentries Husher could remember, in and out of shuttles. Attitude stabilizers had gotten a lot better in the last twenty years. Then there was the time he'd executed an emergency orbital insertion inside a faulty reentry suit...

"Sir, we have the go-ahead to touch down on top of Piper Hall," the shuttle pilot radioed to Husher's com.

"Acknowledged. Take us down."

"It's a beautiful winter day down there. I recommend keeping your jumpsuit zipped up nice and snug, Captain."

"Thanks for the tip."

Ten minutes later, he followed two squads of marines into the airlock. Two more squads had already deployed on top of Piper Hall and were busy securing the rooftop.

The shuttle airlock's outer hatch hissed open, and Husher stepped out into a cutting wind that pelted his face with ice. Through the blizzard, he could see silhouettes of marines running around the roof, generally behaving as though they were in a warzone.

He wondered how the governor would react to him bringing eighty marines along to dinner, edgy after years with nothing to shoot but practice targets. *How do I let Fesky talk me into these things? To think Admiral Iver was about to send me on a diplomatic mission...*

A hulking form in winter combat gear appeared out of the storm. "All clear, Captain, other than this blasted ice," the form said in a slow drawl.

"Thank you, Major Gamble."

Major Peter Gamble was commanding officer of the marine battalion assigned to the *Vesta*. The man had a flair for leadership that Husher sometimes envied, as well as a strong grasp of tactics, as evidenced by the combat simulation scores that Husher reviewed regularly, for all his marines.

"Shall we head down into the hall?" Gamble asked.

"By all means."

A rooftop elevator opened at their approach, either manually operated or programmed to recognize Husher's likeness. It only fit a squad at a time, and so Husher had to wait on the ground floor with the first squad for the other three to join them.

A Tumbran appeared nearby, its spherical, hooded eyes peering up at the marines from atop its oblong head. "My," it said as the third squad piled out of the elevator. "There certainly are a lot of you."

"You don't have to feed us all," Gamble said. "Just the captain. My marines have already eaten."

"I'm certain our chefs can find a way to accommodate anyone who wishes to dine," the Tumbran said, turning to waddle down the hall. "Follow me, please."

As soon as the fourth squad of marines made it down, they all trailed the Tumbran through a series of corridors filled with commemorations and tributes to the life of a Tumbran who'd been called Piper, after whom the hall was named. It had been his sacrifice, along with that of Captain Keyes and his CIC crew, that had wiped out the majority of the Ixan fleet, a move that proved instrumental to winning the war.

As he passed a portrait of the stoic Tumbran, Husher could almost hear Piper's voice in his head, delivering one of his trademark digs—so dry that it sometimes took minutes for the recipient to realize they'd been insulted.

I miss that little bastard.

Keeping pace with the Tumbran, going was slow, which made sense given the alien was around half the height of the average human. But at last, they reached the banquet hall, where long dining tables faced each other across meters of empty marble floor.

A lone Tumbran stood at the opposite end of the hall, hands folded in front of her stomach, which poked out a bit from underneath her tunic. She stood in front of a broad, floor-to-ceiling banner, blood-red in color. Several identical banners hung all around the hall. The garish wall hangings didn't seem in keeping with Tumbran sensibilities, but maybe they'd wanted to do something a bit different with the hall dedicated to one of their most cherished heroes.

"Governor Jomo!" Husher called across the hall. "It's good to see you. Apologies for the heavy marine presence, but my XO can be a bit—"

"Captain Husher, be on your guard," Jomo cried.

Drawing to a stop, Husher tilted his head back, studying the Tumbran more closely.

Without warning, the blood-red banners fell to the floor, revealing enormous alcoves behind them. *Those* were more in line with Tumbran tastes, and so were the statues and artwork they featured.

But Husher didn't have much time to study the decorations. He was too distracted by the hulking, three-meter-tall figures that lurched from the recesses.

Eyes narrowed, body rigid with shock, Husher stared at the alien behind Jomo, his mind churning as it tried to make sense of what he was seeing.

Other than its incredible size and musculature, the giant closely resembled an Ixan, with its dark-green scales, its clawed hands, and its creepy, sinuous smile.

Husher gasped, then, as he realized just who he was looking at. *Teth.*

"Hello, Husher," Teth said, reaching down to grasp Jomo's head with one massive hand, its fingers extending down the Tumbran's entire face.

With a casual flick of his wrist, Teth snapped Jomo's neck, and she went limp, falling to the floor.

"*Attack,*" Teth hissed, and the other Ixa darted across the marble toward Husher and his marines, moving with astonishing speed.

CHAPTER 14

Defense Platform 5

Mug in hand, Fesky settled into the command seat for what she expected would be a long, uneventful watch.

At least I don't have to deal with Kaboh, she reflected as she sipped from her still-piping coffee, which she took with a dash of cream and nothing else. The smarmy Kaithian Nav officer ruffled Fesky's feathers, that was for sure, but he was being allowed to rest in case the captain's visit to Tyros ran long enough to warrant a second watch to take over. In that event, Kaboh would have the command.

Unlike Captain Keyes before him, who'd often stated that he had no desire to allow his CIC to become a cafeteria, Husher allowed his CIC crew beverages, as long as they were kept in tight, plastic mugs that amounted to adult sippy cups. His one other stipulation—besides no alcohol, of course—was that each officer was responsible for making sure the cup's lid was sealed between sips. The first time they spilled hot liquid on themselves, other officers, or on sensitive equipment, he said, was the last time they would find themselves in his CIC. So far, Fesky hadn't had the opportunity to witness whether that was true.

In her peripheral vision, Ensign Winterton's whole frame went rigid. "Ma'am, sensors have just picked up a warship matching the profile from the data package sent to us by Admiral Iver. It's coming around Tyros' moon."

Fesky's gaze locked onto the ensign, marveling at how level his voice was, given this dumbfounding revelation. "That shouldn't be possible," she said, punctuating her words with a clack of her beak. "The system's sensor web is still active. It should have picked up an unidentified ship on the dark side of the moon long ago."

With a curt nod, the sensor operator returned her look with one of calm. "Regardless, Commander. The ship's there."

Fesky gathered her fragmented thoughts with a significant effort of will. It was Winterton's job to use the *Vesta*'s sensor suite to document the environment and report it to the commanding officer. That was what he had done, in as efficient and professional a manner as she could possibly have asked for. Now, it was her job to figure out what the hell to do with the information he'd given her.

"Coms, call Lieutenant Commander Kaboh to the CIC." As much as Fesky disliked the Kaithian, he knew his station well, and Husher would want all of first watch on for a developing combat situation. "Tactical, prep four Gorgon missiles with telemetry parameters and order them loaded into forward launch tubes." Four was a lot, but she didn't want to take any chances with a destroyer of unknown capabilities. "Coms, let's try a transmission—"

"Ma'am," Winterton cut in, "the unidentified vessel just launched two dozen missiles."

"Two *dozen?*" Fesky shrieked, causing the Helm officer to start. She strove to settle herself. For a moment, she'd been annoyed at Winterton's interruption, until she'd realized that it rendered the order she was about to give entirely pointless.

"Coms, get me the officer in charge of Defense Platform 5," Fesky snapped, mentally cursing herself for not having established contact with the platform already. It was at that moment it dawned on her that seventeen years of peace had softened her, and now there was a chance she'd pay for her mistake with her life, as well as the lives of everyone aboard.

No. One destroyer will not take down the Vesta. "Tactical, fire Gorgons."

"Aye, Commander."

"That's not all. Set point defense systems to engage at maximum range, and reassign forward tertiary laser projectors to point-defense mode as well."

"Should I order Banshees prepped to help take down some of the incoming missiles?"

Fesky considered the proposal for a moment. The latest generation of the Banshee missile was a faster, sleeker version of the ones used during the Second Galactic War, though it was still a fairly classical armament, all things considered. "No," she said. "Prep four more Gorgons instead, and six Hydras. We're going for the kill."

"No response from Defense Platform 5, ma'am," Ensign Fry said.

"That's fine." *We'll deal with this on our own.*

"Ma'am," Winterton said, and Fesky found herself glaring at him while resisting an urge to batter him with her wing.

He's just doing his job. "Yes?" she said, managing to sound mostly collected.

"The enemy vessel just launched two more missile volleys in quick succession. Both were equal in number to the first."

The impact of the sensor operator's news made Fesky rock backward in the command seat by a degree or two, and she started to vibrate. Over the years, she'd gotten much better at controlling the Winger tendency to wear emotions on the wing, but her usual self-control had officially abandoned her.

"Helm, full reverse thrust. *Now!*"

CHAPTER 15

Progenitors

Two squads of *Vesta* marines ran forward, fanning out in front of Husher and dropping to one knee, firing round after round at the reptilian berserkers speeding across the hall toward them. The other two squads formed up behind, firing over their fellow marines' heads and effectively creating a wall of speeding lead that crashed into the oncoming aliens, again and again.

It didn't slow them. The first Ixan reached the kneeling marine rank, knocking one soldier to the floor while plunging a claw-tipped hand through the exposed armpit of another. The alien's movements were swift and sure, like the reptiles the Ixa resembled.

Husher's windpipe closed, and his mind's eye was filled by a burning star that streaked across a night sky and lit up his family's home like a summer bonfire.

He felt a hand close over his forearm, snapping him back to the present, and he glanced sideways to see Major Gamble, wide eyes overscored by a crooked, throbbing vein. "We're getting you out, now," the major screamed into Husher's face. "Marines, fall back!"

Four marines were down already, bleeding out on the floor and utterly incapable of falling back. The others—those who'd heard Gamble's order, anyway—attempted to obey, stutter-stepping backward while firing on the hulking aliens full bore, slapping fresh clips into their guns as needed.

"Get back to the elevator!" Gamble roared.

"Belay that," Husher yelled, shaking the major off his arm.

"What? Why, sir?"

"Because it can only fit a single squad. The rest of you will be pinned against the elevator doors and slaughtered. We're going out the front."

"But we don't know what way that is."

"We'll figure it out." Husher drew his P600 service pistol and emptied it into an Ixan sprinting toward them along the side of the room. "We're leaving, now. To me, marines!"

Thank God for embedded ear pieces. If it weren't for those, it would have been impossible for the marines to hear his order over the tumult.

By the time they extracted themselves from the hall, they'd lost about a squad's worth of marines—a quarter of the soldiers that had come inside with them. And he hadn't seen a single Ixan go down.

What have the Ixa done to themselves? But the aliens were leaving him with no time to speculate, as they pounded into the hallway after their prey.

The marines in the rear turned to fire upon the beast in the lead, and at last, it dropped—only to one knee, but it dropped. Its fellows charged past, apparently unconcerned.

"Chief Haynes," Husher said after switching to a two-way channel with their shuttle pilot.

"Captain?"

"I need you to have our ride waiting for us outside the front doors. We're under attack. Tell the marines to deploy defensively around the shuttle."

"Yes, sir," Haynes answered, the shock clear in his voice.

In the seconds before their shuttle had touched down on the roof, Husher had used his Oculenses to access the sensors arrayed along the craft's underside. Now, he tried to square the maze of hallways and doorways confronting him with his dim recollection of the Hall's layout as seen from above. All the while, panic lapped at him like waves against the side of a capsizing boat.

"I think it's this way," he said, gesturing down a side hall and meeting Gamble's eyes.

The major nodded. As always, the marine commander yielded to his captain's judgment, even though his training and specialization made him better suited to this particular situation than Husher, in theory.

But despite starting out as a Condor pilot, Husher had seen his fair share of ground combat back in the messy days of the UHF, and Major Gamble knew that.

Captain Keyes had often wanted him deployed with the *Providence* marines, actually, and not just for his situational awareness, but also for his principles, which Husher had stuck to no matter the circumstances. Even when it had meant flying in the face of Command.

Have I strayed from that? A smaller voice began to answer the question, from deeper inside him, but he quashed it.

The brilliant glow of natural light caught his eye as they rushed through a corridor, and Husher skidded to a stop, glad that his fifty-four-year-old body could still turn on a dime.

"We're here," he said. They'd lost at least another squad as they tore through the corridors—insanely brave men and women who'd spent their lives without hesitation, just to stall the Ixan charge and buy their comrades a few seconds more.

Ixa. Alive, and on a Union world. It still made Husher feel like he was dreaming.

They poured out of Piper Hall's glass doors, rushing down a short flight of steps and then across the snow-covered concrete. The marines wore combat boots whose nanoscale spikes served them well, here, though Husher wore parade boots, and so had to take more care.

The waiting marines around the shuttle fired overhead at the Ixa who crashed through the glass, not bothering to squeeze through doors made for shorter beings.

Husher switched to the two-way channel again. "Haynes, you do fly a combat shuttle, do you not?"

"Sorry, Captain!" the chief said, and within seconds, the shuttle's hull-mounted turrets were swiveling back and forth, firing on the charging foes.

They reached the shuttle. When Husher slammed a fresh clip into his P600's handle and turned to engage the Ixa again, Gamble placed an arm across his stomach, pressing him gently toward the airlock.

"Captain, I really have to insist you get inside. The heroism's appreciated, but my people won't get safe till you are."

Nodding, Husher stepped inside the airlock, and the major sent two squads' worth of marines in to join him. The outer airlock slid closed.

Husher once again connected his Oculenses to the shuttle's sensors in order to continue watching the engagement outside. The added fire of both the combat shuttle as well as the marines who hadn't entered the Hall finally seemed to give the aliens pause, and they withdrew back up the stairs and into the building. Only then did they produce firearms of their own and begin to return fire.

As the last marines piled into the airlock, with Major Gamble among them, Husher saw one of the Ixa—Teth, unless he missed his guess—produce a rocket launcher and aim it at the shuttle.

Husher's hand flew to his ear. "Haynes, takes us away, now. *Now!*"

Haynes did, and the shuttle's landing gear parted from the snowy ground, tilting away from the rocket that screamed from its tube and veered upward, seeking its target.

Lightning-quick, Haynes engaged lateral thrusters so that the shuttle lurched in the opposite direction, *toward* the incoming missile, but at an upward angle that caused it to miss by inches. Husher knew it really was a matter of inches, because through the magic of Oculens, the rocket seemed to pass right before his nose, and he even tricked himself into thinking he felt a breeze as it screamed by.

The inner airlock door opened, and the marines who'd been in the airlock during takeoff scrambled to strap themselves into their crash seats before the steep climb into orbit. Once they were settled, a silence descended on the shuttle—deeply uncharacteristic of marines, who were known for their brash banter before, during, and after a fight.

We're all peacetime soldiers, now. Walking contradictions, wholly unprepared for what's coming for us.

An unsourced transmission request came in over his Oculenses, and he thought he knew who it would be. When he willed acceptance of the connection, and Teth appeared as though towering over him inside the shuttle, his suspicion proved out.

In order for Teth to appear like that, he had to be the beneficiary of either in-depth intel about Oculens technology or enough luck that whatever tech he had access to had developed in precisely the same way. Husher considered the former infinitely more likely.

"How are you alive?" Husher said. Several marines glanced his way, though none of them would have access to Teth's words.

"Lieutenant Husher," the Ixan said, his voice breathier than Husher remembered, and more sibilant. "Or rather, Captain, now, isn't it? We've always enjoyed such exquisite conversations, you and I. Yet here, you open with a disappointingly banal question." Teth's forked tongue made a brief appearance, flicking past his teeth and lips before vanishing into the dark hole of his mouth. Now that he was getting a closer look, Husher saw that several of the bone protrusions characteristic of Ixan faces had escaped Teth's flesh and now showed as white knobs and spikes in symmetrical patterns along the sides of his head. "How am I alive," Teth said, repeating Husher's words. "Hmm. Perhaps you imagined that your mentor's sacrifice was meaningful—that his death put a final end to the force poised to extinguish humanity. Is that what you thought?"

"I thought he killed you."

"He did not. I was far enough from the blast wrought by the collapsing wormhole to survive, as were tens of thousands of other Ixa."

"Sounds like you had some good luck, then."

Teth's thin lips widened into a smirk. "Call it whatever you wish."

"Baxa turned the Ixa into automatons. Mindless slaves. After we killed him, every Ixan we found had basically become a vegetable. We connected them to life support, but they all died within the year."

"So it was with the crew of my destroyer, as well as those of the surrounding Ixan ships. I was only able to save those aboard my ship, and that with great difficulty."

"How?"

Teth's smirk became a wide smile, revealing a pair of elongated fangs that definitely hadn't been there when last they'd met. "So many banal questions. Let me answer several of them at once: the Progenitors. They found me in time, allowed me to resuscitate my crew, and they gave me access to the superior weaponry currently battering your new supercarrier. They also augmented my brethren and I in the way you have seen."

"Who are the Progenitors?"

"Who do you suppose they are, Captain Husher? Why don't you use your vaunted Oculenses to look up the meaning of the word. Maybe that will give you a clue to work with, as an alternative to pestering me with your endless questions."

"What's your aim, here, Teth? What do you want?"

"My aim is tied up with that of my creators. To tell you the truth, Captain, I've gained a certain humility to go with my new power. I am merely the opening volley in the war for which you've been struggling weakly to ready your pitiful Union. There is a path to peace, however brief that peace ends up being. If you would like any quarter for your people at all, there is something I require of you. I would like both you and Jake Price to present yourselves on the Ixa's homeworld, Klaxon."

"I don't know a Jake Price."

"Then I suggest you seek him out and meet him. Quickly! This has only just begun."

With that, Teth's grotesque likeness vanished from the shuttle.

CHAPTER 16

Surface Tension

Before the shuttle touched down on Flight Deck Omicron, Husher dragged himself away from his muddled thoughts long enough to commend both the marines and Chief Haynes for getting them all home safely.

"We lost a lot of good soldiers down there," Husher said, meeting each marine's eye in turn. "There's no sugarcoating that, nor would I want to. But I can promise you one thing. We're going to take it to those bastards hard for what they did."

A hearty cheer answered that, and Husher was glad to see his soldiers' spirits were far from broken. "Major Gamble, I need you to take your people to Cybele, to maintain order and help anyone negatively affected by the Ixan attack. We're not through this yet, but I want you to do everything you can to put those citizens at ease without lying to them about the reality of the situation."

"Yes, sir," Gamble said, all business. He was a jovial hand around the Poker table, or so Husher had heard. While taking everyone's money, the reports went. But in the middle of an ongoing op, the major's sense of humor withdrew to somewhere deep inside him. "Where are you headed, Captain, if you don't mind my asking?"

"The CIC. I intend to start taking our losses out of Teth's hide."

Gamble nodded. "All right, then. I'll have two marines escort—"

"Belay that."

The major's eyebrows rose. "Sir?"

"I'm not about to start suffering escorts on my own ship."

After a brief hesitation, Gamble nodded again. "Yes, sir."

Husher positioned himself at the front of the first group out of the airlock. The task he'd given the marines was important, but it wouldn't count for much if the *Vesta* was bested by Teth's destroyer. He trusted Fesky to do a good job, but he'd much rather sit in the command seat himself at a time like this.

The outer airlock opened, and he dashed across the flight deck, grateful he no longer needed to bother with pressure suits to do so. In the old days, flight decks had been open to space, but with improved airlock technology it was quicker to have combat shuttles and Pythons undergo a brief pressurization and decontamination before entering the flight deck proper.

As he jogged toward the CIC, he found the crew corridors almost empty, which made sense. With an engagement in progress, everyone currently on duty would be intent on their respective tasks, and a change of watch wouldn't happen until they were certain the action had ended.

A groaning, scraping noise from up ahead reached his ears, and he paused, his hand going automatically to his pistol. By now, he'd captained this vessel for thirteen years, and he knew her sounds by heart. A groaning, scraping noise wasn't one of them.

He listened for a few seconds more, hearing nothing. Then, something flayed open the metal of the bulkhead five meters in front of him, emerging into the corridor and tracking Husher immediately with its head.

If it could be called a head. It certainly had no face to speak of, and the "head" was smooth and curved, extending forward as well as backward. The thing was made from some dark-gray metal, and its metallic arms and legs resembled shields that had been stretched along the vertical axis.

The intruder came no higher than Husher's stomach, but it had also just torn through his ship like tissue paper. Deciding to take it seriously, Husher flicked open the clasp holding his P600 in place, whipped it out of the holster, and proceeded to empty its clip into the monster's torso.

The thing scrambled to cross the distance separating them. Husher began walking backward, and when the gun clicked instead of fired, he loosed the empty clip and slammed in a new one.

By now, he was running backward to keep ahead of his assailant, which caused his sidearm's muzzle to waver more than he would have liked. Sucking in a ragged gasp, he tightened up his aim and succeeded in planting the entire second clip inside the intruder as well.

The last bullet made the thing stagger at just a few feet's remove, buying Husher enough time to load his final clip into the gun and finish the job.

He put the fourth bullet into the robot's head, which rendered it inert. For good measure, he brought his boot up hard under what he supposed could be called the thing's chin.

It still didn't move, and Husher took the opportunity to curse loudly, causing a bead of sweat to lose its surface tension and slide down his cheek.

"You're still alive," he told himself. He knew better than to expect more than that from any given day.

At least, he'd once known better. *Maybe I've forgotten. Seems I'll have plenty of opportunity to relearn.*

Opening a com channel with Gamble, he said, "Major, I need you to mobilize four more platoons and get them patrolling the ship's corridors in squads. Assign one squad to guard each of the primary engines, two to Engineering, as well as one squad apiece to patrol our major capacitor banks. Are those orders clear?"

"Clear as day, Captain." The major didn't ask for any explanations, which was one of the reasons Husher considered the man invaluable.

That done, he jogged on toward the CIC, leaving the metal attacker in a heap for collection and study later. As he ran, the turbulence of space battle made the *Vesta* buck around him, and he focused on keeping his footing.

CHAPTER 17

Superheating

"I have the CIC," Husher barked as he passed through the main hatch and strode toward the command seat.

"You have the CIC, Captain," Fesky said, sounding not at all reluctant to relinquish command. She settled herself into the XO's seat, alongside his.

"Sitrep," Husher said as he settled into his chair.

"The enemy vessel launched three massive barrages consisting of twenty-four missiles each. Only a handful got through, though I would have expected them to do far more damage than they did. Sensors showed multiple hull breaches, and I isolated the corresponding sections, but damage control teams found rents they characterized as surprisingly small."

"Those weren't missiles—not traditional ones, anyway," Husher said. "They were robots, designed to infiltrate our ship and target her primary systems and components."

"How do you know that?"

"Because I killed one on my way here. No further questions, if you please, Commander. What explanations I have for you will come later."

That caused Fesky to tremble with what was no doubt embarrassment. Husher could tell the battle had thoroughly flustered her, in a way he'd barely seen from her since before the Gok Wars. He sympathized, but there was no time to hold her talons, either. He needed her best, as well as that of everyone else in the CIC.

"What's the enemy's posture been since the third barrage?" he asked.

Fesky clacked her beak, and her shaking lessened as she seemed to get a better grip on her emotions. "They've mostly been sitting back, swatting down whatever we send their way. One of our Gorgons got through, and that seemed to take out a cluster of point defense turrets, but they've been relying on lasers to compensate."

Husher nodded. "They're probably waiting for us to show signs that their robots successfully tore up some vital systems. Maximum efficiency was always Teth's MO, and I have reason to believe he wants to take us alive if he can."

"Wait, what?" Fesky squawked. "*Teth?*"

He could have kicked himself. "Explanations later, Fesky."

"Yes, sir."

Keenly aware of the tens of thousands of civilians he had aboard, Husher said, "Tactical, prep a barrage of six Banshees and standby to deploy them one at a time, with ten seconds between each." Gorgons or Hydras might have been more likely to connect with his adversary, but he meant the Banshees to serve a diversionary function, so for this, the sleek, fast missiles were his best choice. He turned to Kaboh. "I want you to devise a route that takes advantage of a gravity assist from Tyros' moon, flinging us toward the outer system. Send it to Helm the moment you have it."

"That will take us even closer to the hostile vessel, Captain," Kaboh said. "I would remind you of the people in Cybele, who are likely afraid for—"

"I gave you an order and I expect it implemented immediately, Lieutenant. I did not request your feedback."

"I'm well within my right to give it," the Nav officer said, in the closest he'd ever heard a Kaithian come to grumbling. Nevertheless, he turned back to his console and began to work.

Kaboh was right, of course. Current doctrine did invite subordinates to raise any criticisms they felt warranted. But that doctrine had been developed during a protracted peacetime, and lengthy debate didn't square well with surviving an engagement with a powerful enemy.

"I haven't forgotten the civilians in Cybele," Husher said. "Nor have I forgotten the ones on Tyros, protected by orbital defense platforms that appear to be nonoperational. It's why I'm attempting a measured retreat, in order to lure the enemy away from the planet and deal with them farther out, if we can—ideally, at a remove that also keeps our civilian occupants safe. Our Air Group should be able to help with that."

Husher hated his impulse to justify himself to Kaboh, but he knew the bureaucrats would comb over everything he said today, and he remained far from certain that even a new war would secure his position as commander of this ship.

"Captain," Chief Tremaine said, "Banshees are armed and loaded with their courses, which compensate for our trajectory toward the moon."

"Fire on my mark."

"Yes, sir."

"What's our total capacitor charge?"

"Nearly ninety percent."

Husher nodded. *Enough to fire the primary twice.* That was good to know. IGF captains had less cause than their historical counterparts to frantically fire their primary lasers at the earliest opportunity an engagement presented. In the past, a fully charged main capacitor could cause a catastrophic release of energy given a big enough impact, but modern capacitors were designed to be much more impact-resistant, suspended as they were in shock-absorbent frames that kept them more or less isolated from any shaking suffered by the ship.

Husher had been keeping a close eye on the tactical display, and when they reached the proximity he'd already deemed optimal, he said, "Fire the first Banshee, Tactical."

"Aye."

"Sir..." his sensor operator said slowly, as though he'd noticed something anomalous in his readouts. Then Winterton spoke again, urgency making his voice strained: "Sir, we're getting superheating along the starboard bow. The hull is already breached!"

As soon as Winterton finished speaking, the explosions began, rocking the CIC even in its location deep inside the supercarrier.

Husher's heart skipped a beat. "Helm, adjust our attitude downward relative to the ecliptic plane, twenty degrees, and bring engines to full power."

"Aye, Captain!" said the Helm officer, a Winger named Vy.

"Coms, tell Damage Control to seal off all affected sections." Husher's gaze fixed on Tremaine. "Hit them with our primary, Tactical, and standby to do it again."

"Yes, sir."

"Enemy destroyer is already taking evasive maneuvers," Winterton said.

"Acknowledged. Give me a damage report."

"The hull was breached along sections eleven through twenty-two, in a horizontal gash that stretches from deck eight right up to deck nineteen, in some places."

"Has the superheating effect subsided?"

"For now, it appears to be in the process of subsiding, Captain. But the temperature's high enough in some sections that the hull is still sloughing off."

"What *was* that?" Fesky asked, turning toward Husher, eyes wide.

"If I'm to guess, I'd say it was a particle beam," Husher said, his voice tight. *From what we've seen, Teth is at least a generation ahead of us in terms of weapons tech, possibly two.* Then there were the biological modifications that he and the other Ixa had made to themselves, or which someone else had made. *I'd be in over my head even if the Interstellar Union* didn't *have a firm grip on my leash, as though restraining a rabid dog.*

"Sir," Tremaine said, "our primary laser missed its mark—the enemy ship is moving too fast along a trajectory that's almost the exact opposite of the *Vesta*'s. Now that we're closer, though, I think we can train it on the enemy long enough to inflict some damage."

"Do it."

"Firing primary a second time," Tremaine confirmed. Seconds later, he blinked at whatever he was seeing on the main display, brow furrowed.

Winterton spoke, and his words clarified Tremaine's look of confused dismay: "Sir...sir, the enemy ship has vanished."

Blinking, Husher studied the man's face. "Are we experiencing a sensor malfunction, Ensign?"

"I have no reason to believe we are."

"Could this be the result of advanced stealth tech?" Husher was grasping at straws—he already knew the improbability of what he'd just suggested.

Nevertheless, Winterton answered. "Unless the combined physics knowledge of the four species that comprise the Interstellar Union is woefully inaccurate...no, I don't think that's possible, sir."

"Vanishing isn't either," Husher said flatly.

Winterton had no answer for that.

CHAPTER 18

On the Local Galactic Cluster

Husher called a meeting of his top officers as well as high-ranking civilian officials from Tyros, to be held as soon as possible.

Unfortunately, "as soon as possible" wasn't nearly soon enough, for his tastes. The delay had mostly to do with the necessity of waiting for the civilian officials to take shuttles to orbit, rendezvous with the *Vesta*, and make their way through her labyrinthine corridors.

In the meantime, Teth could be anywhere. The system's sensor web should alert them if he reappeared, but then, it hadn't alerted Fesky of his presence behind Tyros' moon. Or rather, it *had* notified the *Vesta* of an unidentified vessel's presence, but comically late. One of the main purposes of a sensor web was to foil any ships attempting to sneak into a system under stealth, but given the time lag involved in communicating across star systems, the web simply wasn't designed to account for ships capable of appearing out of thin air—or, thin space.

"This isn't how I like to open meetings," Husher said as he entered the conference room, which was populated at last with everyone whose presence he'd requested, "but what the *hell* just happened?"

He tossed his com onto the broad conference table, and it chose that moment to light up with a transmission. The display said "Penelope Snyder," so he ignored it.

"Let's start with you," Husher said, nodding toward Tyros Deputy Governor Pat Siegfried, who'd become governor the moment Teth snapped Jomo's spindly neck. "What happened to your orbital defense platforms? Why didn't they prevent Teth from getting to the planet's surface, and why did Jomo cooperate with the Ixa to lure my marines and I down there?"

Siegfried folded her hands together on the desk, returning Husher's gaze with one of calm. "Your first question is simply answered, Captain. The Ixan warship appeared *underneath* the orbital defense platforms. For reasons that would have been obvious until this week, the platforms have no weapons that point downward, and if they did, their use would involve significant risk to the population below."

"So they would," Husher said. "And Jomo's actions?"

"Were coerced, of course," Siegfried said. "The Tumbran and her aides were held at gunpoint and forced to do as they did."

"A Tumbran met us at the elevator," Husher said. "Unaccompanied. Instead of warning us, he led us straight to the slaughter."

Shaking her head, Siegfried said, "All I can tell you is that we were all terrified of the Ixa and their capabilities, Captain. They seemed to know things they couldn't possibly know, including many things we'd done in their absence."

"It's like the Prophecies all over again," Fesky said.

The Ixan Prophecies had been a series of texts the Ixa had begun publicizing throughout the galaxy after the First Galactic War. They'd predicted a number of events, including humanity's downfall, and as the next galactic war unfolded those events had started coming true.

It eventually came to light that the prophecies were the work of a superintelligent AI, whose ability to run simulations of the universe had granted it a pretty good handle on the future. *Not perfect, though.*

"It *is* like the Prophecies," Husher said. "Which makes sense. We can expect Teth to be working with AIs who are at least equal in power to the one that devised the Prophecies, probably greater."

"Sir?" Fesky said.

Husher glanced at the Winger askance. "Uh, yes?"

She held up her com. "I...just got a message from Penelope Snyder asking to speak with you." With that, her com started buzzing. "Now she's calling."

Husher held out his hand, and Fesky passed over her com. Answering it, he barked, "*Not now!*" Then he ended the call and tossed the com back to Fesky.

Clearing his throat and ignoring the heat creeping up his neck, Husher pressed on: "We'll get to the return of the AIs a little later, and what it means for us. For now, I'd like to hear from you, Governor Siegfried, about how Teth managed to disable your entire planetary net, given it's a decentralized technology, and designed to be resistant to an outcome like this one."

It was Siegfried's turn to look uncomfortable. "Governor Jomo and I collaborated on implementing a kill switch for the entire planetary net, late last year."

Husher squinted at her. "Why in Sol would you do that?"

"We saw it as a safety precaution."

Snorting, Husher said, "You're going to have to enlighten me on that one."

"In the event of widespread planetary unrest...we wanted the ability to exercise control over the, uh, narrative, that the public was getting in an emergency. If we needed to."

"Well, it turns out your kill switch made you uniquely vulnerable. If you hadn't implemented it, we would have heard about the Ixan incursion from your planetary net, and Jomo might still be alive."

Siegfried had the decency to look abashed, but apparently Fesky wasn't satisfied. "Planetary nets, the old micronet, the internet in its earliest form—these are considered the saviors of democracy by more historians than I can name. And you decided to subvert all that with a *switch?*"

"That'll do, Fesky," Husher said, and the Winger fell silent, though her feathers still stood at attention. He returned his gaze to Siegfried. "Governor, is there anything else you'd like to share with us? Anything you think we'd benefit from knowing?"

"There is," the new governor said after a brief pause. "In the weeks leading up to the attack, we kept experiencing random blips from the sensor web, which was telling us that craft were periodically appearing then vanishing throughout the system. We assumed the web was malfunctioning, but..."

"But now we have a theory that fits a lot better than that."

"Yes."

"These blips. Did they represent ships as big as the one Teth just used to pummel us?"

"No," Siegfried said. "Not nearly as big. They were closer to com drones in size."

"Interesting," Husher muttered, then sniffed. "Teth spoke of a species he called the Progenitors. This is basically speculative, but I have a strong feeling that they're the same species Baxa mentioned before we nuked him into oblivion—the same species that created the AIs themselves."

"Captain," Siegfried said. "If the AIs truly have returned, why have they sent only one destroyer to attack us?"

"Well, that assumes the Gok attacks are unrelated. But I take your point, and again, I can only speculate based on what we already know about the AIs that Baxa claimed have been loosed on the local galactic cluster. We know they operate on an extremely long timescale, and we also know they're obsessed with efficiency. Maybe they think if Teth manages to apply enough pressure in the right places, he can debilitate the IGF—make us an easy mop-up job for whatever comes next. He told me that if I 'want all this to stop,' then I should present myself at the former Baxa System, which we now call the Concord System. Not only that, he wants me to bring someone named Jake Price along with me. Does anyone here know that name?"

As he looked around the table, no one seemed to, but Fesky spoke up anyway. "It seems like an obvious trap, sir. This might be exactly how Teth thinks he can debilitate us: by killing you."

Husher chuckled. "I'm flattered, Fesky, but I think you're giving me way more credit than I deserve. I am not the IGF—the IGF is made up of millions of hardworking service members.

"I'm going to deploy a com drone to the Damask System, which Admiral Iver named as his next destination, to seek his guidance on how to proceed. Hopefully, he'll see the wisdom in recalling the *Vesta*'s battle group to rejoin their capital ship, instead of having them continue pursuing a relationship with a species who are known allies of the one that just attacked us."

Fesky was nodding, as were Amy Fry and Peter Gamble. Governor Siegfried looked resolute. Kaboh's childlike fingers drummed silently on the conference table, and he beheld Husher with an appraising look, but said nothing.

As everyone filed out, Fesky paused next to him. "Captain, Teth's demand that you present yourself at the Ixa's old home system...it seems to imply he's set up base there."

"It does," Husher said, feeling pretty sure he knew what was coming next.

After a pause, Fesky said, "As far as we know, Ek is still there. She might be in danger."

Husher nodded. After they'd defeated Baxa, Ek had remained on the Ixan homeworld. Her years of spacefaring had taken too great a toll on her aquatic body, and if she'd continued her interstellar travel, she likely would have died. So she'd remained on Klaxon instead, to live beneath its ocean.

"She likely is still there, Fesky. But as much as it pains me to say, she's not our primary concern. We can't embark on a rash foray into Concord just to save our old friend. It's a noble sentiment, but acting on it could very well put the fortunes of the entire galaxy at risk."

A tremor ran through Fesky. "You're right." Bobbing her head, she left the conference room.

CHAPTER 19

It Rings True

After shuffling through the dimensions a thousand times, a million times, Teth's destroyer emerged into what he'd come to think of as the Prime Reality. And why not think of it that way? He came from this reality, after all, and it would certainly serve as his crucible. For him, no other reality truly mattered.

As for where they might *be* inside that coveted universe, which he believed himself destined to dominate, it was very difficult to say. That they might be billions of light years away from the Milky Way was more likely than not, and thanks to the shifting relationships between the various universes, it would take no shortage of trial and error to figure out how to return to the galaxy that was his target, not to mention the time it would take to recharge the *Apex*'s capacitors enough for another interdimensional journey.

But that's the price we pay for being forced to flee, isn't it?

He slammed a massive fist onto the arm of his throne-like command seat, causing most of the bridge crew to jump. Not

Breka, though. No, his Strategy auxiliary was as calm as always. A sturdy Ixan, Breka, of the purest bloodlines.

The engagement with Husher had not ended the way Teth had envisioned. He hadn't expected the captain to perish, of course, though he certainly would have welcomed that outcome. The AI that had been assigned to Teth advised him not to expect Husher's death this day, and he hadn't, no matter how hard he'd tried to achieve it.

He *had* expected to leave Husher much more...*diminished* than they had, however. Teth had meant his Cleavers to tear up the *Vesta*'s innards, and his particle beam had been intended to find something vital.

His intel had claimed Husher was weakened, a shadow of the bold young lieutenant who'd faced him during the Second Galactic War. He'd certainly seemed pathetic inside Piper Hall, and also during their remote exchange from aboard their respective shuttles. But the human's swift reaction to the particle beam, which was technology he couldn't possibly have known about...

...well, that reaction had reminded Teth of Captain Keyes, his old nemesis, who'd died in the attempt to kill him.

Clearly, Teth needed to readjust his expectations, and also to apply his intel on Husher in a more intelligent way.

That began with motivating his crew.

"Communications auxiliary."

"Yes, Immaculate One?" the auxiliary said, cowering a little.

"Be not afraid. Summon my entire crew to the Deployment Bay. I wish for my eyes to feast on their strength while I address them as one."

"W-what of ship functions, Immaculate One?"

"We're in the middle of the void," Teth said gently, forked tongue playing over his fangs. "There are no enemies to face here, no navigational hazards to concern us. We can rest, if only for a brief moment." When he finished, Teth removed his ceremonial broadsword from the rack that held it fast to the back of the command seat, secure in its sheath. He affixed that sheath to his waist, toying with the idea of stopping in his quarters to behold his reflection before continuing on to the Deployment Bay.

No. He would deny himself that pleasure, as he denied himself many pleasures. That was part of what kept him honed.

Ixa darted past Teth as he strode through corridor after banner-hung corridor. They took great pains not to disturb him as they rushed by, but they also feared the consequences of being out of place once he arrived inside the bay.

Most of the corridors' banners were scarlet, like those he'd ordered hung around the Tumbran Hall, though some were the white of purity, and others were the black of space. Teth enjoyed the grandeur they brought to his vessel—he felt they lent his cause the weight it was due.

When he entered the vast Deployment Bay, his thousands of Ixa were deployed in perfect ranks, just as he'd known they would be. The augmentations the Progenitors had made had turned his brethren into exquisite soldiers; lightning-quick, their physical might now unrivaled even by the Gok. The enhancements had come out well enough that the Progenitors had since expressed an interest in cloning tens of thousands more Ixa, with the intention of making them their main infantry unit in the coming war. Teth had given them his blessing.

In the front row stood his Primary Officers, the purest and most cunning from among the Ixa that had survived the last war with the humans. All of those Ixa were now arrayed before him.

"Strategy auxiliary Breka," Teth called, his voice amplified via a device woven into his uniform's collar.

"Yes, Immaculate One?" Breka responded, meeting Teth's gaze without flinching.

"Come to the fore and stand at my right hand."

With crisp form, Breka marched forward, about-turned, and stomped his foot, coming to attention beside his Command Leader.

"This," Teth said, spreading his hand toward Breka, "is an Ixan. He was the architect of the plan that finally succeeded in exterminating all the half-breeds and purifying our species. The Ixa form a body, and that body was once plagued with disease, but now we are healthy once more. Is that not so, Strategy auxiliary Breka?"

"It is so, Immaculate One!"

"And tell me, to whom does victory offer itself?"

"Victory offers itself to the strong, Immaculate One!" Breka called.

"Yes, but how did the strong *become* strong?"

Breka fell silent, presumably while he puzzled over the answer.

"I will tell you. The strong won their strength by denying themselves what they wanted in the moment so that they could have what they desired for the future—power. In a word, the strong became so through sacrifice. Does that ring true for you, Strategy auxiliary Breka?"

"It rings true, Immaculate One!"

"And if two strong beings enter combat, who wins?"

"He who is willing to sacrifice most, Immaculate One!"

"Not only that, Breka. Victory belongs to he who is willing to make even the ultimate sacrifice, if that is what victory requires."

"Yes, Immaculate One."

"Strategy auxiliary Breka. You are unarmed. If I drew my broadsword—" Steel rasped against leather as Teth exposed the gleaming blade. "—would you die as a coward, or would you kneel, willingly sacrificing yourself to me, if that was what I required?"

Without hesitation, Breka knelt, pushing down the collar of his midnight uniform in order to better expose his neck.

"You are the best Ixan before me, Breka," Teth said, and he swung his sword overhead.

The blade flickered downward, and Teth paused with the razor-sharp edge just kissing the back of Breka's neck.

"Rise, Breka," Teth said, with some mirth. "You have reaffirmed your worthiness."

The Strategy auxiliary stood tall. With that, Teth put his entire body into swinging the broadsword at Breka, cleaving the

Ixan from his neck to just below his right pectoral. The hulking Ixan slid from Teth's blade to the deck, spasming.

"Do not fail me again," he told the remaining Ixa as he marched out of the Deployment Bay.

CHAPTER 20

Fairly Specific Intel

In a rare empty moment, Husher found himself fishing Keyes's wooden crucifix from his desk drawer and letting it dangle from his fingers by its leather thong.

Admiral Iver's reply had arrived via com drone on the fifth day after Husher sent the request for orders. It informed him that the order had already been sent for the *Vesta*'s battle group to rejoin her with all possible speed, and that they should be underway within the next three days. That would mean a week or more before they joined their capital starship in the Wintercress System.

At least it gives us time to avail of Wintercress' shipbuilding facilities for some much-needed repairs after our scrapes with Teth and the Gok.

The drone had also contained orders concerning what to do once the *Vesta*'s battle group returned: together, they were to patrol the Union's most far-flung systems, or at least the ones closest to the Ixa's old home. Iver had apparently drawn the same conclusions from Teth's demands that Fesky had: the Concord System, formerly the Baxa System, was almost certainly his base of operations, and so that was where they could expect new threats to originate from.

For two decades, the Interstellar Union had been working with the Integrated Galactic Fleet to make member systems as safe as possible. Planetary colonies with populations over two million enjoyed a full complement of orbital defense platforms, and every system saw regular patrols, either from capital starships and their battle groups or individually operating warships.

Even so, the systems nearest the former Baxa System were among the smallest and most under-defended in the Union, and so it was the decision of the admiralty to deploy three of the fleet's eight capital starships to exclusively patrol those systems.

Husher had to hand it to the admiralty—their orders were decisive, which was somewhat uncharacteristic for them. Normally, they were just as...*concerned* with placating politicians and bureaucrats as Husher was, as evidenced by Iver's willingness to sign off on his termination if he hadn't agreed to the Awareness Training.

As per IGF protocol, Husher ordered the com drone stowed with the other four that comprised his supercarrier's automated communications fleet. Building, maintaining, and storing the drones added up to an expensive proposition, and after exchanging messages it was standard practice for both parties to simply keep each other's drones for future use.

The drone had also arrived with an unencrypted partition containing civilian files from the Damask System's interplanetary net. It would include messages from loved ones as well as the latest media and software updates, so Husher had to assume morale in Cybele had been lifted at least a little.

He laid the crucifix on the table, its bottom pointing toward Husher's left. Why had Keyes chosen to leave it to him in his will, and only that? Husher had heard of people sending vindictive messages using their wills, leaving their "beneficiaries" weird or useless items. But he knew that was far from Keyes's style. Husher had been close with the man, or as close as a young upstart and his commanding officer could get. Over the course of the Second Galactic War, they'd won each other's respect.

No, if Keyes had left him the crucifix, it was because he considered it valuable.

Even so... Husher couldn't make heads or tails of it. He opened the drawer, dropped the wooden cross in, and stood up with the intention of visiting Cybele and checking on Ochrim's progress.

At that moment, his Oculenses notified him of a voice-only call from Major Gamble, and Husher willed them to put the call through.

"Captain, my marines just caught some type of activist who managed to make her way inside the crew section."

This never ends, does it? "Did you get the name?"

"She declined to give her name, but we did find her in the database easily enough. Name's Maeve Aldaine, a Sociology undergrad at Cybele U."

Ah, an old friend. "Is Ms. Aldaine aware she's now officially a federal offender?"

"I may have mentioned something along those lines."

"Good. Give her our best cell in the brig, and make sure she knows it's the coziest one we could find for her. I'm on my way into Cybele now, but I'll have a chat with her when I get back."

"Will do, sir."

"Husher out."

It was difficult not to smile to himself as he made his way through the *Vesta*'s crew corridors and toward the hatch that let out into the simulated desert. Trespassing on a military vessel—or in the *Vesta*'s case, the crew section of a military vessel—was a federal offense, good for either ten years in prison or a hefty fine. In fact, it was one of the few things about the military that civilians *hadn't* been given unfettered access to.

Who knows how long that'll last, though. The way things are going, I could easily be giving guided tours by the end of next week.

He continued on toward Cybele, trying to banish the mental image of Vin Husher the Smiley Supercarrier Captain waving a gaggle of tourists through corridor after corridor, charming them with endearing anecdotes about the ship and her crew.

When he reached Ochrim's house, a knock didn't bring the Ixan to the door, nor did the bell. Husher sent a transmission request.

"Ochrim," he said once the alien accepted. "You're in the lab?"

"I am."

"I'm coming down. Send your door the command to let me in."

The front door clicked, and the call ended. Husher stepped inside, making sure to secure the entrance behind him. That done, he proceeded to the rear of the house, pried up the floor tile, and activated the panel, which slid aside for him. He began climbing down the ladder.

"Nice day out," he remarked as his foot met the lab's floor.

Ochrim glanced up from where he was standing over a table, using a screwdriver to fiddle around with something. The Ixan peered at him over small, round spectacles that perched on the end of his faded muzzle. "A joke."

"You should try one sometime," Husher said. "Damn, I forgot to bring down beer. Do you have a mini-fridge down here or anything?"

"I'm afraid not, Captain."

"Just my luck. Have you heard about the visit your brother paid us?"

"My...brother?" Ochrim's hand paused mid-screw.

"Teth."

Ochrim blinked. "I follow shipboard news on the narrownet, and I've read rumors about what happened, as well as complaints that our military isn't telling us more. I also felt the tremors from whatever it was we were struck with. But I was unaware our attacker was someone claiming to be my brother."

"Not just claiming, Ochrim. I ran into him myself, down on Tyros. He's bigger, now."

That brought a silence from the scientist, as well as a baffled expression that Husher found pretty gratifying. It was a rare thing to behold.

"Teth seemed to have a couple pieces of fairly specific intel about us," he went on. "And that was just what he let on. You wouldn't happen to be the source of that intel, would you?"

"Of course not."

Husher gave a dry chuckle. "You say that like it should be obvious, but a glance at your history tells us it's anything but." He marched toward the Ixan, and to the scientist's credit, he didn't flinch. When Husher neared, he yanked the metal stool from behind where the Ixan stood, dragged it back a meter or so, and took a seat. "Let's see how good I am at reading you," Husher said, grinning. "You're even more reserved than usual today, and that tells me two things. One, you have something new. And two, the reason you haven't *notified* me about having something new is that you're reluctant to share it with me. You'll claim that the reason for that is your reluctance to violate the Union's strictures on developing weapons for military use."

"I *am*—"

Holding up a hand to forestall him, Husher said, "Stow it. That's what you'll claim, but you do know what it's actually going to seem like to me, don't you? Your reluctance to share any and all advancements with me will seem *very* suspicious, in light of your brother's reappearance. Now, assuming for a moment that you're sincere in your misgivings, I want you to know that I plan to submit any usable findings to the admiralty first. If they don't like that I even went about supporting this research, then I'll take full responsibility. I won't even mention your name. But Ochrim, our society is stagnating as a military power, and I *have* to do something about that. Now, with all that said, why don't you tell me what you've found?"

A brief pause from Ochrim, punctuated by a sigh. "I believe I've discovered how inter-dimensional travel might be possible. If I—"

"Just tell me what you need. I'll get the explanation of how it works from you in the event that you actually manage to make it work. Sorry, I don't think I have the fortitude today to make it through a lecture like the last one you gave me."

"Very well. I need the latest design and drafting software from DeskChain. Not what is commercially available, but the edition they offer to corporations and governments able to pay, which has the more robust simulation capabilities I require."

"Not a simple request. But all right, Ochrim. I'll see what strings I can pull." Husher turned to walk toward the ladder leading up to Ochrim's residence, then stopped, glancing back at the Ixan. "The rumors you heard about our engagement...did they include how the enemy warship seemed to just vanish?"

Ochrim inclined his head. "A couple of them did."

"Do you think it's possible that Teth has learned how to flip back and forth between universes?"

The Ixan nodded. "Very."

CHAPTER 21

Head Fascist

"I see a bright young lady with potential oozing out her ears," Husher said as he drew level with Aldaine's cell. "What's she doing in a military vessel's brig?"

Aldaine stood, fists balled at her sides as she turned a cold glare on him. "Fighting fascist human supremacists."

Husher raised his eyebrows. "Wow. That's quite a charge. What was your plan, exactly, for fighting these fascists?"

"I'm talking about you. You're the head fascist."

"I see. What was your plan?"

Aldaine fell silent for a moment, but she must have decided there wasn't much point in withholding, because she said, "I planned to access the ship's emergency broadcasting system so I could speak to everyone on board the *Vesta*, including the crew."

"Misusing an emergency broadcasting system—yet another federal offense. Do you even know where the equipment is located?"

"I would have found it."

"I tend to doubt that, considering you were apprehended within three minutes of making your way in here. How did you manage to get in, by the way?"

The young activist fell silent, and Husher sighed. He hadn't expected her to give up that information on simple request, or even to indicate whether she'd been helped by a member of the crew. He'd already decided what measure he would take to prevent this from happening again, though: from now on, each crewmember would be given a unique passcode, which they'd have to manually enter whenever they wanted to visit or leave Cybele. Everyone would be responsible for keeping his or her code secure, and also for deactivating it and requesting a new one if they thought it had been compromised. The next time a code was used by an activist seeking to make a point, Husher planned to hold the owner of that code responsible.

"Can I ask what exactly it was that you meant to protest?" he said.

"A lot of things, but mainly your refusal to allow nonhuman crew to participate in Nonattendance Day."

If Husher had ever assumed his capacity for awe would dwindle with age, he was wrong. "If I'd encouraged them to participate in Nonattendance Day, the *Vesta* would have been undercrewed during the Wintercress engagement. You do realize we're now officially on wartime footing, don't you, Ms. Aldaine?"

"That's exactly the time to hold closest to our principles, isn't it? If Captain Leonard Keyes is to be taken seriously, that is. He made public statements to that effect all the time, and so did you, when you were younger."

"I still do," Husher said, feeling a flush creeping up his neck and trying to will it back down. "The principle I'm adhering to currently is that in order to keep everyone on this ship as safe as I can—and, by extension, everyone in the galaxy—I need all hands on deck."

"If this were your only misstep, I could almost believe you. But we already know you're prejudiced against nonhuman species, Captain. Both your actions and your recorded testimony at city council meetings make it obvious."

Giving his head a brisk shake to clear it, Husher said, "Ms. Aldaine, I count several nonhuman beings among my most respected colleagues and friends."

"Ha," Aldaine said. "That's exactly the argument supremacists *always* use. 'I have plenty of Winger friends,' they say, every time they're about to do something that marginalizes Wingers even more."

"That may be true, of supremacists," Husher said. "But it doesn't mean it's never a valid thing for anyone else to bring up, especially when it happens to be correct. My XO and best friend is a Winger, I have a Gok corporal who has my eternal gratitude for saving my life, and I have a Kaithian Nav officer who...well, I won't get into my feelings about him right now. The point is—"

"I don't know how you can do it," Aldaine said. "I don't know how you can stand there and pretend you're the perfect exemplar of interspecies relations, when I *know* you're the opposite. I already know that, Captain, and nothing you say can convince me otherwise."

Nodding, Husher said, "Exactly. That's exactly what the matter is with people like you, Ms. Aldaine. *Nothing can convince you otherwise.* You're not interested in letting other perspectives or even facts convince you. It would be pointless for me to bring up how research has shown that spending time around other species is *actually* the antidote to biased attitudes, not this misguided Awareness Training you keep pushing."

Husher pressed on, before Aldaine could start shouting him down: "You just accused me of thinking I'm perfect on interspecies relations, but I don't think that. I'm well aware I'm far from perfect. We all make mistakes about how to treat each other, and some people truly are hateful. But the honest mistakes, at least, are part of the process. They're part of life. And you refuse to acknowledge that. You hold other people to a standard of perfection that you aren't capable of sustaining yourself, and I can guarantee you, someday that'll come back around to bite you in the ass."

"Was that a *threat?*" Aldaine demanded, and with that, Husher grew tired of wasting his breath.

"Escort Ms. Aldaine to Cybele and release her," he told the guards as he exited the brig.

"I'm going to make your life a living *hell,* Husher!" she yelled just before he drew out of earshot.

CHAPTER 22

Asleep to Awake

The evenly trimmed grass was damp, and it soaked through his creased pants as he knelt there. He'd paid someone to keep the lawn tidy while he was away on deployment, but right now it was far from tidy—beset by flaming timber, it would take months to restore.

Husher would not be the one to restore the lawn. Even at that moment, as he watched the inferno consume his family's home, he knew that. He would leave this place and never return.

The heat bathed him, but he didn't care. Instead, he longed to charge into the conflagration, to rake through the white-hot cinders of his house, to topple beams and smash through burnt walls. He wanted his daughter, and if he couldn't have her, then he wanted to join her.

His uncontrolled sobbing rose in pitch, and soon it reached unnatural heights—notes his voice should not have been capable of. It also gained the regularity of a machine, shrieking again and again in measured soprano.

He woke to a Priority-level call coming through his com, which vibrated madly atop the table next to his bed. Snatching it, he groaned when he saw the name. *Penelope Snyder.*

He answered, growling, "Cybele better be burning down, Ms. Snyder."

A brief pause, followed by, "Excuse me, Captain?"

He strove to regain control of himself, ignoring his racing heart. "Unless this is an emergency, you're abusing your ability to make Priority calls to my com, and that's unacceptable."

"This *is* a priority, Captain Husher, or at least it should be."

"What is it?"

"According to the records my Awareness Trainers have supplied me with, some of your human crew are *skipping* the prescribed training. You *do* recall that if you're to remain captain, every human in your crew must complete this program, don't you?"

We're in a war, Penelope. That's what he wanted to say, but despite the emotional state his nightmare had left him in, he managed to restrain himself. He knew it was entirely pointless to raise that fact.

His voice came out as flat, but he forced himself to say it: "I'll make it known that all human crewmembers must complete Awareness Training or face disciplinary action."

"I'm relieved to hear that. My schedule tells me that you aren't on watch right now. Unless there's been a change?"

"No change." *Unless you count my change from asleep to awake.*

"Then I trust you'll make your promised announcement straight away. I truly believe that time is of the essence, with matters like these."

"Yes," he said, in a tone just as flat as before. "As a military captain in the middle of a war, I can certainly appreciate time-sensitive matters."

"Splendid, Captain. Cheers." Snyder terminated the call.

He pushed himself to issue the required notice on the Board, which was accessible using the crew-only narrownet. With that, he crawled back into his bunk and tried to put the rest of his off-duty time to good use.

He must have succeeded in falling asleep, because forty-five minutes later, he awoke without the ability to account for the intervening time.

There were still two hours left till his next watch began in the CIC, and his com blinked with a message from one Corporal Toby Yung. Yung was requesting an audience with the captain at his earliest convenience.

Sighing, Husher messaged Yung to meet him in his office. He started getting dressed.

CHAPTER 23

Respect for Competence

Yung was already waiting outside Husher's office when he arrived. The marine came to attention once he spotted his captain's approach.

"Corporal," Husher said with a nod as he palmed the hatch open. "After you. Take a seat."

Husher made his way around the desk to his chair. Even before he was settled, the marine said, "Permission to speak freely, sir."

Under current protocol, it was essentially a requirement for superior officers to grant such permission, as often as it was requested. Husher would likely have been inclined to grant it anyway, under most circumstances, but it rankled to be strongarmed into doing it. "Granted," he said nevertheless.

"Awareness Training doesn't work. That's been proven, time and time again, for every form it's taken over the last several centuries. Are you aware of that?"

Drawing a deep breath, Husher said. "I have to speak with some care on this subject, Corporal Yung. If anything I say ends up in opportunistic hands, it could easily compromise—"

"Sir, are you a politician or the captain of a military vessel?"

Husher felt his lips tighten. "While I did give you permission to speak freely, that doesn't unburden you of the requirement to treat your commanding officer with respect."

"I apologize, Captain."

"I understand your reluctance to undergo the Training. I understand if you think it's pointless, and I'd even understand if you had a personal or political reason for opposing it. But the fact is, under the current environment, I have to play ball with the bureaucrats in order to be left alone long enough to properly run my ship. Right now, that means requiring you and every other human in my crew to undergo that training. It is, in fact, an order, Corporal, and you're paid to follow orders."

Yung's nostrils flared, but he managed to moderate his tone as he raised his next point: "There are rumors that you plan to sign on to this new Positive Response Program that's sweeping the fleet, too. Is that something you're considering, Captain? Allowing military assignments to be determined by what species someone belongs to over their level of training and skill?"

Husher tried to suppress a wince but was pretty sure he'd failed. The tightrope he had to walk in a conversation like this caused him almost physical pain. "I understand your concerns, Corporal, but—"

"Ah, come on, sir! You can't honestly be thinking about giving in to them on this. You keep saying you're appeasing the politicians to preserve our military effectiveness, but this program will do the opposite. Besides, the program's *also* been found not to actually improve things for nonhuman species. Of course, things like facts or findings don't seem to matter much anymore."

Husher's vision began to blur around the edges. The corporal's words were getting to him, mainly because he agreed with them completely. Having to argue a side of an issue opposite the one he actually believed was...irritating.

But Yung wasn't finished. "It's not just the program," he said, leaning forward, eyes widening slightly. "It's everything you've been doing to placate the bureaucrats. You might think you're keeping everything together, but it's tearing the crew apart. They see you favoring politicians' agendas over them and their careers. If you implement this program, what will happen to your loyal human crewmembers who get 'reshuffled?' Is the competence of your crew even a consideration for you anymore, Captain?"

With that, Husher saw a line of attack, and he exploited it viciously. "Competence, Corporal? You want to talk about *competence?* All right. Why don't we have a look at your file?" Husher willed his Oculenses to display a shared view of Corporal Toby Yung's service record. When he glanced at Yung's face, he saw a studied neutrality underscored by palpable anxiety. *Good.*

"Recruit Training," Husher said. "Instructor comments. 'Met the bare minimum requirements to complete training.' Infantry School. Barely sufficient grades across the board. Instructor comments. 'Despite significantly above-average intelligence and aptitude, Yung applies himself only enough to skirt by.'"

Husher willed Yung's records to disappear, and he turned back to the corporal. "Do you still want to talk to me about competence, Corporal? Is a lack of respect for competence something you still wish to accuse *me* of, when you couldn't even be bothered to educate yourself to the level of your own competence?"

Yung's brow crept lower. "When did you look at my record?"

"I've never given your service record more than a cursory glance, Corporal, despite being well within my rights to examine it."

"Then how did you know to pull it up just now?"

"Oh, that was no leap of logic. You're clearly a brilliant young man, but you're just a corporal, when we both know you should have gone to Officer School. And why *didn't* you, Corporal Yung? No need to answer that question—I've known plenty of soldiers like you. It's because you know exactly how smart you are, and a long time ago, before you ever dreamed of joining the Fleet, someone didn't give you something you felt you deserved. Maybe that person didn't think your intellect alone warranted it. But you feel like your intelligence puts you above everyone else—that the world should lay itself at your feet, just because you're such a *smart* boy. When it didn't do that, you got bitter, and you swore you'd only ever do the bare minimum to skate by. Well, here you are. You really showed us, didn't you, *Corporal?*"

Yung's lips were a tight, white line. "Permission to leave, sir?"

"Permission granted. And next time you want to criticize *my* approach to command, try getting yourself in order first."

CHAPTER 24

Warp

At last, the *Vesta*'s battle group rejoined her. Their scheduled patrol would take them to the Viburnum System, which was both near the former Baxa System and home to an important munitions facility that orbited the largest of its three gas giants. It seemed a likely next target for Teth, so Admiral Iver had designated it as the *Vesta*'s first destination, a decision Husher fully endorsed.

Their route from Wintercress to Viburnum involved transitioning through five darkgates, which put their travel time at just over two days, since a couple of the systems along the way featured darkgates positioned fairly close to each other.

At least it won't be necessary to go to warp at any point. That would have given Teth all the time he needed to find and destroy that facility.

"Captain," Winterton said without looking up from his console, "transition through the Wintercress-Tansy darkgate should occur in thirty-four minutes."

"Acknowledged, Ensign. How's our hull looking, after the attention it got from Wintercress' galaxy-renowned shipwrights and their robots?"

"They patched us up pretty good, Captain. I won't say she's as good as new, but she's more than spaceworthy."

"My ship? She'd be spaceworthy even if we'd left the hull as it was. She's a sturdy old girl."

"Yes, sir."

"The battle group captains just completed their sound off, sir," the Coms officer said. "Captain Eryl of the *Lysander*, Captain Arbuck of the *Thero*, Captain Lee of the *Golgos*, and Captain Hornsby of the *Hylas* are all reporting systems in the green."

"Steady as she goes, then," Husher said—an ancient seafaring phrase he enjoyed dredging up from time to time, which had once been used to tell the Helmsman to maintain the present course.

"A com drone just transitioned through the darkgate, Captain," Ensign Fry said. "It transmitted a message addressed to you from the *Selene*. Audio-only."

"What's the security designation?"

"Confidential."

Husher nodded. "Play it." Confidential information could be known by almost anyone in the IGF, so long as they didn't share it with the public.

"Captain Husher, this is Commander Ternon of the *Selene*, currently patrolling the Saffron System. The sensor web here has been getting some strange readings, lately. According to the sensors, small craft keep appearing suddenly in random locations throughout the system, then disappearing just as quickly. The web's operators have been calling them anomalies, but when they passed the data on to me, I noticed that the profiles of these 'ghost ships' are identical to the ones detected by the Wintercress sensor web before the attack there." Ternon cleared his throat before continuing. "We are not equipped to repel an attack on the level of what Wintercress suffered. From what I understand about that, only a capital ship can withstand the power Teth now has at his disposal, and you're the closest capital ship to Saffron. This message is to request your aid. Ternon out."

In the wake of the message, a silence settled over the CIC.

"Darkgate transition in twenty-nine minutes, Captain," Winterton said, breaking the silence with his trademark neutrality, which seemed to come fairly naturally to him.

Kaboh spoke next. "The quickest route to Saffron is to effect a warp jump from the system we're about to enter, Captain. I have the departure point coordinates at the ready."

"What makes you think we're going to Saffron?" Husher said slowly.

"Commander Ternon's transmission was—"

"Commander Ternon is unaware of our current mission, which is to protect the munitions facility at Viburnum."

Kaboh turned his entire diminutive frame to face the command seat, wearing a scowl that mixed shock and disgust. "Sir, you can't possibly be considering choosing *munitions* over civilian lives!"

"We're the only ones close enough to reach Viburnum within a meaningful timeframe, Lieutenant. If we don't go there now, we'll be leaving a vital military resource wide open for Teth to destroy or appropriate for his own uses."

"Yes, but we're also the only ones close enough to answer Commander Ternon's distress call."

Clacking her beak, Fesky interjected, in what she probably thought was a calming tone. "What if the *Vesta* makes for one system while we deploy the battle group to the other? That way—"

"Not happening," Husher said. "The last time we allowed ourselves to get separated, Teth nearly melted half our hull off. We're staying together."

Kaboh shook his head, head-tail swaying back and forth. The Kaithian had a facility for employing human body language when it suited his purposes. "I must insist that you think through the implications of your proposal, Captain."

"It's not a proposal," Husher ground out. "If I decide we're going to Viburnum, then I'll give you the order to set a course for Viburnum. I'm sure you know the term for when subordinates refuse to follow orders aboard a warship."

"I'm prepared to follow whatever orders you give me, of course," Kaboh said. "But would you just take a moment to consider how you'll feel if we go to Viburnum, discover there's no threat to the munitions facility, and then learn of an attack on the two colonies of Saffron?"

"In that event, I'll hope that Commander Ternon had the good sense to evacuate the people of Cebrene to Edessa. The former's a fairly minor colony of little more than a hundred thousand, but Edessa's population approaches two million, and last year they were successful in lobbying the Union to install defensive platforms around their planet, despite being several thousand short of the usual population quota. Those platforms are fully operational, and with the two warships on patrol there as well, it should be possible for the Saffron System to mount a reasonable defense. If they fail, that will be tragic, but it will also be the type of thing that results from making expedient military decisions designed to save billions of lives, even when doing so means risking millions."

Several officers around the CIC were wearing expressions of grim approval, and Husher caught a nod or two as well. *That should be the end of it.*

But Kaboh hadn't turned back to his station, and his slim, blue-white shoulders rose and fell. "Captain," he said, his voice meticulously level, "know that if you make this decision, I intend to file a formal complaint on the grounds of moral dissent. As you know, Admiral Iver is a close personal friend, and I'm confident he'll take the appropriate measures once he learns of what transpired."

Husher's eyes locked with Kaboh's for a protracted moment, each refusing to look away until the other faltered. Cheek twitching, Husher was hyper conscious of the CIC officers observing the exchange, waiting to see how their captain would react.

Without taking his eyes off the Kaithian, Husher said, "We'll go to Saffron." His voice came out much softer than he'd intended, and that made heat creep up his neck until it reached his cheeks.

"I'm relieved to hear you say so, Captain," Kaboh said, breaking eye contact and turning briskly to his console. "I'll alter our planned course into the Tansy System so that it takes us to the warp departure point as quickly and efficiently as possible."

As Husher looked around the CIC, his officers' eyes flitted away, and they focused on their respective tasks with unusual intensity.

Fesky held his eyes for little more than a second, and then she averted her gaze as well. That hurt most of all.

CHAPTER 25

Bash Back

"We're clear of system debris, Captain, and safe to accelerate to warp velocity," Winterton said, apparently unaffected by the tension that still clogged the CIC like an invisible smog, even eight hours after Husher's standoff with Kaboh. "All four battle group ships have already completed warp transitions and are en route to Saffron."

Husher gave a curt nod. "Helm?" he said, his voice clipped. He was none too happy about having his will as a captain subverted, and even less happy with himself for letting it happen.

Luckily, Ensign Vy was smart enough to know what her captain wanted. "Opening hatches and extending distortion rods now, sir."

"Very good," Husher said, plunging back into his dark reverie. *What's the point of placating bureaucrats, even bureaucrats disguised as Fleet officers, if it means sacrificing our military effectiveness?* Still, he was convinced he'd done the right thing. Just as Snyder and Chancey had the power to burn down his career, Husher knew Kaboh did as well, but only if Husher agreed to provide the flint and tinder. That was something he refused to do.

To defeat Teth, I need to be in command. I can't let them yank me from the command seat.

But what was the point of sitting there if he couldn't get the correct decisions past the haze of feel-good nonsense? Husher was sure bureaucratic folly came from a place of good intentions, but that wouldn't make the people it got killed any less dead.

"Warp bubble generating," the Helm officer said. "Stabilizing now. Approaching superluminal speed in proportion to declining energy density."

"Acknowledged," Husher muttered.

"Negative mass achieved, Captain. We're in warp."

"Acknowledged," he repeated, and silence fell as his CIC crew checked over critical systems to make sure nothing had been negatively affected during the transition.

Once they were finished, the CIC would become one of the most boring locations on the *Vesta.* Even though the feat performed by the warp bubble—contracting the space in front of the ship while expanding the space behind it—was conceptually astounding, while inside the bubble, there was virtually nothing for the CIC crew to do. The chances of a hostile ship entering the bubble were zero, and it was likewise impossible to steer the ship, since no interface existed for communicating with and controlling the warp bubble itself. Warp transitions had to be carefully preplanned, along a route that was vanishingly unlikely to contain debris of any kind, since impacting anything bigger than a pebble would likely result in the molecules of the ship and her crew getting strewn across the void.

Luckily, the chances of encountering anything at all in the spaces between stars really were infinitesimal, and since the advent of the warp drive, there had been no mishaps involving collisions with errant debris.

Husher's com vibrated, and he slipped it from its holster to find a message from Ochrim inviting him for a beer.

For a moment, he considered which would have been more damning, once IU officials inevitably reviewed his text exchanges with the Ixan—the chummy fiction he was maintaining with the perpetrator of one of the worst atrocities in galactic history, or the truth: that Ochrim was conducting research for him with likely military applications.

Wait, I know exactly which would be more damning. The second one. Much better to continue pretending he was close friends with the war criminal.

"Be right there, pal," Husher messaged back, standing from the command seat. "Fesky, you have the CIC."

"Yes, sir," Fesky said, sounding as morose as everyone else looked.

This time, the pack of protesters was waiting for Husher in the outskirts of Cybele, instead of sitting right outside the hatch into the desert. Husher assumed that was a strategic choice—they'd get more attention from other residents, this way.

"Why haven't you signed onto the Positive Response Program yet?" one yelled, appearing from an alleyway between two residences.

"Why haven't you joined other Fleet captains in the movement to make military hiring practices more equitable for non-human species?" demanded a second, screaming at him from less than a meter's remove.

Husher opened his mouth to respond, and the protester held an air horn in his face, activating it and drowning out his words with a deafening blare.

Seizing the air horn from the protester's grasp, Husher threw it against the side of a nearby residence as hard as he could, where it ruptured with an audible pop.

Get a grip, he berated himself even as his ears rang. *You're a warship captain, not a temperamental child.*

Deciding to take the tack of ignoring the protesters, he marched straight ahead. That was when a band of them trooped into the street ahead, linking arms, digital signs above their heads flashing righteous messages:

"HUSHER ISN'T HELPING!"

"BASH BACK!"

"STOP SWEEPING ME UNDER THE RUG!"

He continued marching, coming to a halt in front of the center protester, whose angry sneer devolved into a look of uncertainty.

There must have been something suggestive in Husher's eyes, because within seconds, the protester he was staring down decoupled himself from his neighbors and stepped out of the way.

Husher passed through them, tearing his com out of his pocket. The ability to send the Oculenses mental commands was too limited to compose an actual message, so for discretion he was forced to tap one out on his com as he walked.

"Can we get that beer at the Secured Zone instead?" he asked Ochrim. "Would that work for you?" He was actually asking whether Ochrim could discreetly show him what he'd discovered there, which he was guessing he could, since as far as Husher knew the Ixan was now doing most of his work in a simulation anyway.

"That'll work," came Ochrim's reply. "I'll meet you there in twenty."

Holstering the com, Husher stalked through the streets of Cybele, fighting the implacable sensation that he was losing control of his ship.

CHAPTER 26

The Secured Zone

The Secured Zone was one of Cybele's most popular bars. He supposed they were trying to follow a military theme, but that wasn't the vibe Husher got—from the name or the atmosphere.

When he entered, the silence was almost total. He supposed that *did* remind him of certain memories from Basic, when their drill sergeant had left them to stand at attention on the parade grounds while a blistering star cooked their innards into a fine stew.

But this quiet was punctuated by soft clicking and even the occasional grunt or curse. The dim interior, lit only by multicolored neon strips that ran along the walls and floors, consisted of several enclosed booths, where patrons sat staring into space—or rather, staring into the fantasy worlds displayed by their Oculenses. Video games, panoramic vids, other media best viewed in the privacy of one's home...that was what people gathered here to immerse themselves in. This was the new "social," and sometimes it even justified that word, in a sense. Sometimes, the gamers played in shared fantasy worlds.

The enclosure of the booths was almost complete, with only a narrow opening for servers to bring drinks when they were ordered remotely. Otherwise, most patrons kept curtains drawn across those openings. The booths even had their own ceilings. They reminded Husher of clamshells, or maybe the wombs to which everyone likened cities like Cybele.

This is how this generation was raised. During Husher's childhood, which had more or less lined up with the end of the First Galactic War, children had still sometimes pretended household implements were guns and chased each other around the yard, playing Marines and Ixa. Or they pretended they were Wingers taking flight, or pretended their dolls were people, or whatever. For Husher, the point was that those games had required some creative input from the children playing them. The generation he glimpsed through the clamshells' openings—they'd been spoon-fed everything, so that they hadn't had to tax even their imaginations.

Husher walked to the narrow window at the back of the room, placing his paycard on the sill. "I'll have a pint of this week's lager, please," he said.

The man on the other side of the window shot him a strange look—whether because he'd actually walked to the window to order or because he was the captain of the *Vesta*, Husher wasn't sure.

He took his beer into an unoccupied clamshell. While he waited for Ochrim, he ordered his Oculenses to go completely transparent so he could look at the shadows that were his only companions, in here. When Ochrim finally made his appearance, the Ixan was beerless.

"Where's your drink?" Husher asked him before taking a long pull from his own.

"I don't need one," Ochrim said. "If they ask me to order something, I'll get a soda."

"Well, I could have used a second one." Husher downed the remainder of his pint.

"Order one using your Oculenses."

Husher grimaced. "Just start up the simulation. Show me what you have." Reaching beyond the clamshell's curtain, Husher found the privacy shield, slamming it across and casting them in utter darkness for the second it took a neon strip to come on, offering them enough light to drink by. Not that that was necessary, since Oculenses had a night vision feature.

At any rate, when he accepted Ochrim's invite, the simulation washed out everything he could see of the real world.

Husher found himself inside a blank void. Ochrim stood beside him, and suspended in the nothingness was a contraption for which Husher had no name. Four-pronged protrusions jutted from the top of the machine, with blue, bead-like wires running down them. A double row of tight coils marched along the sides, projecting in opposite directions.

For more complex simulations, like most video games, users needed a controller of some sort, but Ochrim was able to manipulate the strange object without one, using hand gestures.

"Hopefully the software I talked the Tyros governor into getting for you can do more than simulate a white void and a prop from a poorly produced sci-fi vid," Husher said.

"Oh, yes," Ochrim said. "The DeskChain program allows me to do what Baxa used to—to accurately simulate the universe, or at least its physics, along with a reasonably large region of space."

"It makes me twitchy when you talk about Baxa in that tone."

"Not to worry, Captain," Ochrim said. "My estranged father actually did simulate entire universes—thousands of them at once. I can only simulate a small fraction of one. Also, I lack the superintelligence to go with it."

"Don't sell yourself short, Ochrim," Husher said. He nodded at the contraption. "Walk me through how this thing works."

Husher had always assumed "creepy smile" was just the default configuration for Ixan mouths, but right now, Ochrim appeared to be frowning. He seemed just as apprehensive to go through the process of explaining advanced quantum physics as Husher was to try wrapping his head around it.

"As is often the way with scientific experimentation, I ended up somewhere quite different from my intended destination," the Ixan said.

"I'm fine with that, as long as the surprise destination has military applications."

"It...should. Though I'm not sure you'll respond positively to everything that's involved in the process I've worked out."

Husher sniffed. "What parts do you think I'll object to?"

"It's probably simpler for me to start at the beginning. You recall the experiment during which I successfully contacted my counterpart in the universe next door, so to speak?"

"I remember you seemed pretty convinced that you had, yeah."

When Ochrim turned toward him, his expression was one of clear exasperation, even on an alien face. "I explained to you why it's *incontrovertible* that I—"

Holding up a hand, Husher said, "Yeah, yeah. I accept that you did what you claim to have done. Not saying I remember *how* you did it, or that I even understood how at the time, but I accept it. Let's move on."

"Very well," Ochrim said, clearly still ruffled by Husher's breadth of ignorance. "The first problem I faced—or, thought I faced, at any rate—was traveling to another reality without my double traveling to our reality at the same time. That could result in some awkward interactions, not to mention pointless, since the next universe over would be configured almost identically to ours."

"Hold on a second," Husher said. "When you told me travel across the multiverse might be possible, the military application that came to mind right away was perfect stealth. Is that what you've been thinking?"

"I'm not military."

"Come on, Ochrim. You might as well be, with what you've gotten tangled up in over the years."

The alien hesitated, then said, "As much as I hesitate to highlight *any* military applications to you, given the consequences almost certain to be brought by the Interstellar Union...yes. That is the obvious application, as I see it."

"So that's why you say it would be pointless for us to travel to the next universe over. We'd just end up swapping places with our doubles, and in a combat situation we'd be under fire from our doubles' enemies, who are equal in power to our own."

"Exactly. The only difference between our universe and the next is whatever quantum measurement caused the two universes to diverge. That's far from enough to change the outcome of an engagement."

"We'd be just as likely to die over there as we were in this universe."

"Yes."

"All right. I think I'm getting the hang of this."

Ochrim looked skeptical about that, but he pressed on with his explanation nonetheless. "After I identified that initial, rather obvious hurdle—" To Husher's ears, Ochrim placed a definite emphasis on the word "obvious." "—I set about trying to determine what would be required for us to 'skip over' multiple universes, until we reached one different enough to be useful to us. That was no easy task. Remember that in the first experiment, we merely communicated with the next universe by observing a single isolated ion. What I hoped to do now was figure out how to transport an incredibly complex quantum system—namely, a starship of some size—several universes over."

"Did you succeed?"

"No. Not nearly. But in trying, I did discover something else. This is what brings me to what scientists sometimes call a 'happy accident.'"

Tired of prompting Ochrim to continue, Husher decided to just wait until the Ixan kept talking.

Eventually, he did. "I began with the assumption that in order to transcend the layers of decoherence separating the universes, I would first need to figure out a way to generate and then leverage a decoherence-free space. It's been common knowledge in the field for some time that decoherence can be prevented by firing a photon at an atom whose spin is aligned in the same direction as its path. I thought that maybe travel between the universes might have something to do with repeating that action along the entire path integral—that is, every possible trajectory at once—from within a decoherence-free space."

"Um...and did it?" That was Husher's best attempt at pretending he was keeping up.

"I don't know. I never figured out a way to fire an atom in infinity different directions simultaneously. Nevertheless, I decided to have a shot at creating a decoherence-free space anyway, within the simulation at least. That didn't happen either, but it made me think—what if such a space already exists in the universe, but simply isn't detectable using regular means? Then I started to wonder how it might be accessed. The idea popped into my head that perhaps negative-mass environments, which we know very little about, might hold the key."

"Like the ones created inside warp bubbles?"

"Exactly. But we've made use of negative mass before, in wormhole generators. And so, since there are no actual consequences inside a simulation, I decided to attempt something that would almost certainly be illegal under current galactic law."

"You opened a wormhole inside a warp bubble?"

Ochrim tilted his head sideways. "No. I didn't bother with warp bubbles. Instead, I generated a new type of wormhole, which encompassed the starship like a sphere."

"What happened to it?"

"The simulation crashed. It couldn't account for what I was attempting to do."

"So..."

"Captain, if my theory concerning the physics involved is correct, then two things are true. The first is that, in addition to the many-worlds interpretation, membrane or 'brane' cosmology also holds true for our particular universe. Basically, the three-dimensional space we live in is just one of many 'branes' or 'dimensions' that make up our universe and are gravitationally interrelated. The second thing that's true concerns our use of dark tech. In short, we employed it in completely the wrong way—to connect different parts of three-dimensional space to each other. That's why the technology was found to have such long-term catastrophic effects; the gravitational load we were placing on our individual brane was too much for it to bear, and if we'd carried on, we would have destroyed it. But I believe that connecting branes is how wormholes are actually meant to be used. That way, the gravitational effects are distributed across branes in a way that is easily borne by the universal substructure."

"What benefits are there to connecting the branes?"

"I'm not sure," Ochrim admitted. "I'd have to try it to find out. On a much smaller scale, of course—I believe I could do the testing in my lab."

"Right. Let me see if I have this straight. You want me to authorize you to use illegal technology so that you can test the benefits of reaching a part of the universe that might not exist and if it does, might not exist in a form that's of any actual use to us."

"Essentially, yes. But it's not only authorization that I require—I'll also need Ocharium with which to fabricate the necessary circuitry."

"I'm going to have to think about it."

CHAPTER 27

Thumbs-Down

It took Maeve Aldaine a few days to make good on her promise to make Husher's life a living hell, but in the end, she delivered.

A petition was making the rounds on the *Vesta*'s narrownet with her name at the top. It called Husher a human supremacist for failing to sign on to the Positive Response Program, and it also demanded that he resign.

Even though he was technically off-duty, Husher's spare moments were typically spent in his office anyway, trying to stay on the speeding treadmill that was keeping his ship running. He hated to take time away from that to put out this fire, but Aldaine's petition was already approaching three thousand signatures—six percent of Cybele's population.

Cybele was in many ways a university town, and so those numbers shouldn't have surprised him as much as they did. But besides the threat the petition posed, the fact that so many had signed it also kind of stung. He'd always tried his best to be a good captain and a responsible steward of what the capital starship had become, as much as he objected to that transformation. But according to this petition, at least, he'd failed.

Husher decided the best way to defend himself was to tell the truth about his feelings on this issue—to present his argument with as much logic and sincerity as he could muster. He slid a datapad closer for easy access, willed his Oculenses to bring up the official social aggregator for the *Vesta*'s crew, and he began typing.

"I believe the hyper-focus on group identity," he wrote, "while well-intentioned, is misguided. I believe it's fragmenting our society even as it's meant to bring us together. The Interstellar Union was built on the idea that the most important thing about a being isn't the species or group they belong to, but the content of their character. No one's species should define them, but initiatives such as the Positive Response Program seek to do exactly that. That makes the program divisive. Do we have problems associated with interspecies relations in our society? Yes. Deep-seated problems. But forcing group identity to the forefront of our discourse does nothing to address them. On the contrary, I firmly believe it makes them worse."

Satisfied with what he'd written, he pushed it out to the various social channels where the crew maintained a presence. Then he returned to using his Oculenses to work through an endless stack of performance reviews, making a note to confer a promotion wherever he thought one was warranted.

A few hours later, he picked a social channel at random and signed on to check how his post was being received. His eyes widened.

There were almost a hundred comments, almost all negative, and a number of thumbs-down reactions that far outweighed the number of thumbs-ups. Dozens of users had also rebroadcast the post, and Husher saw that very few of them had added positive commentary.

When he checked Aldaine's petition, he saw it had jumped to over five thousand signatures. *Over ten percent of Cybele...*

He slumped back in his chair, but the Oculenses made sure his view of the narrownet turmoil followed his vision, and he continued to scroll through pages and pages of outrage.

"By suggesting that nonhuman beings shouldn't value their species identity," said one post that was typical of most of them, "the captain is denying their experiences. Take Wingers. They were slaughtered by the thousands, probably millions, at human hands. Even now, they suffer from institutional biases against them that seem designed to make sure they never do as well as humans. The captain's advice to 'forget your species identity' is a cynical attempt to get beings to stop fighting for their rights, and I find it absolutely disgusting. This captain is a white human supremacist."

Husher laughed at that, more from disbelief than from amusement. The narrownet activists, who seemed to outnumber the ones he'd encountered in the streets of Cybele by orders of magnitude, had expanded their demands since Husher had made his post. They were now demanding that he and his human crew join their fellow humans in Cybele by participating in a Nonattendance Day for humans, to show solidarity with their nonhuman brothers and sisters. On that day, humans would be asked not to go out in public.

A chime rang in the office, indicating someone at the hatch, and Husher willed his Oculenses to go transparent. The narrownet tumult vanished from view, though it seemed to linger in the air around him like an oppressive fog.

He opened the hatch to find Fesky on the other side. "Need a drink?" she asked.

"Kaboh has the command?"

"Yep."

"All right, then."

They went to the Providence Lounge, which was the crew's lounge, named for the supercarrier that had led the fight against the Ixa during the Second Galactic War. Husher found the name a bit ironic, since he knew for a fact that Captain Keyes would never have permitted a place on his ship where crewmembers were officially sanctioned to drink alcohol. But with Cybele right next door, it was inevitable that the crew would go drinking while off-duty. Better to give them a place of their own, where they didn't have to worry about civilian scrutiny—and where any trouble they caused was limited to the crew section.

Crewmembers still went to Cybele bars for variety, of course, and no small amount of trouble had been caused over the years. He never saw too many service members in a place like the Secured Zone, though, despite the militarized name.

When you entered the Providence Lounge, you saw the bar right away—a long counter that ran along the opposite wall.

You could sit there and chat with your neighbors and the bartender, or you could join in at one of the tables, which tended to alternate between card games and lively conversation.

"I'll buy," Fesky said.

"Thanks," Husher said, settling into a chair, his gaze drifting to a Poker game being played at a table nearby. "Time to ante up, everybody," a marine private was saying. "You can't win if you don't have some skin in the game."

A couple minutes later, Fesky returned with a lager for him and a bottle for herself. Wingers had trouble drinking from glasses, and her beverage contained no alcohol, since the substance did nothing for Winger physiology.

"It's pretty rich they're calling me a *white* human supremacist, now," Husher said. "I don't suppose it counts for anything that my greatest hero was Captain Keyes, a black man."

"Of course not," Fesky said, taking a sip. "You've been deemed unrighteous, and by definition it's impossible for you to ever do anything good."

"At least we'll arrive in Saffron soon, and I'll be confronted with actual military matters to take my mind off all this."

Fesky lowered her bottle to the table. "Hopefully the 'actual military matters' don't happen in the Viburnum System instead, to the munitions facility."

Grimacing, Husher said, "I'd assumed you brought me here to cheer me up."

"Captain," Fesky said. "Speaking as a Winger and as your friend—I have to advise against signing onto the Positive Response Program. Even if it worked like it's supposed to, which it doesn't, it would still weaken the bonds of your crew even more than they've already been weakened. Crew solidarity isn't something we should be taking for granted, especially during a time of war. Now is not the time to implement a program like this."

"I'm well aware of that, Fesky."

"Are you?" his friend said, and a tense quiet came between them.

Eventually, Husher drained the rest of his drink and placed the empty glass on the table. "Thanks," he said, and left the lounge.

After that, he and Fesky mostly avoided each other for the rest of the warp transition, which their conflicting CIC watches made pretty easy. For his part, Husher didn't know what to say to Fesky. He didn't know what to say to anyone, these days, not even to himself. The pressures bearing down on him were pushing him in two very different directions—military effectiveness and social acceptability—and he felt like he was failing at both.

Awkwardness aside, when he received the notification that they were about to transition into the Saffron System, he called his entire first watch to the CIC, including Fesky.

There was no way he'd enter a potential engagement situation without her at his side.

CHAPTER 28

A Ship That Size

Just as starships were forced to use warp departure points that were well outside star systems, they also had to transition back into realspace well outside their destinations. That had as much to do with the threat of debris as it did with the risk of destroying whatever was directly in front of the ship as it exited the warp bubble. Doing so released every particle the bubble had collected during transit simultaneously, in a massive shockwave with the power to obliterate space stations and starships alike, no matter the size.

Some systems simply weren't accessible via warp drive. The Sol System represented one such—the spherical Oort Cloud meant that transitioning outside it placed a ship a light year or more from meaningful in-system destinations. Luckily, it still had a functioning darkgate. Even though the Ixa had decimated Sol's population, Husher was glad access to humanity's home system was still possible, if only for sentimental reasons. Shortly after the Second Galactic War, the IU had begun a terraforming project aimed at rehabilitating Earth, but that would take centuries to come to fruition.

"I just received radar confirmation of the safe arrival of the *Thero*, the *Golgos*, the *Hylas*, and the *Lysander*, Captain," said the sensor operator once they'd successfully completed their transition into realspace. "They're forming up a few light minutes ahead of us."

"Acknowledged. Coms, transmit orders for them to continue accelerating in formation toward the system's largest colony. We'll meet them there. How does Saffron look, Winterton?"

"It looks quiet, sir," the sensor operator answered, and Husher resisted the urge to check what Kaboh's reaction to that news would be. "That said, the sensor data we currently have access to is two hours out of date."

"Thank goodness the system wasn't attacked as of two hours ago," Kaboh said. "But we must remain vigilant nevertheless. Our presence could end up meaning everything to the people of Saffron."

"Kindly limit commentary to our immediate tactical situation," Husher snapped, irritated by what sounded suspiciously like political posturing, at least to his ears.

"Yes, sir," Kaboh said crisply.

"Coms, have Commander Ayam stand by to scramble Pythons, just in case." Husher knew that order lent Kaboh's words more weight, but he wasn't about to start putting his personal pride above tactics.

"Yes, sir," Fry said.

The quiet persisted as the *Vesta* rode Saffron's gravity well down-system. As they neared the biggest colony, whose orbit happened to place it closest to the warp transition point the supercarrier had entered through, a transmission came through from the *Selene*'s captain. The frigate was too far off for real-time communications, but Husher had Fry play the audio and video for his CIC crew to hear.

"Captain Husher," said Ternon, who was Tumbran—a rarity among IGF warship captains. "Thank you to you and your battle group for coming so quickly. We've yet to detect any hostile vessels in-system, but I find it highly unlikely that readings identical to those taken in the Wintercress System would not precede a similar attack."

"Send a text reply asking him to come closer so we can have a real-time chat about how best to array our forces," Husher told the Coms officer, not in the mood to record the message himself.

"Yes, sir."

Winterton sat straighter in his seat, eyes fixated on whatever he saw on the main display. "Sir, an unknown vessel just appeared less than a light minute off our port bow. Its profile doesn't match that of the warship we encountered in the Wintercress System. The dark-gray coloration is similar, but its shape is that of an almost featureless oblong spheroid, and it's massive—she rivals the *Vesta* in size."

Husher toggled to a visualization of the ship generated by radar, since they were too far for actual visual inspection. *Good God. That thing's twice as big as the* Providence *was.*

"Coms, send a transmission demanding—"

Winterton interrupted: "Sir, the vessel's hostile. It just began launching missiles identical to those used against us by Teth's ship. It...the missile barrage isn't ending, Captain."

"Full reverse thrust, Helm, now!" Husher said. "Coms, have Commander Ayam scramble the entire Air Group and start targeting down those things. Tactical, set lasers to point defense mode, to supplement our kinetic point defense systems. Standby to load Banshees with guidance directives that prioritize targeting the incoming robots."

The chief hesitated, glancing at Husher. "Captain?"

"Just do it, Tremaine," Husher snapped. He blew air through his nostrils, then tried to soften his tone: "I'm just as reluctant to spend Banshees taking down those things as you are, but I'm even less reluctant to let them rip through my hull and infiltrate my ship."

"Yes, sir."

"Coms, tell Major Gamble to mobilize his entire marine battalion and get them patrolling the outer corridors in squads. I want two platoons assigned to Cybele and two more divided among the *Vesta*'s vital systems."

"Aye, sir."

His first volley of orders delivered, Husher had his Oculenses show him the Tactical display. Over a hundred of the vicious little robots screamed toward his ship, with more being fired from the enemy vessel.

He scrutinized the display for further action he could take. His battle group had already reached Edessa, and was too far away to lend the *Vesta* their aid. However...

"Coms, the *Selene* is close enough to get here within a timeframe meaningful for this engagement. If they pile on enough speed, they can hit the enemy ship from behind and take some of the pressure off. Send Commander Ternon a transmission requesting he do so."

"Composing the request now, sir."

The moment the words were out of Fry's mouth, Winterton's hands left his console in a gesture of shocked exasperation. "Sir, the enemy warship vanished."

Damn it. Husher didn't know what that meant for them, but he doubted it was good. "I want ongoing active scans of the entire system."

"Yes, sir."

Husher's eyes settled on Kaboh, who was facing him, wearing a prim smile. "Is there anything *I* can do, Captain?" he asked, his satisfaction evident.

Husher had managed to keep his emotions under control as he gave out orders to deal with the immediate threat, but the Kaithian's smugness helped unleash his temper. "You can reflect on the fact that if a ship that size tried appearing underneath Edessa's orbital defense platforms, it would doom itself. The planet's gravity well would drag it from the sky. The system could have defended itself from this attack without our help, Kaboh."

CHAPTER 29

Blood on Hands

The tactical display told Husher that when the hostile vessel vanished, it had left two hundred and thirty-nine robots speeding across the void toward the *Vesta*. The strange ordnance, totally new to Husher's experience of space warfare, seemed to have guidance systems at least as sophisticated as his Banshees, and so simply steering the supercarrier out of the way wasn't going to cut it. He had to deal with every last one.

"Coms, contact Commander Ternon and request that he divert his course to Edessa. We don't know where in the system the enemy ship will appear next, but we do know that its largest colony presents the most valuable target."

"Yes, Captain."

"Transmit orders to our battle group that they should remain at the colony as well." Husher squinted at the main display, trying to determine his next move. "Winterton."

"Sir?"

Husher glanced at the man, surprised he had to actually vocalize what he wanted—but then he saw how intently the sensor operator was studying his console's readout. "Do I need to have Tremaine start sending Banshees at those things?"

"I think it's prudent to keep them armed and ready," Winterton said. "The enemy missiles' velocity is such that our reverse thrust can't bring us to parity before impact. That said, it is broadening the window we'll have to deal with them, and we've already cut down the barrage by eighty-three missiles. Eighty-four!" he exclaimed, apparently responding to something he saw on his console. Winterton didn't get excited very often, and Husher took his optimism as a good sign.

"Very good, Ensign. I'd like you to work together with Tactical to arrive at an estimate of how many of those robots are likely to get through to our hull. If it's more than five, I'll give the order to fire Banshees."

Husher didn't like the idea of even one reaching his hull—it meant a minor breach and a chance that it would get access to something they couldn't do without.

That chance was slim, though. Major Gamble's marines were well-trained and vigilant. They'd find and destroy anything that wormed its way into the *Vesta*'s corridors well before it found something vital; Husher felt confident about that.

The ship that had launched the barrage showed no sign of reemerging from wherever it had gone, and within twenty minutes, Winterton and Tremaine had determined that none of the enemy missiles were likely to get through.

At that, Husher breathed a quiet sigh of relief. *If we'd been facing two of those warships, and they'd been more willing to stick around...*

It was a good reminder to keep his battle group at hand whenever possible.

"Sir, contact off our stern," Winterton said. "It's the ship that fired the missiles—she's right behind us. We're accelerating straight for her."

"Tactical, do we have enough charge to use our primary laser?"

"Aye, Captain!"

"Use the central aft projector to fire it at the enemy vessel, center-mass. Do it *now.*"

"Firing laser."

Winterton gripped his console. "They're hitting us with a particle beam. Superheating is occurring across a sizable portion of our stern, sir. It's dangerously close to the left side of our main starboard reactor."

Fingers clamped around his chair's armrests, Husher's gaze locked onto his Helm officer. "Use aft, port lateral thrusters to nudge that reactor away from the superheating. Only ten percent power—we don't want to endanger the next reactor over."

"Yes sir," the Winger said.

"Tactical, let's take advantage of our acceleration toward the target. Use aft railguns to send kinetic impactors right into the hole we're drilling with our laser."

"Yes, sir."

Winterton turned toward him. "Sir, the superheating is deteriorating our hull at an alarming rate. I—" Frowning, he turned toward the main display. "The target's vanished again, Captain. The superheating is subsiding."

"Deploy damage control teams to the affected area and then tell me how bad it is."

Winterton nodded, already at work typing up the orders, his fingers flying across the keyboard. He must have already composed the phrasing in his head, since he continued to speak fluidly. Either way, Husher was impressed by the multitasking. "Nearly every deck between aft sections forty-nine through sixty was affected," Winterton said, "and the hull continues to melt. If the damage control teams don't move fast, there's a chance the reactor could be affected."

"Acknowledged. Fry, send orders to Engineering to shut down the main starboard reactor as quickly and safely as possible."

"Aye."

Shaking his head to clear it, Husher took a moment to wonder whether this engagement was even over yet. He watched on the tactical display as Tremaine continued to mop up the robots flying through space toward them—an effort the officer hadn't let himself be distracted from, even when the enemy ship had popped into existence right behind the *Vesta*.

What an admirable performance. From my entire CIC crew. "Good job, everyone," he told them. "From how you handled that engagement, no one would ever say you're a peacetime crew."

But as he continued to study the tactical display, something began to bother him. "The enemy vessel's reappearance...it was far from optimally timed. It would have been much more devastating to show up behind us while we were in the thick of dealing with the barrage it sent at us."

From the XO's chair beside him, Fesky clacked her beak. "Perhaps it can only appear like that at certain predetermined coordinates, and by accelerating backward we happened to head straight for one."

"Interesting," Husher said. "That would be hard to time properly, unless the enemy somehow had ongoing knowledge of the battlespace from wherever it disappeared to. But maybe that explains the random blips picked up by the sensor webs leading up to these engagements. That could be the enemy mapping the system, figuring out the points where it's able to pop back in. I'll be interested in having a look at the sensor web data from the engagement, to see whether it continued to see any blips. That would corroborate your theory, Fesky—the enemy would need to pop back in to check on our position and coordinate the surprise it had planned for us."

"The thing I'm most curious about," Tremaine said as he eyed Kaboh, "is where Teth is. We didn't face him here, so where the hell is he?"

Husher felt pretty sure the answer to Tremaine's question was on the tip of every CIC officer's tongue: Teth was probably in the Viburnum System.

And if that's true, the blood is on my hands just as much as it's on Kaboh's.

CHAPTER 30

Morality of War

After they finished mopping up the remaining missiles, Husher ordered Kaboh to set a course for Edessa, where he planned to have his battle group hold orbit until he was satisfied the hostile vessel wouldn't return.

By the time they arrived over the planet, the enemy still hadn't shown any sign of making another attempt on them, and so Husher felt comfortable letting second watch take over.

He was halfway to his quarters for a much-needed nap when his com buzzed, and he made the mistake of looking at it.

It was Mayor Dylan Chancey, requesting a private meeting in his office.

Cursing under his breath, Husher decided not to bother changing. Instead, he headed straight for the hatch that led to the city. He also didn't bother telling anyone where he was going, since they'd probably insist on arranging a marine escort, given the recent unrest. Walking around his own ship with an armed escort was something he still refused to do, and besides, he didn't feel like sitting around and twiddling his thumbs while one was put together.

It seemed the protesters were taking a break today, as no one awaited him with signs and air horns, either in the desert or in the city streets. *Maybe they're all just too busy sitting at home, signing petitions and typing inflammatory social posts.*

It took ten minutes for Husher to get through city hall's security checkpoints, since the mayor's office was fairly close to the circular council chamber at the center.

Chancey was sitting at his desk when Husher entered, his back to the convex wall of the building's curve, staring into space as he typed something on a datapad. Apparently the door's opening hadn't clued the mayor in to Husher's presence, so he cleared his throat.

"Ah," Chancey said, his gaze settling on Husher at last. "Captain. Please, have a seat."

Husher did, lowering himself into a leather chair with smooth, metal armrests. He folded his hands in his lap and stared at the mayor.

"You're no doubt wondering why I asked you here," Chancey said.

"Whatever it is, I'm guessing I won't enjoy the experience."

"Oh?" Chancey steepled his fingers, regarding Husher over their tips. "Why do you say that?"

"Because whenever I visit Cybele, lately, I leave with more limitations that I need to observe, which reduce my effectiveness and that of my crew."

"Alas," Chancey said, and his smile looked genuinely sympathetic. "That goes part and parcel with living in modern civilization, doesn't it? To move things forward, everyone needs to be able to live and work together with minimal friction, and that means suppressing certain whims and urges."

"I'm not talking about whims. I'm talking about defeating the enemy as efficiently as possible while minimizing casualties, and that includes civilian casualties. We need to follow a morality of war right now, because that's what we're in. You told me you didn't want to stand between me and doing my job, but that's all you've done."

"I apologize if you feel that way, Captain. But if we conduct ourselves like barbarians during war, then what will we be left with once war ends, other than savagery and the desire to wage more war?"

Husher snorted. "There's a balance to be struck between becoming barbarians and binding ourselves with chains!"

Shaking his head, Chancey said, "I'm sorry I can't bring you around to my viewpoint. It would make this a more pleasant process if I could manage it, but unfortunately, your views on the subject have little actual bearing. They are, in fact, seen by many as outdated."

"Then military effectiveness is outdated, and we're doomed the moment a power comes along that hasn't limited itself like we have. That moment is now."

"Do I need to remind you of the careful balance of power the Interstellar Union has sought to create with its military? As captain of a capital starship, you wield a level of power that's completely unprecedented throughout galactic history. That's why Cybele and its city council exists. We're here to rein you in when you let personal vices and excesses lead you to abuse that power. It's what this meeting is about, in fact."

The mayor was right, Husher knew: arguing really was pointless. This was the same dilemma he'd been struggling with for two decades: to remain in a position to counter the danger he knew was coming, Husher had to give more and more ground to a government bent on coddling not only their constituents but every being in the universe, including any enemies that happened to come along. "Out with it," Husher growled. "What are you forcing me to implement this time?"

"I'd rather not *force* you to implement anything, but I will write this into the law if I have to. As you know, I'm aligned with the council on this matter, and we're ready to work together to enact any policy that becomes necessary."

"Just tell me what you want," Husher spat.

"I want you to sign on to the Positive Response Program."

For a moment, Husher lacked words. Then, he said, "I thought it was voluntary. If a captain thinks it'll impair effectiveness, he can decline to participate."

"It has been voluntary, so far. But as you know, we're given leeway to experiment with our legislation. You might call it our civic duty to do that, so that outside society can benefit from what we attempt here—as the Womb of Civilization and all, you know. You can probably see where I'm going with this. If you refuse to participate in the Positive Response Program, then I intend to ensure that legislation is enacted which requires you to participate."

A dizziness struck Husher—a sense of disorientation so strong that for a moment, it felt like his ship was at sea rather than adrift in space. For the first time, it occurred to him that a man like Chancey was probably the most dangerous of all: a friendly viper, smiling until the moment its fangs found your neck.

"Is there anything you'd like to say at this point?" the mayor said, and unlike with Kaboh's recent victory over him, Husher truly couldn't detect any satisfaction underlying Chancey's words.

Does he really believe he's doing best by society? Or is he just giving his constituents what they want? "There's nothing to say," Husher said, his voice emerging as a rasp.

"Are there any objections you care to lodge?"

"You've already made it clear that it won't make a difference. Just let the record show that I think you're dealing the galaxy a death blow."

"Captain *Husher,*" Chancey said, sounding chagrined. "Really. The Integrated Galactic Fleet is a public institution, and it's incumbent on us to set a good example for organizations and businesses throughout the galaxy. That involves helping the underprivileged to find the employment they so want and deserve."

"Do you realize how damn condescending that sounds?" Husher snapped.

"I'm afraid we differ, there."

Scraping back his chair against the marble floor, Husher stood. Before he made for the exit, he said, "Can I make a request, Mayor?"

"Of course."

"Lobby the Interstellar Union to deploy more warships to this region. I intend to make the case to them myself, but it will likely have more clout coming from you."

"It's not something I can promise. But I can tell you that I'll think about it."

Nodding, Husher turned and strode toward the door, feeling like he'd done all he could.

"Captain, there was one other thing."

Husher turned his head sideways, but his body still faced the door. "Yes?"

"The people of Cybele want the Nonattendance Day for humans. Wingers, Kaithe, Tumbra, humans—they *all* want it, and as mayor, it's incumbent on *me* to insist that you permit and encourage your crew to participate."

"Fine," Husher ground out, and he left, struggling to keep his shoulders squared and head high.

CHAPTER 31

Invertebrate

An hour after his meeting with Chancey, as he walked from the wardroom to his office, Husher caught multiple venomous glares directed his way, quickly masked once his eyes found them.

"Is there a problem, Private?" he asked a marine, who was the third one he caught wearing a sour expression.

The man came to attention, snapping off a crisp salute. "Sir, no, sir!"

"You're certain there's nothing you'd like to discuss?"

"Sir, no, sir!"

"Dismissed," Husher said, suppressing a grimace.

Apparently, the mayor wasn't being very discreet about securing agreement from Husher to sign on to the Positive Response Program. Not that he needed to be—clearly, Chancey could do as he pleased—but Husher didn't think the indiscretion was very considerate. There had been no chance to message the decision to his crew yet, and evidently, they were drawing their own conclusions about it. He needed to move quickly if he was to have a shot at forestalling a major deterioration of his relationship with them.

His hand was on the access panel for the hatch into his office when a scratchy voice reached his ears.

"A word, Captain?"

He turned to behold Fesky, feathers standing at attention.

"You're upset," he said.

"You bet I am."

"We can have a word, but I want you to know the conversation we're about to have will be between a captain and his XO, not between old friends. Be very careful of overstepping your bounds here, Fesky." He opened the hatch.

"It's a risk I'm willing to take," the Winger said, brushing past him and turning around.

Husher's eyes narrowed, and he slapped the interior access panel without looking, closing the hatch behind him. "I already don't like how this is going."

"I don't care," Fesky said. "I *told you,* human. I told you. I said do not agree to that program. That it would tear the crew apart and turn them against you. What have you done?"

"I haven't done anything, Fesky. I certainly didn't *agree* to anything. This was forced on me by Cybele City Council."

"So what? You're in a war, Husher. Isn't that supposed to make you a warrior? Fight this!"

"I don't think you understand how *this* works."

"I understand how having a spine works, actually, yes. Winger aren't invertebrates, and I didn't think humans were, either. Turns out there are some exceptions."

"You're out of line, Commander," Husher barked, and Fesky fell silent, seething. "Listen to me. You haven't captained a starship during these last seventeen years. In fact, you've never captained one. You don't understand how thin the line is that I have to walk each and every day, just to remain in command so that I can take the fight to the enemy we both know has been building up for years."

But Fesky was shaking her head. "Husher, the reason I haven't captained a ship is that when you asked me to be your XO, I accepted. I did that because I thought we'd make a good team. I thought we'd stand up for what was good and right and *effective,* just like Captain Keyes and I did, and just as you did when you served under him." Fesky's voice grew softer. "But look at you now. You're trying to appease everyone, and because of that you're accomplishing nothing. Your attempts to stay in command, to please the politicians scrutinizing your every action—it's making you just like they are, Husher. Captain Keyes was willing to sacrifice his life to save the galaxy. And he *did.* And it worked. But you? You're not even willing to sacrifice your career."

"I need a career to be able to do *anything* about Teth!" Husher yelled, but Fesky was already striding past him. She pressed the access panel to open the hatch, and then she was gone.

Fuming, Husher made his way around the desk, dropped into his chair, and yanked the datapad toward him.

Not even my best friend understands the position I'm in.

Furiously, he began to type.

CHAPTER 32

Not Compulsory

"There's no question that the Positive Response Program represents a change," Husher wrote in what would amount to the official announcement of the program to his crew. "A significant change. The *Vesta* has one of the most passionate and loyal crews out there, and I understand many of you are reluctant to leave her, especially in a time of war.

"I do understand that reluctance, more than you probably know. But I want to offer some words of reassurance. No one is going to 'lose their job' with the Integrated Galactic Fleet because of this program. Everyone displaced will be found other positions, and it's possible, even likely, that your new position will also be in a combat role, especially since the need for such roles will almost certainly increase in the near future. Under the Positive Response Program, no one will be 'let go.' The IGF doesn't fire people. Sometimes it discharges them, but it doesn't fire them, and no one will be discharged under Positive Response.

"One further note. I've been asked to inform you that tomorrow will be an official Nonattendance Day for humans, sanctioned by Cybele City Council. This event is being characterized as a show of solidarity, by humans, with nonhuman beings. I'm told that the intention is to send nonhuman beings a message that they are just as welcome in public spaces as humans are. Participation in Human Nonattendance Day is not compulsory, and I'm not requiring or even requesting that crewmembers participate. I will say, however, that if I receive reports of any violence between crewmembers and civilians as a result of not participating, I will take swift disciplinary action against the crewmembers involved."

Once he finished typing, Husher didn't have the heart to read over what he'd written, because if he did, he likely wouldn't be able to make himself go through with it. He decided to just post it straight to the Board, though his finger hovered over the command key for several long moments before finally descending.

That done, he attempted to focus on reports from Engineering on the state of the aft hull. There were no facilities in Saffron where the supercarrier could be repaired, and so they'd been forced to patch her up as best they could on their own—which mostly amounted to sealing off the affected sections and hoping for the best.

Try as he might, Husher couldn't muster the concentration necessary to make sense of the detailed reports. He would read four lines, realize he hadn't absorbed a thing from them, and then read them again. It took five tries to derive any meaning from the passage he was on, and twice as long for the next one.

His com beeped with a Priority message, and he picked it up, relieved for an excuse to divert his attention somewhere else, even if only for a few seconds.

His relief was short-lived.

The message was from his Coms officer, who was passing along word from the Viburnum System.

The munitions facility there had been attacked by a vessel whose profile matched Teth's. That vessel had succeeded in destroying the facility.

Husher lowered his head into his hands and held it there for a long time.

CHAPTER 33

Nonattendance Day

"So, boys, what should we do with our last day on the *Vesta*?" Corporal Toby Yung asked his bunkmates before slamming his fist into a metal post hard enough to lay it open, spattering blood across a bottom bunk's sheets.

"Damn it, Toby!" Private Zimmerman said, jumping up from the next bunk over to check whether any blood had gotten on it. Satisfied, he turned his glare on Toby. "This isn't going to be our last day, you idiot."

"Might as well be. Who knows which of us are going to get 'shuffled' off. I say we enjoy it."

"What do you have in mind?" asked another private, named Mews. "Other than wrapping up that hand before it bleeds on me and I have to kick your ass."

Toby whipped off his shirt and used it to staunch the bleeding. "I say we go get lit up a bit at the Providence Lounge and see where the morning takes us."

"Put on another shirt, first, would you?" Zimmerman said. "I don't want to have to rescue any more female officers from trying to get in the pants of a marine in their direct chain of command."

"All right." After he bandaged his hand and put on the promised shirt, they rolled out to the *Providence* and ordered a round of whiskey shots. Then they ordered two more.

By the time they headed out for Cybele, they all had a decent buzz going, or at least Toby did.

Just before he entered his access code to open the hatch into the illusory desert, he turned to his buddies, feeling a dumb, alcohol-enhanced smile creeping across his face. "Ah, damn it, guys. I just remembered that today's the Nonattendance Day for human beings. Now, we're not gonna cause trouble by going for a walk through the city, are we? We really should all go back to the bunkroom."

"Well, wait a second," Mews said in his steady baritone, which sounded perfectly sober even after three shots of whiskey. "If we go back to our bunks, how do we know everyone *else* is respecting Human Nonattendance Day? We're three upstanding, civically responsible marines. It's practically our duty to go out there and patrol the streets to make sure no humans show their ugly faces."

"Mews is right," Zimmerman said. "I'm sorry, Toby, but I won't let you stand in the way of enforcing Nonattendance Day. I insist that we go into Cybele right this instance."

"Aw, all right, you guys. Guess you're just both more forward-looking than me. Let's go out there and show them just how absent humans can be!" Toby punched his code into the panel, and the hatch slid open. Unsurprisingly, there were dozens of activists right outside, lounging around in the sand. At first, that struck him as amusing—all part of the joke. *We'll go out and screw with them a bit. Have some fun with them.*

Then, something caught his eye that definitely *wasn't* funny.

Almost half of the people sitting out there were humans.

Cursing loudly, Toby marched out of the crew section and into the fake desert. "What the *hell* is this all about?"

Dozens of heads turned toward him, and he leered right back at them. "What are all these humans doing here? We were told we couldn't come out here, but what about all these *people?*" Toby pointed his finger, waving it around to indicate all the humans.

A woman with bright red hair marched up to him, who couldn't have been more than twenty. She had the audacity to place two slim hands on his chest and try to push him back toward the hatch. He didn't budge, of course, but the *nerve!*

"You're not supposed to be here!" she yelled. Something about her reminded him of the captain—maybe it was how much gall she had.

"What are *you* doing here, then?" he yelled back.

"I'm an *ally.* It's fine for allies to be here, obviously. I'm not someone who's going to make them feel marginalized or like they should forget about where they come from or who they are. An ally is someone who stands by oppressed groups and who's willing to step back and step down if it means giving oppressed individuals the space they need."

Her last words rang in his ears: *giving oppressed individuals the space they need.* It reminded him of the hollow reasons he was being fed to explain the possibility he might get shuffled out of a posting he'd held for years. "I don't know what you just said, exactly," Toby said, jamming his finger toward the humans rising to their feet behind her. "But I do know that this is some bullshit." Behind him, Zimmerman and Mews made some sounds that indicated they agreed.

A man stepped up beside the lady, his face a storm cloud all for Toby. "Could I ask you to stop being so aggressive toward her please?"

"What? I'm just talking." Toby sized the guy up. He looked like he probably worked out, but Toby wasn't too worried. "This is nowhere near as aggressive as I get, man, trust me."

"You know what I think your captain's actually afraid of, marine?" the lady said, attempting to push him again. "I think he's afraid that if he actually steps aside and makes way for equality between the species, then he'll lose the ability to brainwash goons like you into hating other species and seeing them as the enemy."

"Lady, don't worry," Toby said. "All I see behind you is Wingers and Kaithe. I'm not paid to kill *them.*"

The gym rat stepped forward, taking a turn at shoving Toby, and this time he actually fell back a step. "I *told* you to stop being so aggressive."

Toby reacted to that with a mixture of instinct, training, and whiskey. The guy got four knuckles to the face, and that was enough to put him on his back in the sand and keep him there.

"Holy shit, Toby," Zimmerman said, at the same time Toby was glaring around at the group of protesters and screaming, "Anyone else?"

A long moment of shock stretched between the fifty or sixty protesters and the trio of marines. At last, the tension broke, and relief washed over Toby as most of the protesters charged toward him and his buddies. He hated waiting for a fight.

A couple of human men came at him at the same time. He booted one in the stomach, making him stagger backward, winded. The other guy tried to land a punch, but Toby sidestepped easily and nailed him in the jaw, making him cry out all high-pitched before backing off. That gave Toby room to elbow the wheezing guy in the back of the neck, which sent him sprawling to the sand.

Glancing behind him, he saw that Mews and Zimmerman were mixing it up similarly, and that made him glad. They were in this together.

A Winger approached, cawing, wings spread to their full, enormous span. That spoke to something animalistic deep inside Toby, and he chose fight over flight, charging into the alien's embrace, bowling it over, and finding its scrawny but muscular feathered neck. He gripped that as hard as he could, trying to choke the Winger out like they choked out new guys back in the bunkroom.

Something white and blue snaked around Toby's neck. *Oh, shit. That's a Kaithian.*

The head-tail constricted, and Toby's last thought was to marvel at how suddenly the tables had turned.

CHAPTER 34

A Lucky Guess

Doctor Bancroft was late for their Prolonged Exposure session, and Husher had a pretty good idea why. He sat in the waiting room and used his Oculenses to review an inventory of the ship's munition stores until, twenty-five minutes later, Bancroft appeared.

"Your corporal is lucky that Kaithian didn't snap his foolish neck," she said. "When the Kaithe fight, they usually play for keeps."

"I know it," Husher said, remembering his time on the Kaithian homeworld. He'd fought the aliens inside a simulation, then, though he'd since learned that the simulation had accurately represented their ferocity, which was completely at odds with their size and appearance.

"What are you going to do with the three marines that went out there?"

"Exactly what I said I'd do. They were all involved in a violent altercation, and so they'll all do time in the brig."

"I would have expected dishonorable discharges for the three of them."

Husher tilted his head to the side. “Seriously? Marines get into brawls all the time without being dishonorably discharged. I don’t mean to diminish the severity here, but no one was seriously injured, and from the sounds of it, there were extenuating circumstances.”

“Excuse me?” Bancroft said, and her sharpness surprised Husher—it ran counter to her usual caring demeanor. “Extenuating circumstances, Captain? Your marines went out looking for trouble. They willingly violated Nonattendance Day.”

“Which wasn’t compulsory. And when they went out, they found other humans lounging out there on the sand.”

Bancroft shook her head. “Well, you’re the captain. The decision is yours, I suppose.”

“I suppose it is.” He nodded toward her office. “Are you ready to begin?”

Without another word, she walked to the door and opened it, gesturing for him to enter. He did, and she shut the door behind him.

“What atrocity will I bear witness to today?” he asked, trying to lighten the mood a little.

Bancroft pursed her lips. “Before I load the program into your Oculenses, there’s a matter I need to raise with you.”

“Oh? What is it?”

“The complaints from crewmembers who feel unsafe are increasing.”

Shutting his eyes, Husher drew in a deep breath. “Let me guess. They’re all from graduates of Cybele U, or some other capital starship university.”

Now it was the doctor's turn to cock her head to one side. "Have you been abusing your special access as captain to view confidential crew medical files?"

"Is that a serious question, Doctor Bancroft?"

"Yes."

"No, I haven't. I was actually joking, but it seems I took a lucky guess."

At that, Bancroft reddened slightly. "I feel it's my responsibility as this starship's Chief Medical Officer to say this. If you don't take further action to address the fears of your crewmembers, I'll be forced to bring my concerns to Cybele City Council."

Husher looked at the floor of Bancroft's office, and he held his gaze there for several long moments. At last, he said, "Thank you for your input, Doctor. I'll certainly give your concerns the careful consideration they are due." With that, he got up.

"What about today's exposure session?" Bancroft asked, eyebrows raised.

"I've decided I don't have the stomach for it," Husher said as he left the office.

CHAPTER 35

Scythes Through Wheat

After receiving news that the Viburnum munitions facility had been destroyed, Husher gained some new nightmares. In addition to dreams of the night his daughter died, he now started having equally dark dreams featuring giant Ixa who stalked through the galaxy, felling all other beings with impunity. It didn't matter who or what came against them—they tore through opposition like scythes through wheat.

With the munitions facility destroyed, logistics had become much trickier in the part of the galaxy that bordered on the Concord System, formerly the Baxa System. Resupply would now take days, and eventually weeks, if demand from warships operating in the region were to increase.

Judging by initial recon missions into the Concord System, demand probably would increase. The intel gathered there confirmed Husher's worst fears: the system had become a rallying point for Gok warships, and a starship similar to the one they'd faced near Edessa had also been scouted there. Teth was clearly preparing to launch an all-out war against the Milky Way, and he'd already struck a devastating blow.

Husher wasn't expecting the orders that came next from the admiralty, but they also didn't surprise him.

"Captain Husher," said the message from Admiral Iver, which had come in by com drone thirty minutes ago. Husher reviewed it alone in his office. "After deliberations, the admiralty has decided that in light of the munitions facility's destruction in the Viburnum System, and in light of the large amassing of hostile warships in the Concord System, it would now behoove the Interstellar Union to make a sincere diplomatic effort to bring peace to the region."

Husher chuckled bitterly at the suggestion that the threat posed by Teth was limited to just this region of space, then he continued reading:

"The ultimate goal is a long-lasting armistice, however, even a shorter-term nonaggression pact is viewed as a desirable outcome, and worth pursuing. As such, the diplomats accompanying your battle group will be given significant latitude in the negotiations. You'll find a separate data package attached to this message—it includes a list of everything we are willing to offer, depending on the length and quality of peace we are offered in return. These include resource rights to mineral-rich systems. I'm well aware of what your reservations will likely be in this matter, Captain, but the point I would raise to you is this: given the power and numbers already fielded by our enemies, it's clearly a worthy aim to avoid further bloodshed. And if our enemies were to renege on a peace deal at any point in the future, we will have had time to bolster our forces and will be better-positioned and -provisioned to answer such a violation with an attack aimed at retaking the systems we've relinquished.

"A final note: it was remarked during our deliberations that you have the Ixan, Ochrim, aboard your vessel. If he's amenable, it might be worthwhile to include him in the negotiations with Teth. If anyone can placate the Ixan commander, it will be his own brother."

After passing on the data package to the diplomats Shobi and Bryson without comment, Husher indulged himself by taking a moment to lean back and squeeze his eyes shut.

Seeking a ceasefire with the Ixa had been exactly what the UHF had tried during the most desperate hour of the First Galactic War. In fact, the mission Husher had been given felt particularly cyclical, since it had been his father, Warren Husher, who was sent on that first diplomatic mission.

Warren's mission had gone about as well as Husher expected this one to go. The Ixa had taken him prisoner, making it look like he'd betrayed his own species and painting him as a traitor for the next twenty years. Shortly after Warren's return to his species, they executed him for the crime of high treason. And soon after that, it became known that without Warren Husher's actions, humanity would have been doomed.

As far as Husher could see, the main difference between then and now was that Warren's mission had come after a long-fought struggle against the Ixa—after humanity had smashed itself against the implacable alien war machine, and all had seemed lost.

The IU, on the other hand, was giving up with barely a fight.

There was no peace to be had with Ixa. That was just as true now as it had been then. But orders were orders.

Before he passed on those orders, however, he decided to take care of some other business first. That business involved receiving a small transport craft inside Flight Deck Zeta and accepting an unauthorized shipment consisting of one thing: more Ocharium than Ochrim could possibly want or need.

CHAPTER 36

What Toxic Actually Looks Like

The voyage to the Baxa System, now the Concord System, would involve another week-long warp transition followed by several darkgate transitions and a final journey under warp, since the Corydalis-Baxa darkgate had been destroyed during the final battle of the Second Galactic War.

On the second day under warp drive, Husher found himself sitting in the Cybele City Council chamber, getting stared down by Maeve Aldaine, who'd been invited to attend the meeting as a representative of the students of Cybele U.

"You are called here, Captain Husher," Penelope Snyder said in the ringing tones she reserved for this round, inward-turned room, "to account for the actions of your three marines—Corporal Toby Yung, Private First Class Dion Mews, and Private Jordan Zimmerman—and to give a comprehensive overview of the steps you intend to take to ensure such an incident can never occur again."

Drawing a long breath, Husher spoke. "I can't account for the actions of my marines. They were reprehensible, and in direct contradiction to my urging crew to remain within the *Vesta*'s crew section during Human Nonattendance Day. In the same note, I made clear that any humans who chose to go to Cybele anyway and engage in violent—"

"This is such bullshit," Maeve Aldaine interrupted. "Did you actually believe a love letter to your violent crew was going to accomplish anything? You should have *forced* them to stay out of Cybele!"

Staring at Aldaine, Husher realized that her words had succeeded in raising his usual disbelief to new levels. Clearing his throat, he said, "I was asked to discuss the actions of my marines and the steps I've taken to address them."

"Go ahead," Chancey said, his tone kindly.

"As I was saying, I made clear to the crew that anyone found engaging in violence would face disciplinary action. And that's exactly what I've done. The three marines already named are currently in the brig."

"Have you scheduled any workshops to educate the rest of your crew on the situation?" Aldaine demanded, her sapphire eyes aflame.

"Workshops...?" Husher said.

Tossing her head in exasperation, Aldaine spat, "Yeah, you know, hands-on sessions designed to educate through participation. Topics like the historical oppression Wingers have faced at the hands of humans would be appropriate, in a situation like this."

"Everyone's well aware of what humans, particularly human governments, have done to Winger populations," Husher said. "Tell me, is it so radical to suggest that it could be more *unifying,* more *peaceful,* to not continually bring up our species' past animosity and fling it in everyone's faces?"

"I think we've heard quite enough," Snyder said, her illusory wings waving as she shifted in her seat and stared at Husher, apparently attempting to pierce his soul with her gaze. "Before we discuss policy, there's one more matter I'll bring to your attention, Captain. Are you aware of the horrific sentiments cropping up across the battle group's narrownet?"

Husher's mouth quirked, but he stayed silent. *Horrific sentiments crop up on the narrownet all the time.*

"I take your silence to signify you have not. Allow me to enlighten you. There are growing voices on there who are openly praising Teth and the Ixa. The title 'Immaculate One' has been floating around for Teth—I have no idea where that charming phrase originated—and several have referred to him as their 'personal Command Leader.' Specifically, they praise the genocide of Ixan interspecies offspring, the subtext being that perhaps humans would do well to 'purify' galactic society of beings who do not match human 'prowess.' The same groups spreading these hateful messages also name you as a figure of admiration, because you stand up for humans to the 'powers that be.' What do you have to say to that?"

Husher blinked, opened his mouth, then closed it. "It's awful," he managed at last. "The Ixa's genocide was one of the reasons I fought them during the Second Galactic War. I felt we needed to take a stand against that as a society." The Ixa were the only known species with the ability for females to reproduce with non-Ixan males, a practice reviled by the Ixa who'd taken power during the lead-up to the First Galactic War.

"Whether or not you're telling the truth about your motivations," Aldaine said, "can't you see your actions as commander of this ship have led directly to the toxicity we're seeing on the narrownet?"

Husher shook his head. "If I haven't already made it clear, I *strongly* condemn those ideas."

"What about the people responsible for the talk? Do you condemn them?"

"Yes!"

"Good," Aldaine said, and seemed about to speak again, but didn't. Maybe she hadn't been expecting that answer from Husher.

"I think it's time we arrive at some legislative proposals for addressing these problems," Snyder said. "since Captain Husher has demonstrated that he's either unwilling or incapable of doing so." She folded her hands across her exposed, digitally flat stomach as she continued. "I've already discussed such proposals with several council members individually, but now we'll put them to a vote, as Mayor Chancey suggested just prior to today's meeting.

Snyder lifted her hands, parting them while clearing her throat. Then, apparently satisfied with the level of ceremony, she spoke, her eyes clouded with the fog of someone reading from an Oculens overlay: "I am motioning my fellow councilors to adopt a proposal for the creation of legally enforced spaces within Cybele where only nonhumans and their human allies are permitted—places where they can go with the guarantee they'll be free of oppression, including some of the toxic ideas Captain Husher has propounded here today." Husher assumed she'd adlibbed the part about him, but it was difficult to be sure.

"The question of which humans are to be considered allies and therefore permitted to enter these spaces," Snyder continued, "is to be determined on an ad hoc basis by the nonhuman beings occupying a given space at a given time. The only step necessary to legally require a human to leave the space will be a request by a nonhuman occupying it. Any Tumbra desiring entry to these spaces will also be subject to the occupants' estimation of whether they are allies, and if they are not, then they will be required to leave. All in favor of this legislation, say aye."

"Wait a second," Husher said. "As captain of this vessel, I have a right to speak before the councilors vote."

Snyder's eyes widened in apparent outrage, but Chancey gave a brisk nod. "Go ahead."

"What spaces are you proposing to prevent humans from occupying?" he asked.

"Only humans who aren't allies will be prevented," Snyder said primly. "As for the specific spaces, those were meant to be worked out should the policy be approved."

"I'd like to hear what spaces we're talking about. If we're talking about private residences, that's one thing. But if we're—"

"The aftward half of Cybele University Green, the area between Skyward Mall and the Epicenter, the Starboard Concourse, and one acre inside Santana Park," Snyder said.

"Those are all public spaces."

"Yes. Out of respect for underprivileged groups and the hardship they've faced, I personally think it's the least we—"

"Well," Husher interrupted, "*you'll* no doubt be allowed to enter the spaces, so it probably makes no actual difference to you, except to help you feel even more self-righteous whenever you enter them."

"Excuse me?" Snyder said, her eyes widening so much it was almost comical.

"You always say your aims with policies like these are integration and unity, but this will accomplish exactly the opposite. By excluding people from places they once could go, based on their species, you'll be damaging society in a way that might be irreversible. You're shrinking the world for certain individuals based on their species or on beliefs they hold that you don't like. You're emulating the sort of people you claim to oppose. If Cybele really is the Womb of Civilization, if the rest of the galaxy truly takes cues from what happens here, then I'm begging you—do not vote to approve this legislation. You can't answer discrimination with more discrimination. This is what toxic actually looks like."

Snyder opened her mouth, but Husher wasn't done. "And why in Sol do you keep lumping in the Tumbra? I still haven't figured that out."

With an exasperated sigh, Snyder said, "Because anyone without the sort of blinders you wear can see how steeped in privilege the Tumbra are, mostly because of how willing they've always been to get in bed with humanity. The Tumbra are part of the problem, Captain. They remind nonhuman beings of their past and present oppression, and if they are asked to leave, then *they will be required to leave.*"

Husher shook his head, once again speechless.

"Now, then," Snyder said, her voice tight, though it carried a hint of premature triumph. "All in favor of the proposed legislation, say aye."

They went around the room, and one by one, the councilors gave their votes.

"Aye," said Snyder.

"Aye," said Chancey.

Next, it was the only Tumbran's turn, who hesitated, his gaze flitting from Husher, to Chancey, and then to Snyder.

At last, he opened his mouth, and a quiet syllable emerged: "Aye."

The vote was almost unanimous—all except a Winger councilor, whose name escaped Husher. Faces darkened when she said "Nay," but the vote moved briskly forward, and the law was enacted with an overwhelming majority.

At the final "Aye," Husher stood.

"History won't be kind to you for this," he said, and marched out of the room.

CHAPTER 37

Both Killers

In keeping with the orders he'd been given, Husher had the *Vesta* and her battle group exit their respective warp bubbles well outside the Concord System, so that the resulting shockwaves dissipated harmlessly into the void without damaging anything.

We wouldn't want to hurt our oldest enemies. In saner times, he might have chastised himself for the sarcastic thought, but he didn't bother now. His mood had gotten progressively darker since his last encounter with the Cybele City Council, and he recognized that he was becoming bitter.

What does it matter? This is over. I've failed, and all that's left is to watch the catastrophe unfold.

Another, smaller voice spoke to him, then, from deeper inside him: *You don't really believe that. You fought to keep the command seat because you know you can make a difference.*

Husher quashed the voice and turned to Winterton. "Are you picking up anything?"

"Nothing, sir—not even anything to corroborate the intel we received, about the system bristling with warships."

That didn't mean much. The Concord System was ringed by a massive asteroid belt, with plenty of rocks big enough to conceal three supercarriers the size of the *Vesta*, let alone anything Teth or the Gok were known to field.

The only thing the apparent emptiness of the system told Husher was that Teth had been expecting this visit, and that wasn't surprising, either. It was characteristic of all his past encounters with the Ixa that they possessed intel vastly superior to that which Husher had access to.

"Coms," he said.

"Captain?"

"Broadcast a blanket transmission throughout the entire system. Text is fine. Tell Teth we came to talk, and that we have his brother Ochrim with us."

"Yes, sir."

With that, Husher leaned back as far as the command seat allowed—which wasn't very much, since it didn't recline—and studied the tactical display he'd willed his Oculenses to show. He felt exhausted.

Teth didn't keep him waiting very long.

"Contact directly off the bow," Winterton said. "It's Teth's ship, sir. It's...sitting there, just outside the asteroid belt, without momentum along any trajectory."

"Meaning we'll collide with it if we continue forward," Husher muttered after a glance at the relevant telemetric data. "Helm, full reverse thrust until we're stationary as well." As much as Husher would have liked to continue until the *Vesta*'s nose rested mere meters away from Teth's warship, he knew better than to come anywhere near the Ixan. That would mean death for whoever failed to shoot first, and Husher knew exactly how far he could trust Teth.

"Incoming real-time transmission request," Ensign Fry said.

"Accept it and put it on the main display."

Teth's newly hideous face appeared, with its knobs of bone breaking through a hardened, scaly face. "Did you bring Jake Price?"

"You don't already know the answer to that question?" Husher said, eyebrows raised.

Teth's tongue made a brief appearance between his fangs before receding into the dark maw of his mouth. "All language is performative, Captain, and sometimes questions are used to make a point."

Husher decided not to bother trying to decipher that. "We don't have a Jake Price with us, no."

"Mm. Now, Captain, I know you've always been a great admirer of my work, and I'd be interested in getting your feedback on my efforts in obliterating your munitions facility in Viburnum. Did you appreciate my masterstroke, or did you even grasp it?"

"Cut the shit, Teth. I admire nothing you've done. I've fought to oppose it for decades."

The Ixan twisted his bulbous head to the left, donning a perplexed expression. "We've made war on each other, certainly, but you've always striven so obviously to emulate me. Clearly, successful emulation is well outside your grasp—we agree on that—but the striving is obvious to all, and it's embarrassing to us both for you to deny it."

"We're *nothing* alike," Husher ground out.

"We are *incredibly* alike. We're both killers, and we've both taken on the responsibility of deciding when it's right for others to die. You're not nearly as good as I am at making those decisions, but we both make them. As well, we're both fighting partly out of vengeance. You killed my father, Baxa, and I killed the man you wished was your father, Keyes."

"Captain Keyes sacrificed himself to help defeat you."

"Call it whatever you want. Keyes failed, and you're filled with a bitter thirst for revenge."

"You're nothing but an abomination," Husher shot back, "created and set loose by the masters you call the Progenitors."

"And you're a dog, kept kenneled by the Kaithe until it drove you half-mad. We can do this all day, Captain. Humans are just as engineered as Ixa. You're as much an abomination as I am. You speak to me using a display accessed with your vaunted Oculenses, but you might as well be looking into a mirror. Now that I've made that abundantly clear to you, dog, why don't you follow your masters' command to *speak,* just as they've told you to speak?"

Husher's chest heaved with his breathing, and the sudden ringing in his ears made it difficult to think.

To have Teth diagnose his situation with such arrogance, such precision...it made Husher want to order his Tactical officer to let missiles fly.

That's what he wants you to do. But no matter what Teth says, you have orders to follow.

"We've come to negotiate a peace deal," Husher managed.

"Ah, yes," Teth said. "Losing the munitions facility rendered the Interstellar Union exactly as pliable as I anticipated. And all it took to make you abandon the facility was to frighten one of your precious interspecies colonies."

"We don't gamble with lives," Husher said, even though, on this point, he basically agreed with what the Ixan was getting at. But what else was there for him to say?

"I've always wondered why you don't gamble with them," Teth mused. "When losing in war means slavery or death, is it not far better to spend any coin necessary to avoid defeat?"

"It's not worth sacrificing our principles." Husher truly did believe that, if not in the way Snyder and her lot did.

Teth raised a massive, clawed hand in a dismissive gesture. "I tire of your sophomoric philosophizing. Surely you're not the one who'll conduct the negotiations on behalf of your government. Who am I to speak with?"

Husher nodded at his Coms officer, and she rerouted the transmission to a small chamber situated deep inside the *Vesta*, where Ochrim, Chancey, Shobi, and Bryson were gathered. Teth vanished from the CIC's main display, though Husher could hear his voice through his embedded ear piece, as well as those of the four designated negotiators.

Husher did have the ability to interject, though Chancey had made it clear that his contributions weren't welcome unless they pertained directly to the security of the ship.

"Greetings, brother," the mutated Ixan said.

"Teth," Ochrim said.

"Hello," Chancey chimed in.

"Let's get right down to it," Teth said, "shall we, oh defenders of the right and good? What have you come to offer me?"

"What do you want?" Chancey asked.

"What an intriguing question." Teth let the silence drag on, then.

Someone cleared his throat—likely Chancey, since he spoke again. "We've come prepared to offer much in exchange for your cooperation in working together to achieve stability for the region. There are resource rights to several systems we're prepared to offer, and we're also ready to hear and consider whatever other requests and requirements you think are—"

Husher muted himself, then turned to his Coms officer. "Shut it off."

"Sir?" Fry said, eyebrows raised.

"Shut it off. I can't stomach it."

"Yes, sir." A second later, the voices vanished from his ear, and Husher breathed a sigh of relief, relishing the silence. He toggled to a view of the tactical display, then, scrutinizing Teth's ship for any sign he might be planning to violate the implied understanding that no shots would be fired during the negotiations.

CHAPTER 38

Belay That Order

Husher was so fixated on Teth's ship that he almost didn't notice the asteroid that underwent a slight but appreciable course change, carrying it along a new trajectory that wouldn't have been possible were it being acted on by the laws of physics alone.

Once he realized something wasn't right, he willed his Oculenses to rewind the feed from his ship's forward visual sensors, and he scrutinized the main display during the moment of change. He needed to be sure.

There. The asteroid's trajectory definitely changed, and not only that, the rock was more than large enough to conceal a ship like the one they'd fought in the Saffron System. This close, the barrage of robots such a ship could loose would be incredibly difficult to fend off, especially combined with Teth's arsenal, and that of whatever other vessels were concealed within the asteroid belt.

"Captain..." Winterton said, and Husher's gaze snapped toward the sensor operator.

He was feeling a bit light-headed—like this entire situation felt surreal. It *was* surreal. They'd come to make nice with the *Ixa,* for crying out loud, and they were clearly about to be played. The Interstellar Union had signed off on this!

"What is it, Ensign?"

"Have a look at the position of Teth's warship on the tactical display. It's inching toward us."

Husher gripped the armrests of the command seat until his knuckles were white and his forearms vibrated. "Tactical—"

"*Captain,*" Kaboh said in a warning tone from the Nav station.

Husher spoke over him. "Tactical, calculate a firing solution for eight Hydras targeting Teth's ship and the area around it. Program them to separate at a kilometer's remove from each other, and tell me when they're ready."

"Yes, sir," Tremaine said, bending to his work.

Hydras were inspired by missiles fielded by the Ixa during the Second Galactic War, which had exploded mid-flight into hundreds of thousands of speeding kinetic-kill masses, raining down on a target ship's hull and obliterating it if enough of the masses connected.

Similarly, every Hydra divided into eight smaller missiles, each equipped with a compact nuclear warhead. The Hydras were fitted with sensors and designed to separate the moment they detected an attempt to shoot them down. The eight-Hydra barrage he'd ordered would split into sixty-four warheads.

"Captain Husher," Kaboh said, "I strongly advise against—"

"I'm responsible for safeguarding this ship, Kaboh," he said. "That vessel is moving against us."

"Missiles armed and ready, sir," Tremaine said.

Husher nodded. "Standby to fire the primary laser, either at Teth's ship or at whatever comes out from behind that large asteroid—it'll depend on how effective our Hydras end up being. Fire missiles, Chief Tremaine."

Kaboh stood up from the Nav station. "*Belay that order.*"

"Excuse me, Lieutenant Commander?" Husher said.

"I'm officially declaring you unfit for command on the grounds that your erratic behavior indicates you're mentally unwell."

Tremaine was looking between Husher and Kaboh, brow lowered, clearly uncertain how to react.

"You don't have the authority to do that," Husher said. "Fire the Hydras, Tremaine."

"Do *not* fire them, Chief Tremaine," Kaboh said. "I don't have the authority to do it, but as chief medical officer, Doctor Bancroft does. And I know she'll agree with me based on the way you're behaving. Tremaine, you are *not* mentally unstable, and for you, firing those missiles will amount to high treason. I strongly recommend you refrain from doing so until Doctor Bancroft at least has an opportunity to comment on this matter."

"Teth's vessel is still approaching," Winterton said.

"We don't have time for a medical assessment in the middle of a developing engagement," Husher said. "Tremaine, fire those missiles. Lieutenant Commander Kaboh, you are relieved from duty."

With a toss of his head, Kaboh's gaze swung toward the Coms officer. "Fry, put Mayor Chancey through to the CIC for all to hear."

"Chancey has no authority in my CIC," Husher said.

"No, but he'll likely be able to tell us why Teth is moving closer."

Slowly, Fry's hand moved over her console, and with a couple taps, the mayor was patched through.

"Mayor Chancey," the Kaithian said.

"Kaboh? Yes?"

"Captain Husher is poised to launch eight Hydra missiles at the Ixan Command Leader's vessel in response to her maneuvering closer. Are you able to explain the vessel's movement?"

A brief silence, and then Chancey spoke, sounding incredulous. "We were having trouble with the connection, so Command Leader Teth tried shortening the transmission distance. That seemed to work, and his Navigation auxiliary is slowing down now."

Kaboh's eyes found Husher's.

"Mayor," Husher said, "an asteroid changed its trajectory in a way that shouldn't have been possible unless an enemy ship was hidden behind it."

"Thank you, Mayor Chancey," Kaboh said over Husher. "The captain has been acting irrationally, but you can rest assured that no rash actions will be taken."

"Right. Good. Thank you, Kaboh."

"It's my pleasure. Terminate the call, please, Ensign, and summon Doctor Bancroft to the CIC. Commander Fesky," the Kaithian said, turning toward the XO's chair, "it's not my place to give you orders, but I would recommend preparing to take command of the *Vesta*."

"This isn't about my mental *state,*" Husher said, glaring at the Nav officer. "This is a political coup of a military vessel."

"Doctor Bancroft is far from a political operative, Captain. She's a medical professional of the highest caliber. If she corroborates my assessment, it will be because she recognizes it as the best thing for her ship and everyone aboard." The Kaithian sat at his console and turned toward it.

Five minutes later, the hatch opened to reveal Bancroft, for whom Kaboh played the video and audio of what had just transpired in the CIC.

Husher sat in the command seat, body rigid. Listening to himself, he *did* sound a bit manic, if you were looking for signs he was unstable.

I'm not, though. I'm stable. It's the rest of the galaxy that's insane.

"I'm truly sorry, Captain," Bancroft said once she finished reviewing the recording. Her hands were folded over her waist, and she met his eyes with what looked a lot like sympathy. "I do find you unfit for command. It would be best if you return to your quarters for now, until we can find you more appropriate accommodations."

For a moment, Husher stayed where he was, wholly unable to accept what had just happened.

"Will we need to contact Major Gamble, Captain?" Kaboh asked mildly.

Husher didn't answer. Instead, he rose from the command seat and walked stiffly from the CIC.

CHAPTER 39

The Taste of Sweat and Fear

"I'm sure you agree, my terms are quite reasonable," Teth said from the command seat in the very center of the bridge, while his various auxiliaries sat around him in total stillness. "In exchange for a five-year armistice, to be renewed for a second five-year period at the end of the first, contingent on adherence by both sides...in exchange for that, I want total control of the Baxa System as well as the six nearby systems we've already mentioned. I also wish to speak with Jake Price, in person, as soon as possible, with the understanding that no harm will come to him. I've already explained where you can expect to find Price. Does that cover everything?"

"That about does it," Chancey said cheerfully. "And as a representative of the Interstellar Union, I agree to those terms. It's been a surprising pleasure to negotiate with you, Command Leader. I'll see to it that the *Vesta* returns with young Price, and as we've already agreed, her battle group will remain here to ensure the IU's interests are being served."

"An unnecessary provision, but an understandable one, Mayor," Teth said. "I will treat them as if they were my own."

Chancey nodded. "If what you say about Price's location is true, we should return in a little over a month. Is there anything else you'd care to discuss, Command Leader?"

"That will be all. Safe travels to you, Mayor. And farewell, Ochrim. Rest assured that I will rebuild the Baxa System in a way that does justice to our father's legacy."

"Goodbye, Teth," Ochrim said, and the transmission ended.

The deathly silence stretched on inside Teth's bridge, as it would for days, if he allowed it to. No one spoke, here—to him or to each other—without his prompting. Nothing happened on the *Apex* without his express approval. The remaining Ixa were as close to extensions of his own body as he could make them, just as they'd been his father's appendages right before his death.

Teth's tongue flicked out, tasting the sweat and fear that always lingered on his bridge. An enhanced olfactory sense was only one of the enhancements with which the Progenitors had bestowed him, but it did make dominance a much more enjoyable experience.

"Coms auxiliary," Teth said.

"Yes, Command Leader!" the auxiliary said, as though he'd been waiting with the words on his tongue, as he no doubt had.

"Play Kreigan's Fifth."

"Yes, Command Leader."

Within seconds—admirable haste, for such an unusual request—the beautiful, discordant chords clashed together, like ships firing on each other from across a battlespace, punctuated by percussion as sharp as gunfire.

"Command Leader," the Coms auxiliary said, his voice much softer as he interrupted Teth's enjoyment of the music.

"Yes?"

"Another transmission request has come in from the *Vesta*."

"Accept it, and put it on the main screen." Teth felt comfortable letting his bridge crew in on any and all intel, since they knew that if they shared it with anyone, he would soon learn of it and kill them. Besides, he'd been expecting this transmission.

It was Mayor Chancey, again, and by now, he'd returned to his office in Cybele.

"Was that to your satisfaction?" Chancey asked.

"Other than the fact it was far too easy, yes, I suppose it was. I do find it somewhat depressing that the human who killed my father reacted to our maneuvers in such a predictable fashion. That rankles a little, I'll admit."

"If it's any consolation, he faces a future of irrelevance and disgrace. Depending on how far the IU wants to carry the fiction that he's unstable, he may end up in an institution."

"Well, you already know how much respect I've come to gain for the IU. That's why I intend to take *such* good care of their ships."

"I know you will. So long for now, Teth."

"So long, Mayor. And thank you for your work."

"Don't mention it. In fact—thank *you,* Teth. I mean that."

“I’m honored,” Teth said, motioning for his Coms auxiliary to cut the transmission.

CHAPTER 40

Brittle Silence

Captain Arbuck of the *Thero* drummed his fingers on the armrest as he watched the *Vesta* dwindle to a speck of light on visual sensors. Then, a flash told him she'd made the jump to warp, and her long journey had officially begun.

Arbuck already felt restless. The idea of sitting around the Concord System with a bunch of Ixa didn't do much for his already frayed nerves. He was a bit of an anomaly among military ship captains, in that he had absolutely no desire to go to war, and had always hoped to serve out his career without ever seeing combat.

Of course, that was the whole idea of an armistice, and maybe it would hold. Given the Ixa's track record, he had his doubts about that, but anything was possible, he supposed.

He just wished he could know the outcome now, one way or the other. He'd always hated waiting, and waiting under these particular circumstances promised to be a special kind of hell, if the first few moments were any indication.

Teth hadn't offered the crews of the *Vesta*'s battle group ships accommodations, and none had been requested during the negotiations. As standard procedure, each warship was provisioned to go six months without needing to resupply from either their capital starship or a planetary colony.

As for the abundance of downtime they now all faced...Arbuck wasn't used to that, but he was looking forward to it, in a way. He had a backlog of apps and virtual "experiences" he'd been meaning to check out with his Oculenses, and he certainly wouldn't turn down the opportunity to do so. In fact, unbeknownst to the rest of the CIC crew, he'd already started watching a vid using the main display, with the sound coming through his embedded ear piece...

"Sir, I'm getting multiple contacts emerging from the asteroid field," the sensor operator said, and Arbuck jerked upright in the command seat, clearing his throat.

"Hmm? Sorry, could you repeat that, Chief?" He'd heard what she'd said perfectly well, but he wanted to buy some time for his brain to process it.

"Eleven Gok ships just emerged from hiding places behind asteroids." The chief fell silent for a moment as she scrutinized the main display, then said, "Eight more contacts just appeared. All Gok."

"Acknowledged, Chief," Arbuck said, ashamed at the tremor that had crept into his voice. "Coms, send Command Leader Teth a transmission request."

"Transmitting the request now, sir."

A brittle silence descended as they waited for the request to be accepted. After several minutes—much longer than it should have taken for the signal to be received and answered—the

Coms officer said, "No response, sir." That much was obvious, but the young officer was clearly as anxious about the new arrivals as his captain.

Arbuck took his Coms officer's redundant statement as a signal that he needed to do something, and he wholeheartedly agreed. *But what?* He cleared his throat again. "All right. Coms, contact the other battle group ships with a recommendation that all four IGF ships should begin making their way toward the warp departure point, while standing by to accelerate to warp velocity. I'm not saying we're actually going to depart the system, but this behavior is highly unusual, and I'd like to take every—"

"The Gok ships have just launched guided missiles targeting all four of our ships, sir!" his sensor operator yelled.

"Calm down," Arbuck admonished, though he could hear the panic in his own voice. "How many missiles?"

"According to the computer's count...two hundred and nineteen."

When Arbuck glanced toward his sensor operator, he saw that the color had drained from her face. Judging from the way he was feeling, he had likely paled as well.

"F-full reverse thrust, helm, and Tactical, ready point defense—"

But his tactical officer's arms had fallen to her sides, and she was slowly shaking her head.

"They're already here, sir."

Arbuck had enough time to realize that he'd left his vid playing on the main display before the bulkhead that held the display caved in, admitting flame and sound to engulf him.

CHAPTER 41

Evil

Husher took Bancroft's recommendation that he return to his quarters, but only long enough to put on one of his two plainclothes outfits and stuff the other into a small duffel bag. Grabbing some toiletries, he stuffed those in as well, and then he left, marching through the *Vesta*'s corridors and ignoring the baffled looks from his former subordinates.

His prayer was that no one in Cybele would recognize him, considering he was never without his captain's uniform. When he opened the hatch into the false desert, he found that so far, at least, his prayers were being answered. There were no protesters sitting in the sand, waiting to harangue him for his oppressive ways.

Now that he'd escaped from the crew section, he realized he had no plan. Escaping had *been* the plan, the only plan, and now that he'd done it, he had no clue what to do next. So he spent ten minutes walking to the farthest corner of the compartment that contained Cybele and he dropped to the sand, his back landing with a thud against the bulkhead. To his eyes, he appeared to be leaning against thin air, since the simulated snowcapped mountains were still far in the distance, inaccessible. And to anyone who spotted him out here, because of the distance-warping effect at play in this desert of illusion, he would appear as a speck in the middle of a sandy expanse.

What would follow, he didn't know. He also didn't know how to react to his situation. He'd fled the *Vesta*'s crew section because he thought there was a decent chance Bancroft would try to have him committed to a locked section of the sick bay. But was there any hope of escaping the *Vesta* herself? And where would he escape to? He'd have to make his attempt in a populated star system for it to have any meaning, unless he merely wanted to kill himself, and somehow he still didn't have that in him, despite his present state of dejection.

Would finding Sera be a worthy goal? Could she ever bring herself to forgive him for what his role in the Gok Wars had brought? Seventeen years had passed without her forgiveness, but what if he went to her? What if he begged?

For the second time this month, he lowered his face into his hands. It occurred to him that now would be a good time to weep, but he didn't have that in him, either. Too many years of exerting iron self-control, he supposed—of doing exactly what he thought he needed to in order to ready the galaxy for the coming onslaught.

The end will come soon enough. That knowledge could be freeing, if he wanted it to be. Stripped of command, stripped of responsibility...he could actually live, for however long he'd have before the galaxy burned down around him. When was the last time he'd truly lived?

He found himself on his feet and trudging across the sand dunes, up one slope and down the next, one foot in front of the other. The lack of demonstrators to harass him persisted, even as he entered the city. Who knew what they might be glued to at home, staring into space as their Oculenses treated them to fabricated sights.

He soon found himself outside Ochrim's door, and he rang the bell. Moments later, the front door slid aside to reveal the Ixan.

"Captain," he said.

"Not anymore. Not of the *Vesta*, anyway."

"I know. It's on the narrownet."

"Figures."

"What can I help you with?" the alien asked, his expression as neutral as ever.

"Feel like harboring a strong candidate for commitment to a mental facility?"

Ochrim raised three clawed fingers to his chin, as though considering Husher's request. "Given your new status, you no longer have power over me. You can't pressure me to share the results of my research with you. In fact, you can't require me to do anything at all."

"Is that a no, then?"

"It's an accurate characterization of the market value of my yes." The Ixan stepped aside, and Husher hesitated for only a moment before crossing the threshold and making his way to the living room, where he deposited himself into Ochrim's favorite chair. "Do you have any beer?"

That elicited a rare chuckle from Ochrim, and Husher heard the fridge open, followed by the clink of two bottles being taken out.

The first swallow was the best thing Husher had ever tasted. “I think things are looking up,” he said. “How’s the multiverse doing?”

“Didn’t I just remark—”

“You said I can’t require you to share your research. But I can still ask.”

Ochrim settled onto the couch across the room, peering at Husher with his lamp-like eyes. He’d yet to sip from his beer. “I’ve made progress,” he said at last. “Even so, I have to question whether it’s worthwhile to discuss my discoveries any further, or whether I should continue pursuing my research at all. As we both know, scientific research and I have a fraught past, and it’s tempting to join you in your current position—that is, relinquishing control of the future, whether voluntarily or not.”

Husher grasped his beer bottle with both hands and sat forward in the armchair, staring at the threadbare rug Ochrim kept around for some reason. The residence could be set to whatever temperature the alien preferred, at minimal cost, and the rug certainly wasn’t serving any aesthetic purpose.

Husher sat in that position for some time, not speaking. His mind flitted from thought to thought, seemingly at random. It wasn’t until he raised his head and met Ochrim’s eyes that he realized he’d been piecing some things together.

“Did you know I lost my daughter?”

After a pause, Ochrim inclined his head. "I had heard. I'm sorry."

"Sure." Husher cleared his throat. "Did you know I'm being treated for PTSD from the night I lost her?"

"I did not. Were you...?"

"There? Yeah. My cab was pulling up to the curb as the house was getting bombed."

Ochrim had nothing to say to that.

"I'm not bringing this up to shock you. But I...I think I just realized something. Losing my daughter made me even more determined to make sure the galaxy's ready for the coming war, because I had almost nothing left, after it happened. Sera divorced me, and all I had was the mission I'd assigned myself with shortly after Keyes died."

"And so, you think we—"

"I'm not finished. Losing Iris made me more determined to make sure we're ready, but it made me more anxious, too. More afraid, of losing the little I had left. It made me want to protect everything, absolutely everything, from anything that could possibly hurt it. My ship, my crew, the civilians living on my ship, the galaxy...everything."

"Do you believe that's what brought you to this point?"

Husher nodded, though he hadn't realized that until Ochrim had just said it. "I do. I tried to hold on to everything, and I ended up with nothing."

"The Fins made a study of PTSD."

Husher raised his eyebrows. "Oh?"

"Yes. Like so many things, PTSD is something that's common to every sapient species we've encountered. It's probably common among nonsapient species, too. In fact, my bet would be that every species experiences some form of it. Now, why do you suppose that is?"

Slowly, Husher shook his head, though an inexplicable knot of excitement had made its home in his stomach as he listened to the Ixan.

"I'll tell you what the Fins concluded. They came to believe that PTSD is an ongoing mechanism—a subroutine, if you will—evolved to alert an organism that it has experienced a threat it can't properly account for. That raises stress levels, because the subroutine is sounding the alarm that the threatening event that caused the initial trauma could easily happen again, and if it does, the organism has no plan for contending with it. You've experienced those elevated stress levels, obviously."

Husher nodded, rapt, and Ochrim continued: "The way to deal with those perpetually elevated stress levels—the way to alleviate the PTSD, even to cure it—is to provide the subroutine with a proper account of the threatening event, and to provision it with a plan for dealing with a similar situation, should it occur in the future. You were the victim of a terrorist attack, and the question you're likely asking yourself now is, how can you come up with a rational account for another intelligent being murdering your three-year-old daughter. Correct?"

"Yes."

"Well, here it is: evil exists in this world. Maybe you knew that already, maybe you truly accepted it, or maybe you subscribe to the more modern notion that there's no such thing as evil. That everyone is basically good. Well, that's nonsense, as your traumatic experience demonstrates. The beings who killed your daughter committed an evil act, because they are, in fact, evil. But even supposing you've accepted the existence of evil in the universe, that isn't enough. Because in order to provide a true accounting of what happened to you, Husher, you also need to recognize that *every living being* is capable of the level of evil that was required to murder your daughter. In fact, they're capable of even more evil than that. Much, much more. And that includes you. You, too, are capable of that much evil."

Slowly, Husher shook his head, but still said nothing. His breathing came slow and steady, though the air rushed through his nostrils, and his chest heaved and fell.

"I heard your conversation with my brother, when he suggested that you're both alike. The thing is, he's right. You *are* both killers, you *are* both motivated in part by vengeance, and you *have* both taken it upon yourselves to decide when a being should live and when they should die. If you want to arrive at a proper account of your daughter's death, if you want to overcome your PTSD, you have to realize that Teth was right. You are just like him. Recognizing that would make you more effective, because it would allow you to strip away your naivety, and it would let you act with the knowledge of just how horrible you're capable of being. Then, and only then, would you be capable of making a truly moral choice: to act rightly, with full awareness of just how possible it is for you to do otherwise."

Ochrim chucked softly. "The peculiar thing about your situation is that in a sense, Teth represents exactly the situation your PTSD has been trying to warn you about, again and again, for seventeen years. Someone has come once more to take from you what you hold most dear. The question is whether you're able to figure yourself out in time to stop him, or indeed whether it might be far too late for you to do so."

Trembling with emotion for the first time that Husher could remember in...well, *ever,* he rose to his feet.

"I think you just made a pretty good case for why we should try to do something about this mess."

Ochrim rose, too. "Then we will try."

CHAPTER 42

Innumerable

"How was speaking with your brother?" Husher asked as Ochrim knelt to lever up the removable floor tile and open the hidden panel into his lab.

The Ixan paused, crouching on the floor and peering up at Husher thoughtfully. "It wasn't an experience I would have predicted having." Flipping up the tile, he activated the moving panel. "Teth brought you up quite a lot. He kept trying to use you to pressure the diplomats into giving him what he wanted."

Husher narrowed his eyes. "What did he say?"

"He kept mentioning how he knows you're pushing for an increased Fleet presence in this region of the galaxy, and how that makes him skeptical of the negotiators' actual commitment to an armistice. In my view, it had the effect of pushing the diplomats to offer more systems to Teth than they otherwise would have."

Ochrim rose from the floor, and he looked like he was about to lower himself onto the ladder when he seemed to notice the expression on Husher's face. "Something I just told you bothers you."

"Did Chancey tell Teth that I'm pushing for a greater Fleet presence?"

"I didn't hear him say it."

"And were you there from the beginning of the transmission?"

"Yes."

Shaking his head, Husher spoke slowly: "Only two people on this ship know that I was pushing for more warships to come out here. My Coms officer and Mayor Chancey."

"This makes you suspicious of Chancey."

"I guess it could just as easily have been Ensign Fry. But she hasn't been working against me ever since this whole thing started. Chancey has."

"There's another possibility: the mayor may have let it slip to someone else that you advocated for a greater presence—someone who's the actual traitor, or who unknowingly passed it on to the traitor."

"Yeah. That's possible, too." Husher had already assumed that Teth would have superior intel, but the idea that it might have come from someone aboard his ship as opposed to an AI's projections...it made him wonder what other sorts of treachery might be at play on the *Vesta*.

It also made him fear for the battle group they'd left back in Concord.

"Do you really think Teth can be trusted to abide by anything he agreed to during those negotiations, let alone an armistice?" he asked.

"No," Ochrim said. "But you're the one who brought us to Concord to negotiate."

"I was following orders. I made very clear that I thought negotiating with Teth was worse than pointless."

Ochrim seemed to be studying his face intently. "Why don't you tell me what you're thinking?"

"I'm thinking I want to turn this ship around and get back to our battle group."

"Success in turning the *Vesta* around is unlikely, as I believe we both know. As for getting back to your battle group...well, follow me." With that, Ochrim began descending the ladder toward his lab.

The knot of excitement in the pit of his stomach made a return as Husher lowered himself to follow.

When he reached the chamber below, he found Ochrim already leaning against the table. As Husher looked around the lab, nothing jumped out at him that looked like an obvious solution to their problem. "You conducted the experiment, then?"

"I did."

Husher realized that Ochrim was wearing a wider smile than he'd ever seen from him—which, coming from an Ixan, was a bit unsettling. But his anticipation of what Ochrim might have found overrode that. "And? How did it go?"

"I have no idea." The smile broadened.

"What do you mean, you have no idea, Ochrim? Why are we down here, then?"

"I fitted a compact drone with a generator governed by an electromagnetic field restrictor so that it would produce a self-contained wormhole, spherical in form."

"Okay. So what happened?"

"Again, I have no idea. All I can tell you is that the drone vanished from view and didn't return. I didn't have time to set up the experiment before we left Saffron, and so we were under warp drive at the time, meaning that wherever the drone ended up, it was still traveling at warp velocities. If, indeed, it ended up anywhere. But even supposing it did go somewhere meaningful to us, and supposing I'd had time to program it to return to realspace at the exact coordinates the *Vesta* would occupy, I didn't have the resources to collect the drone from space. I wouldn't have wanted to, anyway, since that could draw unwanted attention to my research, which is now officially illegal."

Husher was shaking his head. "How does this help us, Ochrim?"

"Because I have a theory about where it ended up, which I consider fairly likely."

Husher sighed. He hated science. "What's your theory?"

"I think it went to another brane inside our universe. And I also believe that brane is a decoherence-free subspace, the attainment of which I consider the ultimate goal of my research. The applications of harnessing such a space are innumerable—within ten years, I could envision—"

"*What are the applications right now?*" Husher yelled.

The scientist blinked. "You said you wanted to rejoin your battle group."

"Yes."

"Well, I have two theories about the subspace's spatial relationship to the brane we occupy. If one of them proves true, it should allow you to reach the Concord System in just a third of the time it takes to reach it under warp drive."

"What if the other holds true?"

"Three times as long. It's also possible that you won't end up anywhere, or that the subspace's physics won't support the integrity of biological structures. That is, you'll disintegrate." Ochrim cleared his throat. "Our dilemma, of course, is that we do not enjoy an overabundance of time."

Husher nodded, pursing his lips as it dawned on him exactly what attempting this would require—namely, nosediving into the abyss and hoping for the best.

But Teth and the other strange warships had to be going somewhere when they disappeared. At last, Husher said, "We'll also need a craft to carry me there."

"Indeed. It will need to be quite small, since it turns out spherical wormholes require quite a lot of energy to generate. Frankly, I have no idea how Teth can create one large enough to encompass his destroyer, if indeed that is how he's managing to vanish."

"Would a Condor be small enough? We still have a few, kicking around Hangar Bay Theta. No one goes down there, so we can do all the work we need right there in the hangar bay. And no one's going to miss a rusted old fighter that's been obsolete for a decade and a half."

"That will be perfect," Ochrim said. "I've already begun work on a spherical wormhole generator for a craft large enough to hold a being, and with some modifications, it should accommodate a fighter the size of a Condor. Let us get to work."

CHAPTER 43

Staring Back in Shock

As Husher worked on the Condor he'd identified as closest to spaceworthy among those stored in Hangar Bay Theta, Ochrim set about modifying the wormhole generator he'd already been working on.

Repairs on the Condor took almost twenty-three hours, during which they both worked without sleep. Ochrim finished the generator seven hours in, which surprised Husher, until he considered that Ochrim had invented the wormhole generator he was replicating at a smaller scale. With the generator finished, the scientist began work on a warp drive modeled after the *Vesta*'s, but small enough for the Condor. Even assuming Ochrim's subspace compressed distance the way he thought it might, Husher would still need to fly under warp in order to travel to Concord and back in time.

Since the *Vesta* was already inside a warp bubble, it wouldn't be possible to generate another one inside the hangar bay—you couldn't generate a negative energy field inside a field that already had negative energy—but Husher *would* have to produce one the instant he left the supercarrier's, otherwise his Condor would be torn apart.

The fighter would also need to be able to attain the velocities necessary to enter warp—in order to return to the *Vesta* once he was finished in Concord, for example. That would require steady acceleration over a much longer distance than the *Vesta* required, since the Condor's engines weren't nearly as powerful. That said, the fighter still had the ability to use what was known as Ocharium boost, whereby it used the rare element to propel itself against ambient axions and achieve speeds that otherwise wouldn't have been possible. That would help, though it made the use of the Condor also illegal. Of course, Husher and Ochrim were well past letting that bother them.

At the end of the day, they retired to Ochrim's living room with a couple of beers. Husher awoke the next morning to find that Ochrim had laid his partially finished beer on the carpet before stretching out on the couch, while Husher was still in a sitting position in Ochrim's favorite chair, his miraculously unspilled drink nestled between his legs.

"So, how will I know when it's time to transition back to this brane?" Husher asked three hours into their second day of work. "How can I figure out what realspace coordinates correspond to a given subspace location?"

Ochrim's head jerked up from installing a rivet to fasten a distortion rod onto the Condor's hull. He reminded Husher of a squirrel who'd just overheard a potential predator. "Oh. Right! I'll need to include a universal positioning system that assumes a three-to-one realspace-to-subspace relationship in all directions. Thanks for reminding me."

"Uh, yeah, my pleasure," Husher said, sarcasm drenching his voice. Ochrim didn't seem to notice.

Fifteen hours later, the Condor was finally ready—either to transport him to subspace or to kill him in a really specific way.

Either way, at least I'll be a pioneer. For some reason, what he was about to do reminded him of the time he'd been the first to survive an emergency orbital insertion using a Darkstream reentry suit—the same model that had killed the only other person to attempt it. *How do I get myself into these situations?*

"So...do we have to get the Condor to a flight deck? That could be tricky."

"No need," Ochrim answered. "You should transition to subspace once you generate a spherical wormhole. I would recommend lifting the Condor off the hangar bay deck first, to avoid taking a chunk of it with you."

"So I won't slam into the side of the wormhole and get torn apart?"

"No, you'll transport the moment you generate it. As for remaining at warp velocities as you enter subspace, don't worry, I've connected the warp drive to the Condor's sensors and programmed it to generate another bubble the moment you leave this one. From there, the drive will cycle down."

"Why don't I feel confident about my safety right now, Ochrim?"

"Because you have no reason to be."

"Right," Husher said with a nod. "I'd forgotten, for a moment."

On the third day of their work—the fourth day of the *Vesta*'s warp transition—Ochrim finally finished installing the modified warp drive inside the fighter. With that, Husher told the Condor to open its cockpit, and he climbed into it.

The moment he was inside, he flashed back to sitting here on one of the *Providence*'s many flight decks, waiting for the go-ahead to launch. Husher missed those days...bantering with Fesky and the other pilots, coordinating ill-advised maneuvers, subjecting their bodies to far more Gs than they should have. His ascent through the ranks and getting his own command had taken him away from all of it. That was the funny thing about success—you spent your life obsessing over it, and the moment you got it, you started missing where you came from.

As the cockpit closed around him, Ochrim's voice came through his ear piece: "If it's all the same to you, I'm going to leave the hangar bay. Unless you require a countdown, or something like that?"

"That's fine, Ochrim," Husher said, not able to muster a chuckle through the anxiety that gripped his heart and quickened his breath. "Either this works or it doesn't. There's not much more to it than that."

"Good luck, Captain."

Husher opened his mouth to correct him, but then he realized the mistake had probably been intentional. *It isn't a mistake, anyway. I still have my rank, unless it's been stripped from me for some reason, without my knowledge.* No one had notified him of much of anything, during the past three days. He wasn't certain they even knew where to find him.

"Thank you, Ochrim."

He waited for the Ixan to leave the hangar bay and close the hatch. They both knew that being in another part of the ship likely wouldn't make a difference if something catastrophic happened. That said, Husher probably would have left, too, if he didn't need to be here.

Once he was alone, he activated the wormhole generator. Abruptly, the Condor disappeared around him, replaced by an infinity of himself; countless versions of Husher stretching out in every direction, every one of them staring back at him in shock.

CHAPTER 44

Copper Taste

The Condor's cockpit reappeared, though Husher had no idea why it had vanished in the first place. He'd nearly fainted from shock as he'd gazed into the cosmic mirror, but it had only lasted a second, and now he found himself in a featureless, black void—at least, according to the fighter's visual sensors.

Also according to the sensors, in conjunction with the universal positioning system Ochrim had fitted the Condor with, he was moving at incredibly fast speeds. That made sense, given he was still flying under warp drive.

Without warning, the drive cycled down, and the Condor exited the warp bubble. Transitioning to realspace—or in this case, subspace—meant an immediate and sharp drop in velocity, but that still left him with a lot of forward momentum to contend with.

When Husher attempted to decelerate, the force of the gravity that crashed against his body like a tsunami made him cry out, and he stopped, panting as he continued to hurtle in the wrong direction.

He'd always made an effort to keep himself in shape, especially as he got older, to combat the effects of aging. Even so, he was in nowhere near the shape he'd been during the peak of his Condor flying career. His body simply couldn't handle G forces the way it once had.

Gingerly, he tried applying the brakes again, only a little this time. He could handle the G forces in small doses, and the exercises from his pilot days started coming back to him as he worked his abs and limbs to facilitate blood flow and ensure he stayed conscious.

I need to do this faster. If Ochrim was right about subspace's relationship to realspace, then traveling at warp velocities would take him three times farther than they normally would.

Gritting his teeth, he laid on more pressure.

Soon, his body was coated in sweat, and his muscles were so sore it felt like he'd left the gym after the hardest workout of his life, turned around, and did the exact same exercises all over again.

It seemed like hours later when he finally slowed to a stop. He wanted to take a long nap, but it wasn't the time for that. Letting himself rest now would amount to a betrayal of his battle group captains.

I need to start the warp transition toward Concord. Then I can rest.

That meant enduring the exact same G pressures—from the opposite direction. It meant turning around and doing it all over again.

With a sigh, he started laying on speed, until he reached a point past which only Ocharium boost could make him accelerate any faster. He activated it, and his body paid the price.

An eternity later, the Condor's accelerometer communicated to the warp drive that his velocity was sufficient to transition to warp. He did so, instructing it to inform him when he was approaching Concord, according to Ochrim's theoretical reckoning.

He felt sluggish, almost feverish from the exertion he'd just subjected himself to. The entire cockpit was slick with his sweat, and the copper taste of blood clung to the back of his throat from the effort merely getting oxygen into his lungs had required, toward the end.

He was too tired even to feel anxious about whether Ochrim was right about subspace—about whether he'd end up at his destination or in the middle of nowhere. And yet, enduring the transition to warp did instill him with an incredible sense of accomplishment and pride as he tumbled into a deep sleep.

A little over thirty-two hours later, the computer notified him that it was time to start decelerating, unless he wanted to blow past Concord.

Before he began, he activated the wormhole generator. He was ready for the countless copies of himself, this time, and all the Hushers looked back at him with set jaws and eyes underscored by black lines.

Maddeningly, even though he'd returned to his native dimension, he still had no idea where he was inside it. The Condor's outdated sensors hadn't been designed to make sense of the universe from inside a warp bubble, and visual sensors told him nothing. They only showed a mess of blue-shifted stars whipping by, with some red-shifted stars to either side of him and an empty void behind, since he was outpacing the light traveling from that direction.

At last, Ochrim's universal positioning system told Husher it was time to exit warp, and he did. Immediately, he expanded the Condor's tactical overview so that it showed him a light year in every direction.

Once the sensors had finished populating the display, and he saw what he was looking for, he raised two stiff arms and yelled in triumph.

He was just outside the Concord System, screaming toward its great asteroid belt.

His celebration didn't last for long. As light began to reach him from the battle group's last known location, it showed not the warships he'd been praying to find, but a wide field of debris that was slowly spreading along the system's ecliptic plane.

"No," he rasped, double- and triple-checking the tactical display to make sure of what he was seeing.

It was time to start decelerating again, and so he did, laying on as much as he could handle. Thankfully, it wasn't necessary to come to a complete stop this time, so it was less intense than his initial deceleration in subspace.

There was no sign of Teth's ship—either it had withdrawn deeper into the system or left to launch another attack. So Husher pressed on toward the asteroid belt, desperate for answers.

It soon became clear what a bad idea that was, as a Gok destroyer emerged from behind one of the asteroids and fired a volley of four missiles.

Immediately, Husher engaged the Condor's gyroscopes to point his thrusters toward the missiles. He gunned the engine, and the immense G forces flattened him against the seat. His cheeks peeled back from his teeth, twisting his face into a forced snarl.

Determined not to pass out, he flexed the muscles throughout his entire body. A few minutes later, he managed to overcome the momentum carrying him toward the missiles, but as he accelerated in the opposite direction he realized that there was no chance of outstripping them. Worse, they were now too close to try to detonate using kinetic impactors or missiles of his own.

He did the only thing he could think of. He activated the spherical wormhole generator, and after a brief rendezvous with an infinity of reflections, found himself back in subspace.

As he breathed a heavy sigh of relief, something occurred to him. If he'd had the energy to spare—which his Condor didn't, but which a fully charged Python would—he could have done incredible damage to the Gok warship using just a single fighter, flitting out of subspace long enough to fire missiles and impactors and then flitting back in to avoid return fire.

Then, he imagined an entire *squadron* of Pythons, outfitted with spherical wormhole generators, weaving in and out of a battlespace and terrorizing a disoriented enemy.

Just as he'd always hoped, the military applications of Ochrim's discoveries were incalculable. But the realization was tempered by the loss of four captains and their loyal crews.

I need to get back to the Vesta.

Husher again began the long, arduous acceleration required to attain warp velocity. With any luck, he would catch the supercarrier just as it was transitioning out of warp.

CHAPTER 45

Supposed to Feel Like That

"Fesky."

It took several minutes for his old friend to reply to Husher's brief transmission, even though they were close enough for real-time communication. But at last, her voice came through, lowered as though she was trying to prevent others from overhearing.

"Husher. I just gave Kaboh the command seat and ran out of the CIC to speak with you. Where are you? Search parties started scouring the *Vesta* for you three days ago!"

"I'm in a Condor, underneath an overhang of Himera's smallest moon, so that the sensors don't pick me up."

A long pause followed that. At last, Fesky said, "There's been talk of having you committed to a locked chamber because of mental instability. I've been arguing that you're *not* unstable, but you're not helping me make my case, here."

"Listen to me, Fesky. I'm not unstable, and I really am in a Condor on Himera's second moon. I'm asking you to trust me, because what I'm about to say is going to sound even crazier."

"What is it?" Fesky said, sounding as though she was bracing herself.

"I just returned from the Concord System, using new technology that I was the first to test, mainly because I supplied the materials to develop it. I can't talk too much about that at the moment. What's most relevant right now is that our battle group's been destroyed, and I have the sensor recordings to prove it."

He got another long silence in response, and he sensed Fesky was grappling with what he'd told her. Finally, she said, "All right, Husher. I'm trusting you. What do you need me to do?"

"Go back into the CIC and order them to open one of the airlocks into Flight Deck Sigma. Tell them that one of our outdated fighters is outside the ship and needs to be allowed entry. Say you can't offer any more details than that. Give the command back to Kaboh and leave the CIC again. As soon as you do, contact Major Gamble and ask him to meet you on that flight deck with some of his marines. Just two should do it."

"Can you at least tell me what the plan is?"

"I have good reason to believe that Mayor Dylan Chancey is working with the Ixa, and has been doing everything in his power to debilitate us. We're going to search his residence."

"That's not quite good enough, Husher. I need to know what your reasons are for believing that."

"During the negotiations, Teth mentioned something that only Chancey could have known. Other than Ensign Fry, that is, and I trust her a lot more than I trust him. Also, the fact that the battle group we left in Concord is destroyed, and that Chancey played a big part in leaving them there—that's pretty damning too, wouldn't you say?"

An audible clack came over the connection and Fesky snapped her beak together. "This feels like it could be either the best decision of my career or a complete disaster," she said. "Is there anything you can tell me that makes me feel better about the chances of the first one?"

"No," Husher said. "But I can say that I think it's supposed to feel like that. And Fesky, this whole situation is already a disaster. You know that, and you also know that if there's even a small chance we can turn it around, we have to take it."

"I was afraid you'd say that."

"Why?"

"Because that's how you've always brought me around to these crazy ideas—by telling me things I already know."

CHAPTER 46

Every Crease

As the commanding officer of the *Vesta*, Husher had always had the ability to access private shipboard communications, provided there was cause to believe the security of the ship depended on knowing their content.

For him, extreme consideration and forethought were necessary before examining anyone's messages. Given his removal from command, however, that was no longer his call to make.

It was Fesky's call. And after making it, she reviewed Chancey's communications and found records of multiple encrypted exchanges with an unknown party off-ship.

Working together to search Chancey's residence, it didn't take long for Gamble, Fesky, Husher, and the two marine privates to find a drive secreted inside a mattress containing several decryption keys. The third one they applied to the suspicious transmissions unlocked them.

The messages Chancey had sent contained exactly what Husher had expected: intelligence on him and other prominent Fleet officers aboard the *Vesta*, information originating from the Interstellar Union, and frank discussions of Chancey's efforts to destabilize the *Vesta* by increasing polarization between the people of Cybele and her crew.

When he and Fesky were finished reviewing the messages, Husher turned to Major Gamble. "Find Chancey, arrest him, and throw him in the brig."

"Yes, sir," the major said before heading straight for City Hall with his marines in tow.

When they were gone, Husher exchanged glances with Fesky. "You're not going to be too put out when I retake command of this ship, are you?"

"Only if you don't screw it up this time," she said, holding his gaze.

Husher considered his friend's words for a bit. Then, he nodded. "That's fair enough. I'll try my best not to."

As they strode across the illusory desert, toward the hatch that led into the crew compartment, something caught Husher's eye from off to the right.

He stopped dead in his tracks as he stared at the man standing perfectly still, wearing the old United Human Fleet uniform.

"You see that?" Husher said.

"What?" Fesky asked, but the moment she spoke, the man disappeared.

"Never mind. Oculenses playing tricks on me." They continued into the crew section, but Husher couldn't get the image of Captain Keyes out of his head. Right before the man had disappeared, he'd nodded at Husher.

As he marched into the CIC, with Fesky right behind him, Kaboh practically gasped: "*Husher!*" The alien was wearing the closest thing to a surprised look that Husher had ever seen from a Kaithian.

"Ensign Fry, I just sent a vid to your console," Husher said. "If you would kindly play it on the main display and grant everyone access, I'd appreciate it." He wasn't used to having to ask for things in his CIC.

"You don't have the authority to give orders here anymore," Kaboh hissed.

"I didn't order the ensign, I asked. But I'm about to retake the ability to give orders, the moment she plays the vid for you."

Fry did play the vid, and everyone in the CIC watched Husher's trajectory through the Concord System, past the wreckage of the *Vesta*'s battle group, and right up to the asteroid belt, where a Gok destroyer emerged to attack.

"How did you come by this footage?" Kaboh asked.

"I took it."

"Impossible."

"Quite possible, in fact, Lieutenant Commander. You may be Kaithian, and your species may have created mine, but even so, there are a lot of things you don't know. I expect that this technology—which I used to both reach the Concord System and return here in time to meet the *Vesta*—is about to become vital to the war effort. But that's not the matter at hand. What's *immediately* relevant is that I was correct about Teth's hostile intentions in the Concord System, and also that Mayor Chancey was just arrested for conspiring with the enemy. Evidently, my actions have not been those of a captain unfit for command, and therefore I'll be retaking the command seat. *Get up.*"

"Nevertheless," Kaboh said. "Doctor Bancroft *is* the chief medical officer aboard this ship, and she *did* declare you unfit."

Husher stepped closer. "And *you,* Kaboh, are a bureaucratic weasel bent on twisting regulations to serve your own misguided prejudices. Get out of that chair, or I'll call Major Gamble to *throw* you out."

Kaboh stared up at Husher, his large, coal-black eyes narrowed and teeth partly bared. At last, the Kaithian stood, making way for Husher.

He settled into the command seat. "You're a talented officer, Kaboh, and I'm fine with you staying on as the primary Nav officer, if you can swallow your pride enough to do so. Are there any other objections?" Husher peered around the CIC, but no one spoke. "All right, then. Kaboh, set a course that turns the *Vesta* around for a warp transition back to the Concord System, then send it over to the helm. Coms, patch me through to shipwide."

Fry glanced at him. Her expression told him she wasn't quite sure what to make of all this, but that she didn't necessarily object, either. "The entire ship, sir? Including Cybele?"

"Yes."

"It's done. You're on."

Husher nodded. "Crew of the *Vesta* and citizens of Cybele. This is Captain Vin Husher. In light of recent developments, including the revelations that Mayor Dylan Chancey has been working with the enemy and that the battle group we left behind in the Concord System has been destroyed, I have retaken command of this vessel. I've ordered us to turn around and return to the Concord System."

He drew a deep breath. "I won't try to conceal my reasons for this decision. Teth is clearly attempting to establish a foothold in the Milky Way, so that he and whatever forces he represents can attack us with impunity. We have limited time to stop him from doing that, and if we leave him alone, he *will* continue to exploit our reluctance to engage in direct combat. He'll have us dividing our forces up in an attempt to protect everything, and in the end, we'll have nothing.

"If I were to return to the heart of the Interstellar Union and seek guidance from the admiralty of the Integrated Galactic Fleet, I have every reason to believe that, instead of sending everything we have against Teth, they would instead circle the wagons while they quibble and delay. I also don't consider it impossible that they'd attempt to seek another peace deal with Teth, perhaps by offering him even better terms than they already have.

"I won't stand for that. Thirteen years ago, I was given command of this ship to do everything I could to protect the galaxy, as well as everyone in it. So that's what I intend to do. If we succeed in defeating Teth, and I'm deemed insubordinate when I return, so be it. But I will face every consequence with pride in the knowledge that I did right by the galaxy, whether the galaxy accepts that or not."

Husher nodded toward his Coms officer, and she cut the transmission.

"You essentially just declared us to be in open rebellion against both the IGF and the IU," Kaboh said.

"Lieutenant, you're free to abstain from participating in the coming fight. If you like, you're even welcome to go see how many crewmembers disagree with what I'm doing. Somehow, I don't think you'll find very many."

The Kaithian apparently decided to remain at the Nav station, and two minutes later, Husher's com buzzed with a call from Penelope Snyder.

"Ms. Snyder," he said upon answering.

"This is an outrage," she hissed. "How can you put tens of thousands of civilians in mortal peril on a whim? Are you really that monstrous?"

"Ms. Snyder, I apologize if, when you decided to live on a warship, you were under the impression that ship would never go to war. The capital starship was designed and commissioned under the misguided notion that it would always be so powerful that nothing in the galaxy could threaten it. Just because that's no longer the case does not lessen our duty."

"Do you at least intend to continue observing the policies enacted by the council under Mayor Chancey? The policies under which so many report feeling safer?"

"I'll tell you what. In three hours, once we're under warp drive, I'll address anyone who'd like to hear my plans. I'll address them in person, on the Starboard Concourse."

"That's one of the legally enforced human-free zones," Snyder said, sounding aghast. "Only humans who are allies are meant to go there."

"Then hopefully, once I'm finished talking, everyone there will realize that I truly am their ally." Husher terminated the call, standing from the command seat. "Fesky, you have the CIC. See us through the warp transition."

"Yes, sir."

His first thought was to visit the wardroom to get something to eat, but he decided against it. He wanted a clear head when he went to speak with the students, protesters, and other citizens of Cybele.

Instead, he went to his office to sit behind his desk in deep thought about what he intended to say. As he contemplated it, he removed Keyes's crucifix from the desk drawer, absently winding the leather thong from which it hung around his fingers.

Before he left, he spent an hour carefully ironing his captain's uniform, laboring over every crease. When he was finished and about to leave, he first slipped the crucifix around his neck, tucking it beneath his undershirt, just as he imagined Captain Keyes had done.

CHAPTER 47

War Is Not Safe

"The so-called captain may have his command seat back," Snyder said, gripping a podium set up at one end of the Starboard Concourse, "but his career still depends on how he treats the people of Cybele. That's been the case since he took command of the *Vesta* thirteen years ago, and it's certainly the case now. The IU will decide whether he should face disciplinary measures and maybe even criminal charges the moment we return."

Having made his way through a crowd of hundreds, if not a thousand, Husher positioned himself to one side of the podium, standing at-ease two or three meters to Snyder's right. She spoke for several minutes more, but at last she relinquished the podium to him.

The moment he grasped both sides of it, the crowd erupted into a cacophony of booing, air horns, and protest chants. Husher gazed calmly out at the crowd, waiting for them to run out of steam.

After ten minutes, the protesters were still going strong, occasionally using their air horns to give their voices a break. The crowd writhed against itself, and he spotted some people leaving, shaking their heads in disgust, at whom or what Husher couldn't say.

The crowd was still only increasing in volume fifteen minutes later, but the *Vesta* would spend a week under warp drive, and Husher was content to stand at the podium until they lost their voices.

I will say my piece. Sooner or later, I will get my chance to say it, and then I will.

Something caught his ears. A chant he hadn't heard yet today, or indeed, ever before. It consisted of three simple syllables:

"Let him speak! Let him speak! *Let him speak!*"

It still took an eternity, but eventually, the crowd fell silent. Husher leaned forward and spoke into the mic:

"I'm sorry that you were lied to, and that you lied to yourself, about the peace we've enjoyed for the last seventeen years." He cast his gaze from individual to individual—from angry scowl to solemn frown to smirk. "I'm sorry you believed this was how it would be from now on, despite the indications to the contrary. And I'm sorry you thought we had become so strong that nothing in the universe could challenge us—so strong you could live your life on a warship without any fear of real danger even coming to your doorstep.

"I understand the thinking that led to it. Capital starships have become powerful economic engines, and they offer a way for the species in our Union to connect with each other. I consider those positive things. But capital starships are also warships, and when war comes, they must fight. In addition to the benefits to our galactic economy and to interspecies relations, you were also placed on my ship to limit me. The idea was that maybe if we make our society harmless enough, the universe will leave us alone, and war will never come to our systems again. But that approach leaves something vital out of the equation. We're all about to gain a harsh lesson in exactly what that something is.

"You came to live on my ship, and in doing that, you asked me to make space safe for you." Husher focused on one person at a time as he spoke. He focused on students, professors, doctors, clerks, custodians, lawyers, mothers, fathers, brothers, and sisters. "You asked me to make *war* safe for you. As though war were something that could be sanitized and controlled. I have some sad news for you. War is not safe. In fact, *life* is not safe—it's unfair and harsh and dangerous. The closest we can get to 'safe' is a locked bedroom far from any battlespace, and even then, your safety won't be guaranteed, which I fear will become increasingly clear in the coming years. I have personal experience that speaks to it. I lost my three-year-old daughter to a Gok terrorist attack, when she was at home, supposedly safe."

His voice lowering, which made several people in the crowd lean forward, Husher said, "You're about to experience the horrors of war first-hand, in a way the public has never experienced them before. I wish it weren't so. But in this universe, you do the best you can with what you have, as unfair as that might be. If you're a fighter, then you don't let unfair limitations stop you from achieving your goals. You work to conquer them, one by one. Right now, life has given me a warship full of civilians and a chance to stop a deadly enemy from gaining a foothold in our galaxy's backyard. I'm going to take that chance, because this war will be fought for the survival of every species in the galaxy, and keeping ourselves safe is not worth giving up an opportunity to save them.

"There's been a lot of talk about oppression lately—about how some groups have it worse than others, how they've been treated unfairly, and how they're still being treated unfairly even now. I'm not here to debate which species have it better than others. But I am here to say that trying to tear each other down is not the way we make things better. That only weakens us, and leaves us even more vulnerable to catastrophe. If we're to survive what's coming, we need to put aside our animosities and pull together. We need to *work* together, because right now, we're at risk of not having a society to share at all. But if we can manage to unite, and if we can manage to win, then maybe we can grow. And if we do that, then we can all become stronger and more prosperous, as one people. All of us."

The applause that followed was much more lengthy and robust than Husher had expected. It only came from about half the crowd, and it didn't last nearly as long as the booing had, but it was something.

When it died down, he added, "Given Dylan Chancey's treachery, every policy enacted while he was mayor is now rescinded pending further review, and that review will wait until after the coming battle. As for the creation of zones closed to humans, Tumbra, or any other species—I will do everything in my power to oppose that, and if I am ever blinded or weak enough to allow it to happen again, I will resign. That divisive bullshit has no place on my ship."

Nodding, Husher began to step away from the podium. Before he could, Penelope Snyder's voice blared from the crowd, amplified by a bullhorn: "Does this mean you're instituting a military dictatorship, Captain?" she said.

He leaned into the microphone again. "It means you chose to live on a warship that is now going to war. Feel free to call that whatever you like."

With that, he left the podium and began to leave Cybele.

But Snyder wasn't done. "Your daughter is still alive, Captain Husher," she said into the bullhorn.

Slowly, Husher turned, and as he did he could feel an incredulous grimace twisting his features. *What insane tactic is Snyder using now?*

"That isn't funny, Ms. Snyder," he bellowed, without the aid of the podium's microphone.

"It wasn't a joke," Snyder answered. "Your daughter's alive, and she's standing right here." Her hand lowered to rest on the shoulder of a young woman, and it took Husher a couple of seconds to recognize Maeve Aldaine.

As their eyes met, Husher felt like he was drifting away—as though he were hearing the growing murmurs of the crowd through a long tunnel.

Snyder seemed half-crazed under the best of circumstances, and what she was claiming now was absurd. Yet, as he gazed into Aldaine's widening, ice-fleck eyes, the same color as his own, he knew beyond a doubt that what Snyder had said was true.

CHAPTER 48

Old School

They sat alone in the wardroom, where Husher's officers had done him the decency of giving them privacy. Either they'd heard the rumors about Snyder's claim already, or they nevertheless sensed the conversation's importance. Husher felt grateful to them either way.

"How?" he said, looking from Snyder to Aldaine and back again. He'd already offered them food and drink, but they'd both declined.

"I'm wondering that, too," Maeve said. "Was this really the best way to tell us, Penelope?"

"Apologies, dear," Snyder said. "The captain left me with no choice."

"By which you mean you realized that you were down to your last card to play in your attempts to control this ship," Husher said.

Glaring at him, Snyder said, "If you want information from me, maybe you should start treating me with some respect."

"Well, I already know you're going to tell me the truth. If you don't explain how this came to be, I definitely won't believe you, and the card you've played will have no value whatsoever. So let's stop wasting time. How did this happen?"

Before Snyder spoke, Maeve did, staring at Husher. "My mother always told me she barely knew my father. She mentioned that she was married to you, once, but that you divorced and then she hooked up with someone at a party—that I was her 'happy accident,' and she didn't want my father to know about me because she didn't think he'd make good father material."

Husher narrowed his eyes. "Sera? Hooking up with someone at a *party?*"

"I didn't think it seemed like her either, but I just figured I didn't know her when she was that young and maybe she'd changed. I never once entertained the thought she was lying to me, as she's my mother." Aldaine glanced at the bulkhead for a moment, then back at Husher. "The reason I wanted to sit in on that first council meeting was because I knew mom had been married to you, and I wanted to know what you were like. To see whether what everyone says about you is true, about how old school and regressive you are."

Husher gave a tired chuckle at that. "And?"

"Turns out you are, yeah."

Raising his eyebrows, he turned to the university president. "How did this happen, Snyder?"

Lips pursed, Snyder said, "Sera told me about the night your house was bombed. Maeve's babysitter was inside when it happened, but Maeve was at her playmate's house, down the street."

"Iris."

"Hmm?" Snyder said, head tilting sideways.

Husher looked at his daughter, the slow wonder of this situation still dawning on him. "Your birth name was Iris."

"Yes," Snyder said. "Sera changed that before she was old enough to know the difference, to make sure word of her survival wouldn't reach you."

"That name does seem familiar to me," Maeve said, and she spoke the word slowly: "Iris."

Snyder cleared her throat. "Anyway. Maeve had been invited for supper to her playmate's house, and the babysitter messaged Sera to ask her was it okay, which she said it was. The playmate's mother heard the bombing, of course, and when she saw whose house it was she called Sera."

Snyder paused, and Husher realized he was leaning forward, his eyes fixed on the woman's face. "Sera told her not to tell me Iris had survived," he said.

"Indeed. She knew that if the Gok had tried to kill you once, they could easily try it again. For Maeve's protection, she wanted to get her far away from you. That was the reason for the divorce. To protect your daughter."

Slowly, Husher shook his head. Part of him understood what Sera had done, but another part of him resented her deeply for it.

"Of course, when Maeve expressed her intention to study at Cybele U, Sera was horrified, and she contacted me to explain the situation. She didn't even know me, but she'd been following my work, and she believed she could trust me. Over the years leading up to Maeve's enrollment, Sera and I kept in close touch, and we became friends. I promised her I would do everything I could to make both Cybele U and the *Vesta* as safe for her daughter as I possibly could."

Husher's gaze drifted to his daughter once more. *Iris. Maeve.* She'd helped Snyder in her efforts to change things on the *Vesta*, and while he considered those efforts misguided...

"Thank you, Penelope. Thank you for looking out for my daughter."

Snyder sniffed. "Captain Husher," she said, and her tone told Husher she was about to administer her final blow. "If you won't turn the *Vesta* around to keep the people of Cybele safe, will you do it for your daughter?"

Husher met Snyder's piercing gaze, and then he turned to study Maeve's unreadable expression for a long moment.

He looked at Snyder again. "No."

CHAPTER 49

Unbridled

As the *Vesta* transitioned into realspace beyond the outskirts of the Concord System, Husher experienced an odd mix of grim resolve and...well, excitement.

He'd never enjoyed the act of making war, but he understood its necessity. Certainly, he didn't live under the illusion that every war through history had been necessary or even warranted, but he knew that sometimes war *was* needed to stand up to an enemy who couldn't be negotiated with, who wanted to destroy your way of life or simply to kill you.

Despite what he considered a realist's perspective on armed conflict, today, he felt excited. *And why shouldn't I?* The coming engagement would mark the first time since the advent of capital starships that their unbridled might would be unleashed. The first time a capital starship captain would not be forced to adhere to ROEs that offered the upper hand to the enemy on a silver platter.

Husher knew it wasn't the most noble sentiment he'd ever felt, but he was excited to see what the *Vesta* could truly do. Besides, since he'd already determined the warships in the Concord System were hostile, he was technically still observing the IU's ROEs. *Hopefully, I can get them to see it that way.*

"Multiple Gok contacts just outside the asteroid belt, sir," Winterton said. "Teth's vessel has made an appearance as well."

"How many Gok ships?"

"Twelve, but they're spread thin, with several light minutes between most of them."

"The Ixa and the Gok..." Fesky muttered. "Two species that have never had any trouble getting along properly."

Husher glanced at her. "Neither have you and I, Fesky. Mostly, anyway. We've always had each other's backs. You haven't let Snyder get to you enough to forget that, have you?"

The Winger clacked her beak, then lowered her voice so only Husher could hear. "Well, to be fair to Snyder, you're still pretty annoying sometimes, human."

Husher chuckled, then toggled his Oculenses till they showed him a tactical display. After a few seconds' scrutiny, he saw the obvious angle of attack. It was a bit too obvious, which probably meant it was the one Teth wanted him to take, but Husher was content to play the Ixan's game long enough to feel him out.

For a moment, he wished there'd been enough time to outfit a squadron of Pythons with the ability to enter subspace, but that would have involved a lengthy delay, and probably returning to an IU system. It occurred to him that passing on that game-changing technological innovation to the Fleet would depend on whether he achieved victory, here.

No pressure.

"Kaboh," Husher said.

Slowly, the Kaithian turned to face him. "Captain?"

"Am I going to have any trouble getting you to follow my orders during this engagement?"

"As long we're clear that I am *merely* following orders, and that your actions have almost certainly already destroyed your career—then no, Captain. You won't."

That'll have to do, I suppose. "In that case, set a course straight at Teth's destroyer and the two Gok cruisers flanking it. Bring engines to seventy percent power."

"Yes, sir."

"Tactical, I want port and starboard Hydra broadsides at the ready. Depending on how the other Gok ships react, we may need them."

"Aye, Captain. Commander Ayam just reported that all Python pilots are ready and standing by to scramble."

"Very good. Coms, make a shipwide broadcast advising all civilians to secure themselves and family members inside the safety harnesses provided to each residence." In Husher's experience, people normally kept the restraints affixed to a wall in a closet somewhere, since they didn't like the visual reminder that the *Vesta* was a warship and might actually find herself in battle someday. *I just hope no one threw them out.* If anyone had, they were likely in for a rough ride.

The necessary orders given for now, Husher sat in the command seat, back straight, and watched on the display as his supercarrier neared the opposing ships.

He felt he was doing the right thing, deep down in his gut. And in his experience, whenever you felt that way, you usually were.

CHAPTER 50

What It Means to Tangle

"The Ixan destroyer has loosed a fifty-missile barrage and has begun to withdraw into the asteroid field, sir," Winterton said. "She's yet to come about, though. This doesn't look like a full-fledged retreat to me."

"I'm sure it isn't," Husher said. "Teth's trying to bait us. But we should focus on the immediate problems first. Tactical, let's show those Gok cruisers what it means to tangle with a capital starship that's actually able to fire on them. Loose four Hydras each in a formation that blankets the area around those targets with potential firing solutions—say, twenty kilometers along both the X and Z axes. Make sure the missiles are programmed not to target enemy missile fire. Our point defense turrets should take care of most of those, though I'd like forward laser projectors set to point defense mode, to be safe."

"Aye, captain."

Winterton turned from the main display toward Husher. "Sir, the cruisers just added missile salvos of their own to the destroyer's. Twenty-five missiles apiece have joined the incoming barrage."

"Coms, relay orders to Commander Ayam that he's to scramble Pythons at once. Tell him to prioritize the Gok missiles as targets, and that I'll have further orders for him once he's finished with that."

The CIC officers with tasks to complete bent to their work, and Husher watched on the tactical display as his plan unfolded.

Over the next ten minutes, he saw something on the display that startled him: things were going exactly the way he wanted. Both traditional and laser point defense systems worked together to start mowing down the incoming robots the moment they were in range, and Pythons in tight formations swooped in to pick off the more conventional Gok missiles on the large barrage's flanks. Apparently, none of those had been programmed to prioritize fighters as targets should they appear, given that they just sailed dumbly toward the *Vesta*'s hull until they were obliterated.

"Hydras ready to fire on your command, Captain," Tremaine said.

Husher nodded. "Fire Hydras."

"All Gok missiles have been neutralized," Winterton put in. "The Pythons are starting work on the ordnance from the destroyer now. The chances of any robots getting through to the *Vesta* are extremely low."

"That's what I like to hear," Husher said, though he still felt bewildered. One of the only constants of space combat—and of warfare in general—was that plans *never* retained their original form after coming into contact with reality. A warship captain who was going to survive was one who needed to have Plans B, C, and D ready to go, and a captain who planned to survive for very long needed even more than that. Staying ready to turn on a dime was part of the job.

The Gok cruisers seemed to spot the missiles targeting them, since they attempted to maneuver out of the way, but they weren't ready for the Hydras splitting into several smaller missiles. The Gok had never seen weapons like these, since they hadn't been around during the Gok Wars, and the species' military intelligence was even more useless than the IGF's intelligence.

When the four Hydras split into thirty-two smaller missiles, the enemy cruisers scrambled to shoot them all down, using their own rockets in conjunction with point defense systems.

But it was far too late. The smaller missiles still packed quite a punch, and even two would likely be enough to take down the enemy ships.

Far more than two made it through. Of the first volley, eleven missiles bypassed the target's defenses, and of the second, thirteen.

Both missile cruisers came apart in violent eruptions, the flames of which were swallowed almost instantly by the airless void of space.

The *Vesta*'s CIC erupted into cheering and fists pumping in the air. Husher's heart rose at that, and for the first time, he realized just how long it had been since he'd heard that sound inside a Fleet warship.

"Be mindful of shrapnel from those cruisers," Husher said to Winterton, and when he spoke, the cheering died down. He didn't like to dampen the celebrating, but they *were* the only vessel in a battlespace beset by an unknown number of enemies, after all.

"Aye, sir," Winterton said, though he'd been among the first to resume scrutinizing his console's readout.

"What's the destroyer's posture?" From the tactical display, Husher could see that Teth was still retreating, but the data overview there only told him so much.

"Steadily accelerating in reverse, though she hasn't yet come about to face the inner system."

Husher nodded. *Still not committing to a full retreat.* Again, he wasn't surprised. The asteroid belt was the perfect place to lay a trap for the *Vesta*. "Conduct constant active scans of the asteroid field as we enter it, Winterton. I want to know the instant something pokes a head out from its hiding place. And Coms, order Ayam to have his birds performing recon flybys behind asteroids big enough to conceal a warship within the range we've seen from the enemy."

"Yes, sir," Winterton and Fry said in rough unison.

"The other Gok ships should be similarly unprepared to deal with our Hydras, so the broadsides we've readied should account for any that decide to show up. If we see another of the warships we faced in Saffron, though, we might have to give it some extra attention."

"Sir," Winterton said, "the Ixan destroyer has ceased its reverse thrusting and is now moving toward us under what must be full engine power, or something close to it."

"Is she within range of our primary?"

"Yes, sir."

"Fire primary at that destroyer, Tactical."

"Aye, sir."

"The destroyer is launching another missile salvo," Winterton said, his hands flying across his console. Moments later, he said, "Sir, the primary laser only made contact for a few seconds. The destroyer just thrusted laterally to maneuver out of the way, the moment it finished launching its barrage."

"Cease firing the primary, Tactical. Winterton, how many missiles?"

"Eighty, sir."

Husher swallowed hard. He opened his mouth to give another order, but before he could, the sensor operator spoke up again.

"We're experiencing superheating along the nose of the *Vesta*. The destroyer's hitting us with its particle beam. We're already seeing major hull warping!"

Winterton seemed about to speak again, but massive explosions cut him off, accompanied by violent rocking that threw Husher against his seat's restraints again and again.

CHAPTER 51

Below the Ecliptic

"Answer with our primary!" Husher said. A quick study of the tactical display had told him just how well Teth had boxed him in: to move to port would be to maneuver toward the incoming wave of robots, and a giant asteroid limited movement to starboard.

"We don't have enough power to fire the primary again," Tremaine said through gritted teeth.

Husher furrowed his brow. "Why not?"

"The explosions were a main capacitor bank blowing, sir," Winterton said. "It took our total capacity to around seventy percent, meaning firing the primary once took us below the necessary charge to do so again."

Husher cursed. That also meant even a full charge wouldn't let them fire their primary laser twice in succession. "Helm, reverse thrust along an angle that takes us below the ecliptic, *now!* Tremaine, hit the destroyer with fifteen Banshees and a spray of kinetic impactors along the horizontal axis. Send another spray just below their ship. I want them incentivized to break off."

"Firing missiles and impactors," Tremaine said.

"We're out of the particle beam, Captain," Winterton said with a sigh of relief. "We took immense damage to the nose of the *Vesta*. In addition to the capacitors, we lost visual sensors in the area as well as nine crewmembers who were servicing the main gun."

Damn it. "Let's turn our attention to the incoming missiles." Glancing at the tactical display, Husher saw that the Air Group had already managed to cut them down by seventeen, but without the *Vesta*'s help in dealing with the barrage, most of the speeding robots were still in play. "Tremaine, I trust we have enough charge to put tertiary laser projectors in point defense mode?"

"Aye, sir."

"Do it, then. Helm, increase reverse thrust by fifteen percent. Keep a close eye on those active scans, Winterton. Now would be the perfect time for Gok to start coming out of the woodwork, especially with the Pythons taken off recon."

"Will do, sir. The Ixan ship is making no move to refocus its particle beam on the *Vesta*. It's resumed backing away toward the inner system."

Husher nodded. As reluctant as he was to do so, he had to admire the sophisticated game Teth was playing. The Ixan was walking a fine line between luring the *Vesta* down-system and taking every opportunity to try and neutralize her. If Teth overplayed his hand, he likely figured there was a chance the supercarrier could retreat, or at least maneuver back to a more secure position. But at the same time, if he didn't take some chances, then he might never get a shot at victory.

Clearly, Teth considered vanquishing Husher a worthy goal, and Husher didn't consider it immodest to agree, at least inwardly. Other than preventing the enemy from establishing a foothold, Husher's main reason for attacking Concord was to spur the IGF to action. If he failed, he had every reason to believe the IU would continue equivocating and attempting to bargain. He'd watched them do it for too long to believe they'd do otherwise, unless they were forced to.

"Seventeen enemy missiles left in play, sir," Winterton said. "We should be able to neutralize the remainder before any—" The sensor operator broke off as something seemed to catch his eye on the main display. Husher watched as color fled the man's face.

"A ship identical in profile to the one we fought in Saffron has just appeared from behind the large asteroid on our starboard side, Captain," he said.

It felt like an invisible fist made of ice had clenched Husher's stomach. For a moment, he couldn't speak as he watched the massive vessel belch hundreds of missiles that screamed across the battlespace.

CHAPTER 52

Peacetime Soldiers

Major Peter Gamble moved in formation along a port-side crew corridor with what he considered one of his weakest squads.

Gamble didn't like to waste time with his strongest marines, even in a potential combat situation—they'd already ingested the right principles from their training, and they lived and breathed them. They didn't need him there, holding their hands.

No, the marines Gamble spent time with...they did need a little help. Like most people in the service, these were peacetime soldiers who'd never seen combat outside the sims, which got war wrong more often than not. Of course, even many peacetime soldiers had the right instincts for war, or at least instincts that could easily become the right ones, with enough exposure to battle.

The squad Gamble was with now...it didn't consist of that type of soldier, exactly.

Either way, with Captain Husher back in the command seat, Gamble wouldn't be surprised if none of the robots even made it into the *Vesta*. The man certainly had enough experience, and he had skill oozing out his ears. Plus, Captain Husher seemed pretty reluctant to let any more of those little devils inside his ship to wreak havoc.

Gamble had seen fighting during both the Second Galactic War and the Gok Wars. At thirty-eight, he was old to still be pulling active duty, but he'd do it until his body broke down completely or they crammed a promotion so far down his throat that he had to take some desk job. He knew that would happen eventually, and he dreaded the day it did.

For all its faults, Gamble believed in the Interstellar Union, and he'd spend his dying breath protecting it. Maybe its citizens appreciated that, and maybe they spit on him for it. Probably it was a mix of the two. It made no difference. He'd die to protect them nonetheless.

A blast shook the corridor, then another, then another. The *Vesta* bucked beneath him, throwing Gamble headfirst into a bulkhead.

His combat helmet absorbed most of the impact, but his neck felt sore as he picked himself off the deck. *Somehow, I think that'll be the least of my worries.*

"Everyone all right?" he called to the others.

A ragged chorus of "Yes, Major," greeted his ears, and a quick glance around the corridor found nobody down for good.

Good enough for me.

"Major Gamble," said Captain Husher's voice through Gamble's ear piece. "Come in."

"I read you, Captain."

"You're about to have company. We're getting hit with a surprise barrage of those attack robots, and there's no way to avoid it. A few dozen at least are going to get through."

A few dozen... When he spoke, Gamble tried to keep the shock from his voice. "Sir, should I have Yung, Mews, and Zimmerman released from the brig so they can join in the fight?"

"That's a negative, Major. Under no circumstances are those three to be released. When I take disciplinary action, it means something, and I plan to keep it that way. Wouldn't be much of a punishment if it ended the moment the next battle started."

"Yes, sir." The captain had a point. Those marines would be itching for a fight, and when they realized they were missing out on one, only then would the punishment feel real.

"I want you to personally take a company of marines to Cybele and secure the city," the captain said. "Deploy the rest of the battalion exactly as I had you distribute them before, patrolling the corridors and guarding vital systems."

"I will, sir."

"Husher out."

Gamble immediately switched to a company-wide channel. "All marines in Hammerhead Company, double-time it to Cybele and meet me in front of the Epicenter." He cut the transmission, then looked around at the squad he was leading, a few of whom were looking at him like they were going to be sick. "Get yourselves together, now," he told them. "Let's move."

Under normal circumstances, it was universally understood that only the hatch into the fake desert should be used to enter or exit the large compartment that contained Cybele. But these were not normal circumstances, and Gamble and his squad used one of two port-side emergency hatches instead.

The moment they emerged, it became clear what a good decision that had been. A shriek pierced the air, audible even from this distance, and without prompting, the entire squad broke into a run.

So, some of their instincts are good after all. Gamble wasn't surprised. Even during peacetime, making it through marine training was no joke. If you didn't have what it took to be a soldier at least on some level, you simply didn't make it into the battalions.

Gamble unclasped a pouch at his waste, reached inside, and grabbed three microdrones, which he tossed into the air. While the microdrones had a number of settings, their default was to stay just ahead, checking around corners and zooming up to get a glimpse of upper-story windows and rooftops. That was exactly the setting Gamble wanted, right now. His Oculenses overlaid all three drone feeds onto what he was already seeing, and he could turn the opacity up or down with a thought. He could even give them simple commands that way, or change their settings. With any luck, the drones would prevent his squad from getting blindsided by a pack of killer robots.

They passed a man whose overlay made him look a bit like a mime, to Gamble's eyes. He was lying face-down, a few feet from a residence door that had been left open.

Gamble knelt, placing a hand on the man. "Sir, are you—?" His hand encountered something soft and slick, with too much give to it. When he recoiled, and his hand exited the man's overlay, it came back wet with scarlet.

"Guy's shredded," Gamble said hoarsely. "Something got him with a lot of sharp edges. Let's keep on moving."

They found action well before they met the rest of Hammerhead Company at the Epicenter. Gamble's rightmost drone glimpsed robots rushing down an alley just before they spilled onto the street his squad was on.

"Contact!" he yelled, raising his R-57 assault rifle and putting three rounds into the nearest robot while shuffling backward. "Fall back to the other side of the street, use the alleys!"

Gamble glanced back and spotted the tiny space between residences that he planned to retreat down. The robots were coming at them fast, and he heard the horrified scream as one of his marines went down without firing a single shot. There was nothing to be done for him beyond what Gamble already had—given him the orders that, if he'd followed them fast enough, might have saved his life.

It's do or die time. This is how we get combat experience. Ideally, that happened without loss of life, but loss of life was also an inescapable part of combat.

Gamble's job was to make it happen mostly on the enemy side. *If these robots can be said to have lives.*

A couple of them pursued him down the narrow gap between the residences, and Gamble scrambled back, continuing to slam fresh clips into his R-57 and emptying them into the things' metallic hides.

At last, both his attackers were down, and he leapt over their metal corpses, using the residence walls to propel himself upward to avoid getting cut up on their sharp parts, some of which were jagged, now that he'd finished with them.

Checking down the next alley, he saw one of his marines had almost made it to the next street over, with one of the metal devils in close pursuit. The marine had dropped his gun halfway there, and the robot had simply charged over it, apparently ignoring it.

Gamble raised his gun, took careful aim, and put a round into the thing, center-mass. It went down instantly. *Is that where their brains are...?* It would be good news, if so, since their thin, curved heads presented such small targets, especially when they were facing you.

"Thanks, Major," the marine called as he picked up his gun from where he'd dropped it.

"You owe me a beer," Gamble said, then got on the company-wide channel. "All squads currently in or en route to Cybele, report to me."

They needed to consolidate their position inside the city, and fast. This was already a disaster, and if any more of those things got inside before Gamble could lock down the area, it would quickly become a catastrophe.

CHAPTER 53

Ripped to Pieces

Husher watched on the tactical display as his Pythons advanced on the enemy ship's missile barrage in waves, using kinetic impactors and the latest generation of Sidewinders to neutralize dozens of the robots at a time. The *Vesta*'s point defense turrets were also working overtime, supplemented by lasers whose energy supplies were rapidly depleting.

Then, his breathing caught as he saw an entire squadron of Pythons go down almost simultaneously.

Seconds later, Commander Ayam's voice squawked through his ear piece: "Captain, the robots' are changing their behavior!"

"How? What the hell is going on out there, Commander?"

"A group of them just changed course suddenly and latched onto a formation of my birds," the Winger said. "They ripped them to pieces in seconds."

"They're no longer prioritizing the *Vesta* as the target," Husher muttered as he considered the unsettling development, racking his brain for what to do. "Commander, I want you to use looser formations, or even abandon squadron formations altogether. Judging from the fact we just lost sixteen fighters in the space of seconds, our movements are far too regimented and predictable. Have half of your pilots work together in preassigned pairs, and have the other half fly in finger-fours."

"Yes, Captain."

"Ayam, I also need you to assign some of your pilots to target the enemy ship. That thing doesn't look to be running out of missiles, and if we can't do something about her soon, we're going to have a perforated hull and a ship full of robots."

"I'm on it, sir. Ayam out."

Husher turned toward Tremaine. "Tactical, I want you to arm four Hydras and load them with firing solutions similar to those we used against the Gok. I also want you to arm four Gorgons and distribute them randomly throughout the barrage those Hydras will turn into. I'm sending in some Pythons to attack the enemy vessel—between those and the Hydras, not to mention the mess of robots and fighters already clogging up the battlespace, we should get a Gorgon or two through."

"Understood, sir," Tremaine said. "I'm on it."

While he was waiting for his next gambit to take shape, Husher reviewed some of the data coming in from Damage Control. They'd already called their second watch on-duty, and they were about to get third watch out of their bunks, if the turmoil hadn't already done that.

According to the estimations Husher reviewed, using his Oculenses to flick through updates and absorbing them as fast as he could, thirty-nine of the robots had successfully infiltrated his ship's hull.

Another transmission request came in, from Major Gamble, and Husher accepted. "Go ahead, Major."

"We've finished securing Cybele, but sir...there have been some civilian casualties."

Mentally bracing himself, Husher said, "How many?"

"At last count, there are twenty-nine dead and one hundred and forty-three injured. Most of those have been hospitalized. I'm sorry, sir."

"I'm...I'm sure you did what you could."

"We weren't fast enough. It's as simple as that."

"There are a lot of people at fault for those deaths, Major Gamble, but you aren't one of them. You aren't to try taking that blame for yourself. That's an order."

"Yes, sir."

"Keep me apprised of any further developments. By text, if you please. Husher out." He turned toward the Tactical station. "What's the status of those missiles, Tremaine?"

"Just uploading the finalized telemetry now, Captain. They're already waiting in the tubes."

"Fire at will."

"Firing four Hydras and four Gorgons."

Husher watched on the display as the rockets crossed the cluttered battlespace that stretched between the two warships. Before the Hydras had a chance to split, one of the robot-missiles changed course to target it, but the advanced weapons were programmed to separate in response to a threat, and the robot only ended up latching itself onto one of the eight smaller missiles. It shredded it, destroying both it and itself, but the other seven continued on.

A flash of inspiration made Husher stare hard at the tactical display, and he realized he had enough time to execute. "Send me the missiles' targeting data at once, Tremaine."

"Here it is," the Tactical officer said with a flicking gesture atop his console.

"Commander Ayam," Husher said over a two-way channel with his CAG, "instruct the two finger-fours currently keeping pace with our missile barrage to concentrate fire just below the closest pole of the oblong spheroid. I'm sending you the area I mean now over Oculens. That's where our missiles are headed."

"It will be done, Captain."

Husher watched with his heart in his throat as the enemy ship's point defense turrets pounded away frantically at the incoming missiles and Pythons. Most of the fighters were soon forced to peel away, in order to avoid getting hit, and then the turrets started work on efficiently mowing down the cloud of rockets formed by the fully separated Hydras.

In the end, only one of the smaller missiles made it to the enemy hull. But all four Gorgons did.

Fire blossomed from the opposing vessel, and as soon as the void quenched that, another explosion ruptured her hull dozens of meters down. Two more followed.

If he'd had access to his primary laser, Husher might have finished off the ship then and there. He briefly considered sending kinetic impactors into the breach, but the ship was already moving away, thrusting toward the protection offered by the nearby asteroid.

"Good job, everyone," Husher said over a wide channel, addressing the comment to Ayam and the Air Group as well as his CIC officers. "But this is far from over. Stay frosty and get the job done. Pythons, return to base for now."

Closing the channel, he looked around his CIC, meeting each officer's eyes for a few seconds each. "If we're going to continue, we need to get out of this asteroid belt, so we can see threats coming. In an even match, that...carrier, for want of a better term, would have been obliterated. But because it was able to maneuver so close to us undetected, it almost finished us. I'm not letting that happen again. That said, leaving the asteroid belt for the inner system is probably exactly what Teth wants us to do."

Grim faces and set jaws met his eyes as he continued to shift his gaze from officer to officer. Even Kaboh looked determined.

"Major Gamble just informed me we lost twenty-nine civilians during the attack on Cybele," Husher said. That brought winces from his officers. "One hundred and forty-three have been injured. Our marines were able to secure the city, but we have no guarantee more civilians won't die." Husher pointed to the main display. "On the other hand, victory today could mean the difference between saving the hundreds of billions of civilians that live in the Interstellar Union or allowing them to burn. I need to know something. Are you with me in this?"

"Aye, Captain," Fry said right away, and Tremaine immediately echoed her. One by one, the officers sounded off.

All except Kaboh. Husher turned toward the Kaithian. “Lieutenant?”

“Aye, sir. I’m with you.”

“Time to ante up,” Fesky said.

Husher nodded. “Let’s ante up.”

CHAPTER 54

Teth's Gambits

"Exiting the asteroid field now, Captain," Winterton said. "No sign of any warships moving to stop us. Wherever those ships are, they're well-hidden. The only hostile showing on radar right now is Teth's destroyer, which is halfway to the Ixan homeworld."

"Maybe the enemy's bunched up behind the planet," Fesky said.

Husher had considered that possibility, too. Making a stealthy entrance into a system was next to impossible, especially if the system was equipped with modern sensor webs. Employing stealth on defense, though...

That was a completely different story. All you needed were sensors updating you on the approach of enemy ships—a function Teth's destroyer could easily be serving—and the patience to wait behind a planet, moon, or asteroid until the right moment.

It would take a little over forty minutes for the *Vesta* to join Teth's ship near Klaxon. Husher had endured some excruciating waits during his military career, but he expected this would prove to be one of the worst. The supercarrier's battle group had been obliterated, and she was alone, deep in enemy territory and surrounded by an unknown number of hostile ships.

Husher saw the tension he felt reflected in the postures of his CIC officers as they monitored their respective stations in silence. Seven minutes after they'd begun their descent into the system, Winterton spoke again: "A Gok destroyer just emerged from the asteroid belt, at almost exactly the same place we exited." The sensor operator paused, then added, "A missile cruiser and a frigate are close behind it."

Nodding, Husher waited for several minutes more. Then, he asked, "Have any more ships emerged, Ensign?"

"Negative, sir."

"Coms, tell Commander Ayam that in twenty minutes, provided no more warships have emerged, I want him to scramble the entire Air Group and take them back to deal with those three ships. He has more than enough firepower to handle them, and we have more than enough to deal with Teth."

"Provided Teth has no surprises waiting for us behind Klaxon," Fesky said. "Which we're almost certain he does."

"I said we have *more* than enough firepower, Commander. This is a capital starship class supercarrier, and we have the muscle to crash whatever surprise party Teth has planned."

"Yes, sir," the Winger said, though she didn't sound convinced.

The silence resumed, and so did the waiting. Watching the tactical display, Husher saw that Teth still seemed in no hurry. His ship had less mass, and so it took less energy to propel, making it nimbler. The destroyer could have easily outstripped the *Vesta* if her commander wanted. *Hell, he could do the disappearing trick, too.* This wasn't an authentic retreat, and both Husher and Teth knew it. Had this been a game of chess, they would both be employing obvious strategies—on the surface, anyway. As for how deep this game actually went, that remained to be seen.

"The destroyer has reached Klaxon's moon," Winterton reported at last. "She appears to be making her way behind it, sir."

Fascinating. Teth's gambits continued to come off as incredibly facile. "Alter our course to give the moon a wide berth, Kaboh," Husher said. "If Teth has positioned artillery there, I want the option to break away quickly."

"Aye, Captain. Calculating course now."

The minutes continued to creep past, silent and uneventful. For all they knew, Teth could have slipped behind the moon and vanished. But what would be the point, other than to force the *Vesta* to use up some of her fuel on a wasted trip down Concord's gravity well? *Hardly a devastating blow.*

It reminded him of their first engagement with the Ixan destroyer, in Wintercress, when she'd materialized on the dark side of Tyros' moon, striking before the system's sensor web could warn the *Vesta* of her presence. But this maneuver was reversed, with Teth slinking behind cover like an injured animal wanting only to lick its wounds.

"Circling the moon now, Captain," Winterton said. "The destroyer is coming into view. She's just sitting there in lunar orbit, oriented toward us."

"Let's see if we can't liven things up a bit," Husher said. "Tactical, arm two Hydras and two Gorgons. I'd also like six Banshees loaded in the tubes, either to supplement the more advanced missiles or to help shoot down incoming ordnance if need be."

"Aye, sir."

"The destroyer is maneuvering toward us," Winterton said. "No shots fired yet, and she's moving quite slowly." The sensor operator blinked. "Sir, I've continued to conduct regular active scans of the system, and the results from the latest one just came back. I'm picking up something strange on radar."

"What is it?"

"I'm not sure. It's unlike anything I've encountered or heard about. Whatever it is, it's invisible to visual sensors, but the radio waves are bouncing off it just as though it were solid. It appears to be spherical in form, and centered on Klaxon's moon. We're trapped inside it, sir, with the Air Group trapped outside."

A lump took shape in Husher's throat. It seemed they'd been right about there being a trap, but completely off about its nature.

"Tactical, fire a Banshee at whatever that is from a port-side tube. Record the missile's impact on visual sensors and play it for me, Winterton."

Both officers got to work, but seconds later, Winterton had something else for him, and it wasn't welcome.

"The destroyer has begun firing missiles, Captain. They look to be more robots. Thirty-five in play already."

"Point defense should account for those, but standby to use the loaded Banshees if necessary, Tactical, and to replace them in the tubes."

"Missile impacting now, sir," the sensor operator said. "Should I patch the live feed through to the main display?"

"Go ahead."

Winterton did, just in time to catch the collision. This time, there were visual phenomena—namely, the brief flash of the Banshee exploding, followed by ripples of electric-blue energy that flowed out from the impact site.

"The destroyer just launched forty more missiles," Winterton said. "Radar's showing no effect on the structure's integrity from our missile's detonation. It...oh, God."

"What, Ensign?"

"The sphere appears to be shrinking, sir. It's closing in on us."

CHAPTER 55

No Pressure

"Fire Banshees at the incoming missiles and switch out the programming for the Hydras already loaded in the tubes—I want them taking down robots instead."

"Yes, sir," Tremaine said, his jaw rigid as he focused on his work.

"What's our capacitor charge?" Husher asked.

"Down to fifteen percent. Enough to assign tertiary laser projectors to assist with point defense, but not for long—likely only ten minutes or so."

"A total of eighty-nine enemy missiles currently headed for us," Winterton said, his voice as tense as Tremaine's. "The destroyer is reversing thrust and rotating—it looks like Teth plans to fall back and use the moon for cover."

"That's no retreat," Husher said. "He'll come around the other side and hit us with his particle beam from behind."

Winterton's eyes widened at the possibility, but Husher just wanted to curse. He'd known full well that Teth would have something waiting here for him, but he'd assumed he could always pull out if things got too hairy, even if it meant speeding away at full engine power perpendicular to the ecliptic plane.

Now they were isolated from their Air Group and trapped in a shrinking space where Teth's smaller, more maneuverable destroyer had the advantage. Even as Husher studied the tactical display in bewilderment, he saw eight Gok ships emerge from the asteroid field and head toward his stranded Air Group. Five more followed.

We need to get out of here, immediately. "Nav, set a course to pursue the destroyer that takes us through the missile barrage."

Kaboh looked at him. "I cannot have heard that correctly."

"You heard me. Lock it in and send it over to Helm, now. Tremaine, I want four more Hydras loaded into forward tubes as well as twelve Banshees, all programmed to target down missiles. Spray kinetic impactors into the approaching missile cloud, as well—hopefully we can take down a few more that way."

"Yes, sir. This will reduce our remaining Hydras to the eight we've loaded into the port and starboard tubes for broadsides."

"I'm aware of that. I'm also aware that this will guarantee we'll take at least some of those robots on the hull. Damage Control will have their work cut out for them, and so will Chief Gamble's marines, but better this than letting Teth fire that particle beam up our ass." Husher turned to Kaboh. "How's that course coming?"

"I just sent it to the Helm," the Kaithian said, his voice strained.

"Good. I have another task for you. Assume the enemy destroyer's acceleration tops ours by thirty percent and come up with an estimate for when we'll be on the exact opposite side of the moon from it—that's when I want the *Vesta* brought fully around, followed by bringing our engines up to one hundred percent. Collaborate with Tactical to figure out the moment Teth's nose will appear around the moon's horizon. Tactical, I want you to fill the space we expect the destroyer to occupy with kinetic impactors, as well as four Banshees for good measure."

As both officers hunched over their consoles, Husher turned to his sensor operator. "Winterton, take a good look at that forcefield, or whatever the hell it is. I want you to figure out exactly what it centers on—is it the moon's core, or is it a spot nearer its surface? My guess is the latter."

"Yes, sir."

A series of slight tremors ran through the deck and up Husher's seat—that would be the robots they were taking on their hull. It killed him to picture the metal killers tearing through his ship, but it was what had to happen.

At last, they were through the cloud of robots, after only seventeen of them made it into the *Vesta*'s hull. *Not the worst outcome, but certainly not good.*

"Bringing her around," Vy said, and Husher watched on the display as the remaining forward visual sensors showed a view of the dusty, barren moon, and then of the horizon they expected the enemy ship to appear over. "Engaging engines at full."

"I've located the forcefield's center, Captain," Winterton said. "You were right. The forcefield centers on a point near the surface of the moon, on the side opposite us."

"Then that'll be the site of whatever's powering it. I doubt Teth would be able to carry a generator big enough to power that thing aboard his ship, so the positioning makes sense." Husher opened up a two-way channel with his marine commander. "Major Gamble, are you there?"

"I read you, Captain. My marines are in the process of mopping up our latest visitors."

"Glad to hear it, but I'll need you to take your best soldiers off that task. I'm assigning you with a mission that will probably decide whether we live or die today."

"No pressure, then."

"Nothing you can't handle." *I hope.* "Get two squads comprised of your best marines to Flight Deck Delta as quick as you can. Suit up before you go—combat pressure suits. Take some heavy artillery with you. Your job is to find and destroy whatever's generating the forcefield currently pinning the *Vesta* against this big rock."

"You can count on me, Captain."

"Good man. Husher out."

As he terminated the transmission, Tremaine spoke. "Firing kinetic impactors and four Banshees at the coordinates where we expect the destroyer to appear."

Several long seconds later, Winterton said, "No sign of her, sir. We—oh. There she is—she's cresting the horizon underneath us!"

Husher gritted his teeth as he processed the fact that Teth had played him again. "Helm, engage attitude thrusters to lower our port side twenty degrees."

"Aye, sir," Vy said.

Husher tried not to dwell on the ordnance he'd sent tearing through empty space instead of the enemy destroyer's hull. "Tactical, be ready to fire our port-side Hydra broadside the moment the targeting becomes viable."

"Yes, sir."

Next, Winterton spoke the words Husher had been dreading: "Superheating along our port side, sir."

"Helm, standby to accelerate away the moment those Hydras have left the launch tubes."

An explosion rocked the ship. "That was two rows of point defense turrets exploding, as well as a secondary capacitor bank," Winterton said. Another explosion. "Several laser projectors in the area were just obliterated," the sensor operator added.

"Tremaine?" Husher said.

"Firing Hydras now, sir."

"Full power to engines, Helm," Husher barked. "Squeeze every drop of acceleration they'll give us."

His eyes riveted to a splitscreen showing a tactical overview alongside sensor readouts, Husher watched as the destroyer continued her circuit around the moon, methodically neutralizing the thirty-two missiles screaming her way, one by one.

The missiles' targeting systems were sophisticated, and they'd track Teth until he managed to deal with them all. Hopefully, the volley would buy Gamble and his marines the space they needed to get down to the moon, but Husher didn't think for a second that the Ixan was finished.

The smaller, faster ship had the clear advantage in the ever-shrinking space between the forcefield and the moon. If this fight dragged on much longer, Husher knew they were all doomed.

CHAPTER 56

Major Peter Gamble

Gamble expected no trouble getting his best marines to Flight Deck Delta on time, but getting the shuttle and pilot he wanted there was another story.

As he sprinted through the corridors toward where he needed to be, assault rifle at the ready in case any robots decided to come through the bulkhead at him, he made a snap decision.

"Chief Haynes," he said over a two-way channel, "I want you to leave Flight Deck Alpha and fly around the *Vesta* to Flight Deck Delta and pick us up. Think you can do that? I need you there in seven minutes, max."

"Not what I'd call the safest maneuver, in the middle of an engagement," Haynes said.

"Oh, is that why your callsign is Psycho?" Gamble said as he ran. "Is it because you like to sit around in the comfort of your home and sip tea? Is that why you signed up to fly a combat shuttle?"

A brief pause, and Haynes said, "How did you know my callsign? They gave me that in flight school. I haven't told anyone here."

"I know a lot of things, Chief Haynes, including that I'll kick your ass if you're not on Flight Deck Delta with the *Vesta*'s best combat shuttle by the time I arrive there."

"Yes, sir," Haynes said quickly. "On my way. Haynes out."

Probably the pilot knew Gamble was joking, but there was still a note of uncertainty in his voice. Gamble liked it that way. He didn't enjoy making threats, but he also didn't enjoy lacking what he wanted when he needed it most. In that sense, a climate of healthy fear of what Gamble might do wasn't the worst thing in the world.

As his last couple marines were running across the flight deck, the inner hatch opened on one of the airlocks, and the combat shuttle Gamble had wanted descended from it, landing neatly a few meters away from his people.

It hadn't just been the shuttle itself he'd wanted, even though he expected it to play a significant role in the coming mission—it was a craft with lots of artillery, designed for direct actions against targets where heavy resistance was anticipated. But besides the shuttle, Gamble had also wanted Haynes himself flying it. The man had demonstrated some serious ability during their escape from Tyros; flying that had probably saved the captain's life, as well as Gamble's. *That's who I want taking us down there.*

"Johansen," Gamble said, pointing at one of the marines. "Did you bring what I need?"

"You got it, Major," the marine said, slapping a lidded trolley next to him.

"You're a good man, Johansen."

As he'd left Cybele, Gamble's com had shown Johansen as the closest to Flight Deck Delta—as well as the closest to the nearby armory. He'd quickly instructed the man to get the necessary artillery, including the charges they'd use to blow that generator to pieces.

"You've all been chosen for the weapon you rate highest on," Gamble told the assembled marines. "I put together this direct action on the fly, as I was jogging here. If I can do that, y'all can handle any confusion that arises with minimal fuss. Grab your weapon, sort yourselves out, and get on the shuttle. You have thirty seconds, marines."

Johansen flicked the lid of the trolley onto the deck, and Gamble's marines clustered around the guns, digging through them until they found the one they were strongest on. That done, they sprinted toward the shuttle's open airlock. The last marine piled in twenty-nine seconds after Gamble had given them their time limit. *Not bad.*

"No need to wait for us to get all comfy-cozy, Psycho," Gamble told Haynes over a wide channel. "Let's go now, while the shuttle airlock is still pressurizing."

"Going."

Gamble felt the shuttle leave the flight deck and thrust toward the airlock on its way out of the *Vesta.*

Captain Husher's voice came over a two-way channel. "Major, we're approaching the location we believe the forcefield generator to be. Our plan is to decelerate and remain in the vicinity for as long as we can, in case you need some air support."

"I appreciate it, sir," Gamble said. He would have told the captain not to endanger the ship needlessly, but he knew he didn't need to.

"You're ready to deploy?"

"We're heading for the airlock now."

"Good luck and God speed, Major."

"Thank you, sir. Same to you."

Seconds later, the exterior airlock door opened, and they were rocketing out into the void. None of the marines had taken their helmets off—Gamble was glad he didn't have to tell them that. This flight wouldn't be long enough to justify it, and besides, in the middle of a battle, the chance of losing interior pressure was high.

"Remember, everyone, we're going to be much lighter on our feet down on the moon," Gamble said over a wide channel. "The good news is, so will any Ixa we encounter. That means their fancy new genetic enhancements will count for less when it comes to running us down like they did on Tyros. The bad news is, we can probably expect to encounter some heavy firepower as a result. Stay frosty, everyone."

"Oorah," the marines answered as one.

The staccato of one of the shuttle's turrets sounded overhead, followed by something landing on the hull.

Within two seconds, Gamble had unclasped his restraints and was running for the airlock. He slapped the panel to let himself in, entered, and pressed an inner panel to close the hatch behind him.

Through the narrowing gap, he glimpsed several marines who were clawing at their restraints, as well as Tort, who'd simply ripped his off and was halfway to the airlock.

Too late, Gamble thought as the hatch slid closed. "Psycho, I need an airlock override, and I need it by the time this chamber finishes depressurizing. I know what that sound was, and I know there's nothing you can do about it now that it's made its way past your turrets."

"You sure about this, Major?" Haynes said. "This isn't—"

"What you'd call the safest maneuver? Son, I'm gonna show you what psycho really means."

The outer airlock hatch opened, and Gamble gripped an overhead handle with one hand to swing himself onto the shuttle's roof while keeping a firm grip on his R-57 with the other.

Twisting around, he activated the magnets in his combat boots to secure himself to the hull, and then he tensed his leg muscles to straighten himself.

Just in time—he came face to face with a robot that was turning toward him and brandishing its razor-edged limbs.

One metal arm came at Gamble. He fired, his bullets propelling the limb away. The second arm swung toward him, and he shot that away, too.

Before the robot could make another move, Gamble deactivated the magnets in his left boot long enough to deliver a swift kick to the thing's midsection, quickly retracting his leg before it was sawed off.

The robot staggered backward, and Gamble fired a round into it, sending it clattering across the hull.

The shuttle was approaching the moon, now, and Gamble's legs were aching with the strain of staying upright and balanced.

Gunfire flashed from the moon's surface, and Gamble dropped to the shuttle's hull. The robot scrabbled soundlessly across the metal toward him—he could feel the vibrations.

Flipping onto his back and slapping another clip into the gun, he emptied it into the thing's face, point blank. That did the trick: the robot lost its motor power, floating off the shuttle, which proceeded to land roughly on the moon's surface seconds later.

The flashes of at least a dozen muzzles all across the moon's surface told him they were already getting shot at by a lot of hostiles. Gamble hauled himself over to a squat barrier on the shuttle's roof, intended for exactly the purpose he planned to put it to.

"Get those turrets into play, Chief Haynes," he said over a wide channel. "Marines, deploy around the shuttle and use it as cover. We're already in the shit, here."

CHAPTER 57

Seems Irrational

"The destroyer is coming back around the moon, sir," Winterton said. "It's headed straight for us."

"Acknowledged," Husher said tersely as he studied sensor data from the moon's surface, which showed hundreds of Gok and mutated Ixa moving on Major Gamble's position. With only the two squads Husher had told the marine commander to take, he looked certain to be overrun.

"The forcefield is closing in rapidly, sir," Winterton said. "It's now half the size it was. We'll soon have barely any room to maneuver at all, and the Gok attack force will reach our Air Group within fifteen minutes."

"Acknowledged, Ensign," Husher ground out, barely containing his frustration. "Helm," he said, twisting around in the command seat to look at the Winger.

"Captain?"

"Spin this ship around and point our starboard side at that destroyer. Without delay. It's time to use our last Hydras."

"Yes, sir," Vy said, punching a few commands into her console. With that, the *Vesta* began to rotate on the tactical display.

"Tremaine, fire on my mark. In the meantime, I need you to direct kinetic impactors toward the surface of the moon, using our underside point defense turrets. If we leave Gamble and his marines to deal with all those attackers, they'll be overrun within minutes."

"We'll be offering ourselves to Teth by remaining here," Kaboh said. "He'll use his particle beam to finish us."

"That's what the Hydras are for," Husher said.

"What about when they're depleted?"

"I'll deal with that situation once I'm in it," Husher growled. "One thing at a time. Tremaine, make sure to fire well away from our combat shuttle."

By willing his Oculenses to show him a magnified visual of the moon's surface, he was able to see that Gamble had set up two heavy machine guns in the shuttle's shadow. At the moment Husher zoomed in, a rocket streamed out from near the shuttle's hull, and then another, from the opposite side. In the meantime, the shuttle's four turrets were firing full bore, and doing considerable damage. That was impressive, considering it was only Haynes operating them, though he was likely using AI for assistance.

The marines were mounting an admirable defense, but it couldn't last—not on its own. The Ixa and Gok had them surrounded, meaning the shuttle offered little cover, other than the airlock and fold-out barriers that were now standard issue for combat shuttles. Already, Husher could spot four marines down of the twenty who'd gone to the moon's surface.

Then, Tremaine brought the *Vesta*'s underside point defense turrets to bear, operating them manually. It was an unusual, perhaps unprecedented way to use them, but it had an immediate and devastating effect.

Clouds of regolith dust plumed up from the moon's surface as impactors sheared pressure suits in two, throwing the Ixan and Gok ranks into utter chaos.

"Sir..." Winterton said.

Husher glanced at the tactical display, specifically at the destroyer's proximity. "Hold, Tremaine," he said.

"Yes, sir..." the Tactical officer said, though he sounded as anxious as Winterton.

"Superheating along the starboard side, Captain," the sensor operator said. "One of our flight decks is threatened. I strongly recommend—"

"I said wait for it!"

Long seconds passed as the *Vesta*'s hull sloughed off, the effect creeping closer and closer to Flight Deck Omicron.

"Fire Hydras!" Husher said.

Tremaine did, and the superheating persisted two seconds more before Husher was rewarded for his steady hand. The destroyer veered to starboard in what was clearly a desperate maneuver. Such a sudden course change would be hard on any ship's engines, and what was more, it wouldn't grant the warship the velocity it needed to outstrip the missiles.

The enemy point defense systems blazed to life, and the destroyer fired a wave of robot-missiles, in its first attempt to use them in an intercept capacity.

It almost worked. Two of the Hydra fragments got through, punching sizable holes in the destroyer's hull, which retreated back around the moon at speed.

Husher drew a breath, knowing his next order would likely be the hardest one he'd ever given: "Kaboh, note the destroyer's trajectory and come up with a course that will intercept it, head-on."

The Kaithian didn't answer, and several CIC officers turned to Husher wearing expressions ranging from confusion to consternation.

"If we leave now, Major Gamble will be overrun," Tremaine said.

"There's a good chance of that," Husher replied. "But if this engagement continues, it's a certainty that we'll lose against Teth's destroyer in this confined space, and our Air Group will go down before we do. Teth will expect us to stay and protect our marines, since they're our ticket out. That's why we *have* to do this."

"Seems irrational to me," Kaboh said.

"I agree. But when you're dealing with an enemy able to anticipate every rational option, irrational ones are all you have left." Glancing at the tactical display, Husher saw how his Air Group was now hugging the forcefield as the Gok warships closed in. Taking a deep breath, he said, "This is my order. I expect you all to carry it out."

CHAPTER 58

If the Captain's Left Us to Die

"Major," one of his marines, Roux, said over a two-way. "The *Vesta*'s leaving her overwatch position."

Risking a glance overhead in between laying down suppressive fire against the Ixa and Gok closing in on their position, Gamble grimaced inside his helmet. Next to him, Tort had hoisted a heavy machine gun on his shoulder—something no human could do—and was using it to pound away at the enemy ranks.

"I can see that, Corporal," he said. "You just keep on shooting."

Gamble had climbed down from the shuttle's roof because of how vulnerable it made him to hostiles firing from a hilltop nearby. Instead, he'd positioned himself behind one of the fold-out barriers. Most of his marines were using the shuttle's other barriers for cover. Tort was standing almost completely in the open, using the big gun to shoot at anyone who looked likely to shoot at him, but that was just Tort.

Johansen opened up a private channel with Gamble, then. "Major," the private said, "did you notice—"

"I see that the *Vesta*'s leaving, yes." Something glinted overhead, several meters above the barren, gray terrain. Gamble squinted at it, and he realized it was a grenade, sketching a slow parabola in the low gravity.

"Grenade coming in from my twelve," Gamble barked over a wide channel. "Everyone, take cover as best you can." Around him, marines ducked behind fold-out barriers or into the shuttle's open airlock. Everyone except Tort, that was—the Gok would probably refuse to take cover from the heat death of the universe.

Taking careful aim, Gamble exhaled fully and squeezed the trigger. The grenade exploded meters overhead, raining down shrapnel but doing far less damage than if it had detonated at ground-level.

With that, Gamble opened a wide channel. "Everyone, please stop contacting me privately about the *Vesta* leaving. I understand you're trying not to worry your comrades, but we're marines, damn it." Gamble fired on a Gok who was advancing to a nearer position. The big alien didn't bother to retreat to its previous cover, so Gamble put two more rounds into it, and the third succeeded in ripping open its pressure suit. That sent it fleeing in the opposite direction, probably for the facility that housed the forcefield generator—maybe its suit didn't have the ability to self-seal.

"Let me ask y'all something," Gamble continued over the wide channel. "Does anyone think Captain Husher would leave us to fight this many Gok and Ixa without a damned good reason?"

No one spoke. "Exactly," he said. "If the captain's left us to die down here, you can rest assured our deaths will mean something. No service member wants to die, but if we have to, then making sure Teth doesn't get the foothold he wants to seems worth it to me. Can I get an oorah."

"Oorah!" the remaining marines yelled back at him. It wasn't as loud as Gamble had expected—they must have lost more soldiers in the last few minutes.

"Show them what you're made of, marines," Gamble said, slapping a fresh clip into his gun and emptying it into the encroaching army.

CHAPTER 59

Knots of Tension

Struggling to keep his mind off the plight in which he'd left his dwindling marine force on the moon's surface, Husher focused on something just as nerve-wracking: the visual feed of the moon's horizon as it unspooled before them.

"Eight Banshees and three Gorgons are armed and ready, sir," Tremaine said. "Railguns have also been loaded. I've calculated firing solutions based on where we expect to encounter the enemy destroyer."

"Very good," Husher said. And it was, except that Teth was almost never where they expected him to be.

Indeed, as they neared the location where they'd anticipated the destroyer, Winterton spoke up: "He's not here, sir."

"Full power to engines, Helm," Husher said, gritting his teeth. "Get us back to our marines."

There were two possibilities: either Teth had anticipated Husher's gambit and had looped around to attack the marines with impunity, or he'd altered his course to get a better attack angle on where he'd expected the *Vesta* to be. Both possibilities involved the enemy destroyer returning to where Husher had left his marines to fend for themselves.

"He's not attacking the marines," Winterton said as the supercarrier completed her circuit of the moon. "It—there he is! He's advancing over the horizon off our port-side bow."

"Helm, bring our nose to port until we're lined up with Teth's destroyer. Tremaine, hit them with everything the moment we are."

"Aye, sir," the Tactical officer said, and less than a minute after that: "Firing first four Banshees. I've loaded them with courses that will have them curving around to hit the destroyer's port side."

"Good work," Husher said.

"Firing the other Banshees, kinetic impactors, and Gorgons now."

"The destroyer's slow to react," Winterton said, clutching his console as he stared hard at it. "She looks to be training her particle beam on us—but she's reversing! Teth knows he can't withstand a barrage like that."

Husher's eyes were riveted to the main display as the missiles closed in. "Are we experiencing any superheating?"

"We just started to," Winterton said after shuffling some items around on his virtual display. "It's the same spot on our bow as before—that'll be bad, if it persists. Most of our kinetic impactors are going to miss due to the destroyer's reverse thrust, but Banshees are still on track—*damn it.*"

Husher regarded the sensor operator with eyebrows raised. It was the first he'd ever heard the man curse. "What is it, Ensign?"

"One of the three Gorgons just went down."

Nodding, Husher said, "Continue nosing us to the left, Helm, and Tremaine, don't let up on those impactors. Helm, I want more power to the engines."

Both officers acknowledged his orders, and Husher tried to ignore the knots of tension in his chest and deep in his stomach as he watched their attack play out.

"We're down to three Banshees and two Gorgons," Winterton said. "Another Banshee just went down...another Gorgon...*yes!*"

Husher didn't need the man to tell him what had caused his sudden jubilation, since he'd watched on the tactical display as all three remaining missiles struck home.

"We just took out one of the destroyer's main forward engines," Winterton said. "Their ability to reverse thrust has been cut almost in half."

Just as the sensor operator said it, the *Vesta*'s newly superior acceleration saw her closing the gap and nearing her enemy.

Kinetic impactors from the *Vesta*'s magnetic railguns poured into the wound created by her missiles, and the entire destroyer abruptly ruptured. The CIC burst into cheering.

Watching on visual, Husher saw that one piece of shrapnel from the expanding debris cloud looked bigger and more symmetrical than the others. "Winterton," he barked. "Is that an escape pod?"

The sensor operator scrutinized the display for a moment. "It certainly looks likely to be, sir." Just as he spoke the words, the craft vanished.

"That was Teth," Husher said with certainty, his feeling of satisfaction tempered by the knowledge that he still hadn't finished his Ixan nemesis. "How are our marines faring?" he asked, almost afraid of the answer.

After a few seconds, Winterton answered: "They're still alive and fighting!"

"Thank God. Tremaine, let's refocus on helping them reach that generator. Our Air Group's still in hot water—if we don't rejoin them soon, the Gok will pin them against that forcefield and take them apart."

CHAPTER 60

Shoot to Kill

By the time the *Vesta*'s guns came back into play in the fight for the moon's surface, the marines defending the shuttle were down to Gamble, Roux, Johansen, Tort, and three others—not including Haynes, the pilot.

The shuttle was looking pretty banged up, and the regolith around it was littered with motionless marines. Near Gamble's left foot, out of the corner of his eye, he could see a young private's blackened face through his helmet's cracked faceplate.

It was a grim scene, meaning there was plenty of room for their spirits to be raised. The *Vesta*'s return certainly did that.

Despite that he'd told the marines they'd been chosen for this mission because of the guns they rated highest on, Gamble wasn't actually using the weapon he most excelled with. As much as he liked his R-57 for its versatility and its run-and-gun nature, his heart belonged to his Rk-9 sniper rifle, which he'd stashed just inside the airlock.

When the supercarrier's guns once again started tearing up the moon's loose terrain, sending plumes of dust shooting upward and shrouding the area around the shuttle in a gray haze,

Gamble got on a wide channel. "Roux, you're closest to the airlock. Toss me my sniper. We're gonna leave Haynes to continue defending this position while we get this raid rolling." He pointed to the top of a rise ten meters or so off the shuttle's aft—one of the few places not currently covered in a dust haze, and also one where they'd had the most success putting down the aliens pressuring the shuttle.

"I'm going up there on overwatch while you six push in that direction," he said, pointing the way the shuttle's starboard side was facing. "Wait till the dust settles a bit, so I can actually see enough to be of some help, then rush 'em. By the time you're ready, I should be in position."

Roux passed him his sniper rifle, which he slung across the back of his pressure suit before sprinting toward the rise he'd indicated, assault rifle held at the ready in case any hostiles popped up to contest the hilltop.

Progress was slow in the low gravity, given Gamble had a keen interest in not bouncing too far into the air. Doing so would offer the enemy a nice, clean target. Instead, he inched forward while crossing the distance between shallow craters and low rises as fast as he could manage.

At last, he gained the hilltop without encountering any enemy combatants. *Nice.* The slope formed a natural sniper hide, with a gentle incline on the far side, perfect for steadying himself against the crest while he lined up his shots.

Just as he'd predicted, the dust was beginning to settle to the ground as he was getting situated, and his battle-weary team was getting ready to act.

"How are we interpreting the ROEs, today, Major?" Johansen asked. An important question for any soldier who didn't want a run-in with a conga line of lawyers once he got back from deployment.

"We're on a barren moon with no atmosphere, in the middle of a system that's supposed to be deserted. I don't think we're gonna run into too many civilians," Gamble said over the wide channel, which brought a couple chuckles. "The only beings here are the ones guarding the generator they're using to keep that forcefield up, whose sole purpose was to trap us like fish in the barrel they wanted to shoot us inside. Unless they surrender, which I doubt they will, shoot to kill."

"Can do," Roux said.

"Move out," Gamble said.

The six marines ranged forward with guns at the ready, using the moon's natural formations as cover whenever possible.

Right away, a Gok popped up from a crater that must have been deeper than it looked. The alien's position would have let it get the drop on Tort from behind. It *would* have...and if Gamble hadn't put two high-powered sniper rounds into the seam where its helmet met its pressure suit, that's probably exactly what would have happened.

"Thanks," Tort rumbled. "Owe you beer."

"Don't mention it, big guy."

Gamble continued to scan the moon's terrain for anything out of the ordinary—anything that moved, in other words. He was glad he'd been able to take down the Gok so handily, but he was far from sure it would be that simple if an Ixan popped up, ready to go. Based on Tyros and on today's fight, in their new form, the Ixa were harder to put down than even Gok.

Studying them through the Rk-9's scope, some features of the moon's terrain pretty clearly weren't natural. A couple rectangular rises, about five hundred meters off, were obviously artificial, though covered in heaps of dust, probably so they couldn't easily be spotted from orbit. How the captain had known to deploy them here, Gamble didn't know, but he also didn't bother wondering about it. The CIC had their business, and he had his.

Then, his worst fear came true: an Ixan reared up from a hollow, pounding up the slope toward the nearest marine, Johansen.

Gamble got two rounds into the reptile before it made it to the private, but it made no difference. The Ixan seized Johanson by the shoulders and smashed its forehead into his faceplate. The alien's helmet must have been hardened somehow, because the faceplate cracked.

It didn't stop there. The Ixan held out Johansen with one hand and produced a pistol with the other, firing it twice into the marine's neck.

Two more sniper rounds made the Ixan stagger, but it recovered quickly, making its way toward Corporal Roux.

Damn it. Gamble reloaded smoothly, only decades of training keeping his hand steady as he rushed to try and save his marine.

Too late. The Ixan was there, reaching for Roux—

—when Tort crashed into it, both hulking beings hitting the ground in a tangle.

That meant Gamble couldn't get a clean shot. He silently cursed the Gok as the two struggled on the ground, the Ixan quickly getting the upper hand.

Gamble had noticed a mild hero complex in the big Gok the moment he'd started working with him. Hell, Tort's involvement with humans had started with saving Captain Husher's life, during the Second Galactic War. He'd racked up more saved lives since then, but if his inclination drove him to sacrifice himself along with Johansen, it would make a dark day even darker.

I really don't want to lose that big lout.

The Ixan managed to pin Tort to the regolith, and it swung its pistol toward the Gok's face. Tort caught his adversary's wrist, but their difference in strength quickly became clear as the Ixan's gun progressed steadily toward Tort's head.

Unfortunately for the Ixan, making it on top had also given Gamble a clear shot. He took one, then he took another.

His third shot sheared through the softer fabric at the Ixan's armpit, meant to enable range of motion but also offering a distinct vulnerability for Gamble to target. His shot must have hit something vital, or maybe it was simply enough punishment to put the berserker off its game.

Either way, it keeled over, and Tort pressed the advantage, slamming his ham-like fist into the Ixan again and again. The Gok picked up his heavy machine gun, which had fallen to the regolith nearby, and he sprayed bullets all up the Ixan's body.

That seemed to do it.

After beating the Ixan, reaching the two structures only involved dispatching a couple more Gok, which seemed like child's play in comparison.

"Patch me through a visual as you take the bigger structure," Gamble said.

It took five minutes for a private, who'd been chosen for his hacking as much as for his proficiency with a shotgun, to bypass whatever security was on the entrance.

Once he had it open, the marines began with a flashbang tossed into the front room, and then they piled inside. Gamble continued scanning the moon for targets, glancing every now and then at the feed in the corner of his vision. His soldiers cleared room after room, confirming exactly what he'd suspected: the Gok and Ixa had sent everything they'd had against the shuttle. Thanks to the *Vesta*'s guns and the marines' resilience, it hadn't quite added up to enough.

The generator, it turned out, was down a long flight of stairs, likely meant as another failsafe, in that it couldn't be taken out from orbit. It had required a ground assault to accomplish its destruction.

"All right, marines. Set the charges and get out of there," Gamble said.

CHAPTER 61

No Such Luck

The forcefield went down just as the Gok ships were nearing it, their intention obvious: to pin the *Vesta*'s Air Group against the energy barrier and wipe them out, away from the protection of their base ship's heavy artillery.

No such luck, Husher thought as his supercarrier moved out from the confines of the moon, once more free to go anywhere in the galaxy it wanted.

Here is good, for now. "Coms, tell Commander Ayam that half his Air Group's on missile defense duty, while the other half is to harry the Gok warships and screw with their lateral mobility. Tremaine, what does our arsenal look like?"

"Two hundred and sixty-five Banshees, thirty-six Gorgons, and as many solid-core kinetic impactors as you'd care to send into space, Captain."

"Let's send them into Gok hulls instead. Start with just the closest destroyer for now, but mix in two Gorgons, and send two Gorgons apiece at the nearby Gok cruiser and frigate as well."

Husher's hope was that the kinetic impactors would suggest to the Gok that he was following standard IGF doctrine left over from the Gok Wars: focus on mowing down one target then move on to the next. Ideally, that would make his other targets feel safe for the moment, rendering them utterly oblivious to the stealth missiles headed their way.

"Sir, a squadron of Pythons just neutralized a corvette," Winterton reported.

"That wasn't what I ordered Ayam to do," Husher said. "Reprimand him for me, would you?"

That brought a round of chuckles, but Winterton just blinked at Husher, completely impervious to the air of jocularity that had followed breaking free of the forcefield. The man was probably among the most serious people Husher had ever met, which wasn't a bad thing in a CIC officer, and also not a bad reminder to everyone in the CIC. Restored freedom or no, they were facing down thirteen Gok warships. Despite the might brought by the *Vesta* to any engagement, especially one waged against warships with comparable technology, war should never be an object of amusement.

Keyes would never have tolerated chuckling inside his CIC.

In contrast with his sober thoughts, the engagement soon came to favor the supercarrier and her Air Group. The cruiser and the frigate were both obliterated by the Gorgons that found their hulls with no resistance, and the destroyer lost half its forward guns.

After that, every last Gok ship turned about and began to flee for the relative safety of the asteroid field.

"Should we pursue, Captain?" Kaboh said, voice neutral.

"Yes," Husher said. "I believe we should. Tactical, target down those ships."

CHAPTER 62

Pieces

Husher sat strapped into a crash seat across from Fesky, inside one of the *Vesta*'s combat shuttles, but one meant only for mass troop deployments. This shuttle didn't have anything like the armaments on the craft Chief Haynes had flown down to the surface of Klaxon's moon.

Thinking of that mission made him wince, and he worried for a moment that his friend would take his expression the wrong way, until he realized Fesky wasn't paying him any attention. At the moment, she was deep inside herself, as near as Husher could tell.

Fourteen of our best marines. Gone.

Military commanders spent what capital they had to accomplish vital objectives. Sometimes, that currency took the form of soldiers' lives. The knowledge of how badly it would hurt him to spend that currency—of how it would haunt his quiet moments until the day he died—that knowledge hadn't stopped him from spending it.

This was war, and war was a bastard. It left everyone in pieces, including the survivors.

"You all right, Fesky?" he said, as much to distract himself from his thoughts as to check on his friend.

The Winger was trembling violently, and the intrusion of his voice made her start. "What? No, I'm not fine. She's alive, Husher. She's *alive.*"

"That's a good thing."

"Of course it is. But what am I to say to her? After all this time...after what she's been through..."

"She's just another being, Fesky. And she's your friend. She'll be happy to see you."

But Fesky was shaking her head. "You have no idea what the relationship between Fins and Wingers was like, human. You have no idea what they were to us..."

They'd been searching the planet for the better part of a week. The *Vesta* carried some watercraft, and the marines had been out in them for days, emergency lights on, scouring Klaxon's oceans. Pythons had performed flyby after flyby, scouring the shores and the seas for signs of Ek.

Husher had begun to consider how he was going to break it to Fesky that they'd have to end their search and return to the Interstellar Union's core systems. The admiralty would want a full report on what had transpired here, and the bureaucrats would be eager to make Husher face the music for the decisions he'd made.

Wouldn't want to deny them that.

But just as he'd been about to have the talk with Fesky, Ek had been found. And now, here they were, on their way to speak with her.

The shuttle landed on the shore of a bay, and Husher slowly unclasped his crash seat's restraints. Fesky was still fumbling with hers, and he suppressed a smile.

"Need a hand, there, Madcap?"

"I'm fine, human," Fesky grumbled. At last, she ripped them off her with a jerk and stood, storming past, the breeze from her wings wafting against Husher's face.

He followed her into the airlock, trying to catch her eyes, but she stared steadfastly at the hull while the airlock cycled through the usual processes.

The outer hatch opened, and Fesky took a halting step toward it, then another. At last, seeming to steel herself, she exited the craft.

Just outside, she fell to her knees.

"Honored One," Fesky said with a sigh.

Meters beyond, Husher spotted Ek, sitting in shallow water up to her chin, just above her gill slits. He hadn't been there the day her breathing apparatus had been removed, and seeing the Fin without it didn't square with his memories of her. Her mottled skin continued where her suit had once been—the suit that had kept her body constantly moisturized. And like other Fins before her, she wore no clothes, and Husher had to fight the urge to avert his eyes, reminding himself that this had been considered normal for her species.

"I thought I told you not to call me that, Fesky," Ek said.

"I—I—"

"If we are to have a conversation at all, it will be as equals, and if you do not start acting like mine, then I will turn around and swim back into this ocean. Now, stand up."

Still trembling, Fesky stood.

"That is better," Ek said. "I will not have you groveling the first time you meet my children."

"Ch-*children?*" Fesky said, but Ek didn't answer.

Instead, she lowered her mouth below the water's surface, and bubbles rose as she spoke. Presumably she was speaking, though to Husher it just sounded like burbling.

Ek lifted her head, then, spreading a finned arm toward the water behind her. Six fully grown Fins broke the surface.

"Children, meet my dear friend, Fesky. And this is Captain Husher, another close friend. "Captain, Fesky—meet Sarl, Ohm, Rah, Mei, Ki, and Zin."

"How is this possible?" Fesky asked.

"When we parted ways twenty years ago, I told you I was not doomed to live alone in these oceans. Did you not surmise my meaning?"

"I mean—it did occur—but I assumed—"

"I was artificially inseminated during my last days on Spire, Fesky. I have never had a mate, as I never connected with another Fin on that level, but I still carried a desire to procreate. It was an exceptionally foolish thing to do, considering my status as the only spacefaring Fin, and the deterioration of my health at the time. But all has worked out well, and I am not the last Fin after all."

Fesky's legs seemed to give out, then, and she hit the grassy bank with a thud. "I'm so happy," she said.

Husher couldn't contain himself—he laughed, and the Winger turned to glare at him. But her expression quickly softened, as she no doubt realized that he wasn't laughing at her. He was laughing because he felt just as much joy as she did, at the resurrection of the Fins, and at how earnest and true his friend Fesky was.

He felt his laughter settle into a smile, which faded as his gaze settled on Ek. "I hope you know I can't leave you here," he said.

She inclined her head. "The Ixa knew that we were here. They hunted us for months. That was why you had such trouble finding me...because my family and I were in hiding, deep beneath the ocean. It is by mere chance that I glimpsed one of your fighters as I ventured to the surface to see how things were."

"The *Vesta* won't leave until we figure out a way to safely transport you and your children," Husher said. "Ochrim is with us, and he just made a breakthrough that will likely revolutionize—well, everything. If he can do that, he can surely find a way to bring you home with us. I'll put him on it."

"I thank you," Ek said.

That wasn't all Husher had to say on the subject of Ek and her family joining them, but for now, he held his peace. The truth was, he wanted Ek in his CIC. Her uncanny perception had gotten the *Providence* out of some incredibly tight jams during the Second Galactic War, and they needed her now more than ever.

"I trust you know what the Ixa's reappearance means for the galaxy, Captain," Ek said.

"I think I do. But I'd be interested in hearing your perspective."

"During the Second Galactic War, you defeated a single AI—the one that created the Ixa. That AI's project was to dominate this galaxy, just as its counterparts were assigned with dominating the local galactic cluster. I consider it unlikely that very many of the AIs failed. On the contrary: I believe that this galaxy was one of the very few who successfully resisted them." Ek's gaze drifted to the sky. "If I am right, then in order to complete their domination of this galaxy cluster, they will need to stamp us out, once and for all." Slowly, Ek shook her head. "This time, victory will require more than defeating just the Ixa, or even just defeating an AI. This time, victory demands that you find the creators of the AIs themselves, and it demands that you render them unable to perpetrate these actions against any sentient species, ever again."

"Agreed," Husher said after a brief pause. "But 'render them unable' sounds kind of sanitized. You mean that I'll need to kill them, or enough of them that they become a pale shadow of what they are now."

"We do not yet know what form their society takes," Ek said. "But at the very least, you will have to destroy the parts of that society which enable it to wage war."

Nodding, Husher turned back toward the shuttle. "I think I'd better go talk to Ochrim about getting you back to the Interstellar Union. There are some politicians I'd very much like to introduce you to."

CHAPTER 63

Not the Time

On his way across the desert into Cybele, Husher came across a woman sitting in the sand, her hands covering her face. Sobs racked her body, and she didn't seem to notice him until he spoke.

"Penelope?"

Her hands jerked away from her face, which was red and puffy. "*Husher,*" she said, having apparently dropped her frequent use of his title, which she'd always delivered with a note of disdain, to his ears.

"You're..." He shook his head. He'd been about to remark on how her overlay wasn't turned on, but she no doubt knew that already. In truth, he had no idea what to say. Snyder had caused him no end of trouble, these past weeks, and she'd been one of the main obstacles between him and doing his job. Even so, he took no satisfaction in seeing her like this.

"What happened?" he said at last.

"I added the wings of a Winger to my overlay. I've always had such respect for the Wingers...I've always related to them so closely. I'd been thinking about adding the wings for a long time, going back and forth on them, but finally, I decided they were the truest expression of who I am. So I added them."

He shook his head. "And?"

"And the narrownet exploded. They said I was appropriating Winger culture, making a mockery of it, by acting like I could understand the oppression they've been through. They called for my resignation, and at first I just ignored them, but the pressure kept building and building until there were students outside my door and outside my window, screaming, and *cursing,* and..."

Snyder trailed off, replacing her head in her hands. She resumed sobbing. "Well?" she said, her voice made scratchy and wet by her crying. "Are you going to gloat about this or not?"

"No," he said quietly, and Snyder lowered her hands, frowning. Her red-rimmed eyes met his. "I don't take any pleasure in what's happened to you, Snyder," he continued. "It only makes me fear for the future. With crisis on our doorstep, now is not the time for our society to be devouring itself."

He continued walking, then, toward the city. But he paused, and he spoke again without looking back.

"If you need somewhere to stay, away from Cybele, while you decide what you'll do next...message me on my com. I'll find you somewhere in the crew section."

She cursed him in reply, and Husher nodded, continuing his walk toward the city. His lower lip tightened as he fought the urge to weep as well—not because she'd cursed him, but because of what it signified about humanity: the bitterness and the folly.

The readiness to answer failure by tearing one's self apart, along with anyone within arm's reach.

It reminded him of his conversation with Ochrim in the Ixan's living room, and it made him want to weep, in a way that not even being stripped of command had done.

Brushing the back of his hand across his eyes, he continued toward Cybele. He needed to speak with Ochrim, but first, he would find his daughter, to sit and talk if she was willing.

EPILOGUE

Jake Price

Seaman Jake Price stalked the corridors of Tartarus Station daily, trying to get some good out of the bureaucrats stationed there whenever he glimpsed them out in the open. That was rare, and whenever he did see them, they were usually accompanied by a bodyguard or two, who stared Jake down until the conversation came to an end.

He could hardly believe the way he and his companions were being treated. They'd been required to relinquish their ships and military hardware, which they'd done, as a gesture of goodwill. Then, they'd been shuttled here to "wait on word" to come down from the Interstellar Union, the new governing body for the Milky Way.

But word never came, and the bureaucrats brushed him off with weasel words. Their skill in saying empty things that amounted to artful dodges of every question he asked...it was unlike anything he was used to, after growing up in the Steele System. He'd heard all about the liberals who'd taken over the Milky Way government just before Darkstream's exile from the galaxy, but he'd always taken those stories with some skepticism. People tended to descend into caricature when describing those they viewed as their political opponents, so Jake had never quite believed that the Milky Way politicians could be anywhere near as controlling, wishy-washy, or pretentious as the old-timers said.

But whether their stories had been caricatures or not, the people on this station *exceeded* them. The number of times he'd been condescended to or smarmed in the phoniest ways...it made him want to vomit. He'd never been much for politics, but these people were almost forcing him to cement his position on things, to become just like those old-timers had been.

The civilians Jake and his teammates had saved from the Progenitors' onslaught had been transported and housed at Imbros, a planetary colony nearby. God only knew how they were faring.

Worst of all, the bureaucrats had Jake's mech, and the longing he felt for it contributed in no small part to his constant irritation. He dreamed about it every night, but never about piloting it, strangely. In his worst nightmares, the mech walked away from him, to turn on those he considered friends.

He took lunch every day with Ash Sweeney, his best friend and fellow mech pilot. She'd been one of the original members of Oneiri Team, the eight Darkstream soldiers who'd piloted the first MIMAS mechs. Half of the original Oneiri Team were dead or missing after the war they'd fought back in the Steele System, but the members who remained were closer than ever.

"You remember how Roach used to talk about Vin Husher all the time?" Ash had asked him at lunch earlier that day. Roach had been the original commander of Oneiri Team, before he'd gone insane and murdered one of the pilots under his command. He'd tried to murder Ash, too, and he'd very nearly succeeded—Ash was still recovering from being impaled on Roach's blade. Oneiri Team had abandoned their old commander in the Steele System, which had been in the process of getting torn apart by the Progenitors at the time.

"Yeah," Jake said. "I remember. Liberal pansy, he usually called Husher."

"Well, I heard some guards talking, and apparently Husher is bogeyman number one for the government, these days."

"Are you telling me Roach's 'pansy liberal' is *not liberal enough* for this government?" Jake shook his head. "Roach has to be rolling in his grave."

"Assuming Roach is dead."

Jake's mirth died down, then. "Yeah."

Now, Jake was back to marching through the station. His favorite question was to ask whether he and the other former Darkstream soldiers were being officially detained—and, in turn, it was the question the bureaucrats were getting the best at avoiding answering. He also liked to ask them whether they considered he and his fellow soldiers guilty of any particular crime.

At an intersection of corridors up ahead, a four-legged alien strode into view. Her presence, as well as that of her brethren, probably played a big part in the bureaucrats' reluctance to let the arrivals from the Steele System join the rest of galactic society, but Jake didn't hold that against her. He was finally starting to trust Rug, which was the human word the alien had chosen to name herself. Rug was a Quatro, and Quatro didn't have names.

She glimpsed Jake, then she made for him at once, at a speed that made him think something was probably up. Rug was larger than the largest horse, with a royal purple coat and midnight eyes. She roughly resembled a bear in shape, though her broad head and powerful tail put Jake more in mind of a panther. Not that he'd ever seen a panther in real life, or a horse, for that matter. But when someone had told him that was what Quatro resembled, he'd looked them up, and he basically agreed.

"Jake Price," Rug said once she reached him. "Something has happened."

"Yeah? What's going on?"

"There has been an arrival. Another wormhole has opened."

"*Another* wormhole? The desk-jockeys can't be happy about that." Wormholes were now illegal under galactic law, though Jake could kind of understand that, since their use compromised the fabric of the universe. "Did another warship manage to escape the Steele System?"

"Many warships have emerged," Rug said. "An entire fleet of them. But these are no human warships."

"Who, then?"

"They are of Quatro make, Jake Price. These ships were sent by the Assembly of Elders—by the government whose tyranny I and my comrades risked our lives to escape."

Jake nodded, remembering everything Rug had told him about the Quatro government and their promise of equal prosperity for all, which had ended up translating into starvation and slavery when the rubber hit the road. "Are they attacking?"

"No. Your species has already sent a vessel to speak with them, and to ascertain the reason for their arrival."

"Oh," Jake said, nodding. "Well, that doesn't surprise me. I'm pretty sure your Assembly of Elders is going to get along with the Interstellar Union just fine."

Acknowledgments

Thank you to Rex Bain, Bruce A. Brandt, and Jeff Rudolph for offering insightful editorial input and helping to make this book as strong as it could be.

Thank you to Tom Edwards for creating such stunning cover art.

Thank you to my family - your support means everything.

Thank you to Cecily, my heart.

Thank you to the people who read my stories, write reviews, and help spread the word. I couldn't do this without you.

About the Author

Scott Bartlett was born in St. John's, Newfoundland – the easternmost province of Canada. During his decade-long journey to become a full-time author, he supported himself by working a number of different jobs: salmon hatchery technician, grocery clerk, youth care worker, ghostwriter, research assistant, pita maker, and freelance editor.

In 2014, he succeeded in becoming a full-time novelist, and he's been writing science fiction at light speed ever since.

Visit scottplots.com to learn about Scott's other books.